Tapestry of Dreams
Eight Imaginary Tales
By
Herbert Grosshans

Published by
Melange Books, LLC
White Bear Lake, MN 55110
www.melange-books.com

Tapestry of Dreams, Copyright © 2008, 2011 Herbert Grosshans
ISBN 978-1-61235-022-6

Names, characters, and incidents depicted in this book are products of the author's imagination or are used fictitiously. Any resemblance to actual events, locales, organizations, or persons, living or dead, is entirely coincidental and beyond the intent of the author or the publisher. No part of this book may be reproduced or transmitted in any form or by any means, electronic or mechanical, including photocopying, recording, or by any information storage and retrieval system, without permission in writing from the publisher.

Credits

Editor: Jane Carver
Copy Editor: Mae Powers
Format Editor: Taylor Evans
Cover Layout Artist: A. Bratt
Photo used with permission & taken by Herbert Grosshans

Tapestry of Dreams
Eight Imaginary Tales
By
Herbert Grosshans

Blood of the Virgin:
Only the virgin bride-to-be of the man
he hates can give him what he craves.

Dream on a Hot Day:
A cold drink isn't the only thing the girls are willing to give.

Le-itha:
Four years alone on an alien planet can change a
man. Will Professor Melton still be the same?

Luugus:
Things are not always what they seem on Omega,
the fourth planet in the star system Betelgeuse.

Maggi:
Rick Diamond looks forward to a relaxing trip in his new spaceship.
Relaxing? He couldn't have been more wrong.

Vania Starborn:
Captured and tortured by a cruel enemy,
the girl with the golden skin gets her revenge.

Rhodar:
When the big barbarian buys the little creature
in the golden cage, he buys himself a lot of trouble.

Sarah's Gift:
Seeking shelter in Sarah's cabin during a snowstorm,
Jake finds more than just protection from the storm.

Look for Herbert's books at
www.melange-books.com

The best-selling Xandra series (Three books)
Seeds of Chaos, Book One, Eden's Gate
Seeds of Chaos, Book Two, Hell's Gate
Stardogs, Book One, Return to Redsky
Stardogs, Book Two, Redemption
Orion—The Hunt
Cliffs of Time
Outpost Epsilon
Orion, Symbiont of Passion

Visit Herbert's website: http://hegro.blogspot.com/

Cross the threshold into the World of Dreams and Imagination.
Warning: Adult material. Some people may be offended.
Enter at your own risk.

Blood of the Virgin
By
Herbert Grosshans

Virgin blood so sweet and red.
Drink too much and you may end up dead

She was watching me out of dark, brooding eyes, as she squatted on the small rock shelf, her black, almost transparent wings enveloping her nude body like a thin cloak.

"Are all humans this inquisitive?" she asked, her head tilted slightly to one side. She spoke the common language with a peculiar accent.

"Some," I said, smiling. I could see two needle thin fangs between her full lips gleaming in the failing light of the setting Primary, her body silhouetted against the Red Companion, the smaller, weaker sun. She was young, slim, with small, nicely shaped breasts. A black triangle between her open thighs concealed her sex-organ, but I knew she was a full-grown female, eager to feed.

I had to be careful because a hungry female, especially one as young as she, could kill me in her feeding-frenzy. But I wanted her badly, almost as badly as she wanted me.

Another danger I had to consider…the ones hiding behind the boulders and the rotten tree stumps. She was the bait. The youngest and the prettiest one. The others… I didn't want to think about them.

I looked down at my erection. The enhancer cream I had rubbed into my groin would give me the endurance to satisfy three of the females, maybe four. I was hoping there weren't too many of them. I wanted the Prince. He wouldn't make an appearance until he was absolutely sure the females controlled me.

Her laughter made me look up. She had a beautiful smile, if you overlooked her long incisors. "You are impatient." She mocked me with her laughter. Without warning, she launched herself into the air, and in an instant she hovered above me.

"Lie down!" she commanded me, her eyes glowing softly in the twilight. I realized that the primary sun was slowly sinking below the horizon. Only the red one was still fully visible.

I sank to my knees, moved my discarded pants so my head would rest on them, careful to keep the small needle gun hidden in their folds. The ground was sandy and soft, and I stretched out, waiting for her to straddle me.

From close-up, I noticed that her black pubic hair was sparse, barely covering her thick mound.

Flapping her great wings slowly, she sank into my lap, hovered for a moment, then her sex-organ closed over the engorged head of my penis. I watched her hot sheath swallow it. She felt tight but slippery, and she took me deep into her belly.

Her wings collapsed, covered us like a dark blanket. As she stretched out on top of me, she kept snapping her pelvis. I opened my shirt to expose my chest, and her small breasts flattened against my naked skin, firm and warm. She caressed my face with her breath. It smelled sweet, and when she kissed me, I tasted the yarl-berries she had eaten to keep her breath fresh.

My tongue touched one of her incisors, reminding me to keep up my guard.

"Tell me when you are ready to spill your seed into me," she whispered after breaking the kiss.

I nodded, concentrating on her soft, tight sex-organ. "Will you come then, too?" I asked her.

She laughed, rotating her hips. I could feel the gentle pulsing of her vagina-walls. Her lips touched my neck. "I will," she murmured.

She wanted me to come inside her. She needed my semen to mark me. After this, she would be able to find me anywhere.

As young as she was, she possessed good control. Her breathing started to become ragged, and I knew she was fighting the urge.

"When?" she gasped.

"Soon," I said, taking her slim hips into my hands to steady her movements.

"Soon," she repeated, her voice cracking with the effort to control herself.

I groaned. She gave me pleasure beyond description. The secretions of her vagina sent me to highs I'd never experienced with a human woman, or any other female I ever coupled with. My hands moved to her round buttocks, dug into their firm flesh.

"Come now!" she cried out.

I was ready. The pressure inside me exploded and, with a shout, I lunged upward. The pleasure became so intense that I barely felt her incisors puncture my artery. As my penis pulsed inside her clutching vagina, filling her with my discharge, her mouth began feeding.

When my penis stopped throbbing, she lifted her head and sighed. "Your blood is sweet," she whispered. "It makes my head spin."

I didn't tell her about the drug I had injected into my bloodstream. It wouldn't kill her, but it would make her sleepy and lethargic.

I sensed another presence beside us. The young *Yill* in my arms released my member, rose to her feet. She didn't take to the air, just stepped aside, the tips of her wings scraping my chest.

Both suns had disappeared, but one of the moons had risen, bathing the bleak landscape with its pale light.

Another Yill-female stood above me. She looked older; her breasts sagged on her thin ribcage. Without a word, she sank down, wings spread behind her, one of them ripped and scarred. This female had not been flying for quite some time. She relied on the skills of the young Yill to snare a victim.

Her face was lined but not ugly. Opening her mouth, she displayed her fangs. They were long and thin, healthy. Feeding for her didn't present a problem…yet.

I watched my penis spread the thick carpet of her pubic hair, and it didn't surprise me to find her vagina as tight and soft as that of the young one.

Letting out a soft moan, she sank into my lap, began to gyrate her hips. She showed skill, experience. Contrary to what some believe, her kind does enjoy sexual intercourse as much as any other species. By nature, Yill-females are loving and always sexually receptive, even to males not of their species. That's why human men search them out, but never in their natural environment. Only men with suicidal tendencies did that, or men with ulterior motives.

She had her eyes closed as she moved her pelvis lazily in my lap. Her vagina walls rippled across the length of my penis, caressing, sucking, coaxing it to release its precious load.

I reached up to dig my fingers into her breasts. Even though they had lost their firmness, they were still soft and round. She moaned when I took the thick nipples between my fingers. Then she bent forward and let me suck on them.

"Don't wait too long," she said suddenly, her voice soft,

seductive. Her beautiful, brown eyes studied me with curious interest. "You are different," she said. "Most humans loath us for what we are."

"I'm not *most humans*," I said, letting my hands travel along her body to cup her buttocks. They were fleshy, but still quite firm.

She let out a triumphant cry when she felt the first stream of my discharge jetting into her womb then she sank her fangs into my neck, drank eagerly.

The drug would prevent her from taking too much of my blood.

"Your blood tastes strange but pleasant," she said when she was done, licking my neck with her tongue. "I feel intoxicated."

"Move, Yarla," a raspy voice said beside us. "It should have been my turn."

Yarla touched one finger to my neck, and then she released my penis, leaving it strutting into the air. I felt like closing my eyes when I saw the other female crouching above me. She was not old but hideous to look at, one side of her face a mass of scars, her nose half-eaten by some disease. Her only fang protruded from lips that drooped to one side.

She laughed when she saw the disgust in my face, and then with a deft movement she sheathed my rigid organ. She was dripping. I entered her easily, and I had to admit grudgingly that she gave me a better fuck than the other two. She was wild, passionate and out of control. I came inside her with a roar, almost forgetting where I was. When she sank her fang into my neck, it stung. It quickly brought me back to reality. She might have drained me had it not been for the inhibitor in my blood.

Even at that I had to push her off before she could take more than I felt comfortable with. She tried to resist, but suddenly there were other hands pulling her away.

I looked at the ring of females surrounding me. There were too many. Before any of them could straddle me they moved apart, made room for a tall figure striding toward us.

"Leave him!" a male voice thundered.

The Prince.

He looked splendid in his black pantaloons. His upper body was bare. Corded muscles rippled under smooth, black skin. He moved with the arrogance only a man with great power possesses.

"Why did you seek us out?" he asked, looking down at me. I was acutely aware of the sharp, wicked claws that adorned the tips of his hands. With one swipe he could open up my belly, spill my entrails into the sand.

"I came looking for something," I answered, sitting up.

"What could you find here?"

I grinned and casually pulled my pants toward me.

He looked at my erect penis. "I suppose I could have saved myself that question," he said, shaking his head. "My hunters might have killed you." He turned away. "Bring him!" he ordered the group of females.

I slipped into my pants, shoved the little needle gun into a pocket and grabbed the small backpack that held my meager possessions. "I come freely," I said.

He made a half-turn, looked at me. "Either you are very stupid, have a death-wish, or are just plain ignorant. Whatever it is, it doesn't matter." Spreading his giant wings, he took to the air and soared away, toward the old castle.

Most of the females followed him. Only a handful remained with me. Three of them were armed with bows. They were different from the others, larger and bulkier. Leather protected their elbows and knees. Bands made from metal circled their thighs and arms, and their breasts were covered with strips of hardened leather. They belonged to the caste of Warrior-Hunters; fierce fighters, feared and respected by anyone who met them in battle.

An army of Yill Warrior-Hunters would be a great threat to the humans on this planet, but a large army would need a strong leader, one who could unite all the tiny kingdoms. That would never happen because there was too much rivalry between the princes and their households.

The young female I had first encountered interrupted my thoughts. "Did you enjoy our coupling?" she asked.

Grinning at her, I said, "Look who is inquisitive now."

"And why shouldn't I be? We are not stupid animals who fuck all the time and drink blood, you know."

"I know."

"Humans think that of us. Why is that so?"

I shrugged. "Maybe it's because your kind does not make the effort to communicate with humans."

"Humans shun us. They kill us on sight, given the opportunity."

"*You* kill humans." I gave her a sidelong glance. "What is going to happen to me?"

She was silent for a moment, then, "You'll probably be killed. After your blood is sucked out of you." She sighed. "I enjoyed coupling with you. There are not many males in our clan." She stumbled suddenly. "I feel tired," she said, slurring her words. The drug was beginning to take effect.

The older female, the one with the crippled wing, put an arm around the younger one to support her. "Maybe you drank too much of his blood," she said to her. Then she looked at me. "She is still inexperienced. Controlling the urge to feed before she receives a male's seed takes much willpower. The young ones have to learn to balance the hormones they release into their bodies when they feed."

"I didn't know that," I said, wondering when she would begin to feel drowsy.

Her canines gleamed in the pale light when she smiled. "The less you humans know about us, the better."

"So why tell me?"

She shrugged. "You won't tell anyone."

A lichen-covered stone wall loomed before us. On top of the wall two armed sentries crouched, their bows ready. One of my guards called out to them. Moments later rusty hinges creaked in protest, as a little used iron gate swung open to let us in, protested again when the gate closed. The courtyard lay in semi-darkness. Silhouetted against the disk of the larger moon, the walls and roofs of the castle threw irregular shadows onto the cobbled stones.

We entered the castle through a wide, tall door made out of ironwood. Most castles were ancient but well-built fortresses against intruders from the ground and the sky. Musty air, laced with the aroma of broiling meat and wood smoke, wafted into my nostrils. Yill are not just bloodsuckers. They do eat meat, as well as vegetable matter. Drinking blood to the Yill is part of their sexual need. They didn't do it to survive.

Another fact humans seemed to be ignorant of.

The Prince came walking down a wide staircase. He and his followers had landed on the roof, entered the castle through doors in the tall towers. Oil lamps hanging from the ceiling and set into the rough stonewalls bathed his imposing frame with their flickering, weak light. "Don't you know that humans are not welcomed here?" His voice sounded hollow in the large hall.

"And yet you had a human mate once," I said.

"That was a long time ago." He stared at me. I couldn't see his eyes, but I knew they were black. "How do you know this?"

I chuckled. "It is not uncommon for a Yill-prince to keep a human female as a mate or slave."

"She was never a slave!" He spoke sharply.

"Perhaps not." I looked around for the two females who had been with me, but they were gone. By now probably sleeping on a perch in one of the common rooms. My armed escort had also disappeared.

The soft whisper of a pair of wings made me look up. A slim figure landed silently in front of me.

A young female, dressed in a thin gray gown, the sign of a virgin.

Folding her wings, she came closer, looked into my eyes. "Who are you?" she asked.

"A prisoner. And who are you?" I countered.

She laughed. "For a prisoner you act much too arrogant." She trailed a finger along my throat. "I am Princess Arlia." With a sudden movement, she put one hand behind my neck, pulled my face closer to hers. She smelled of *Laven-dew*. Young virgin females of her species loved to bath in it. Her incisors were short, not fully developed. "I will taste your blood tonight," she whispered into my ear, pressing her tongue into my throat. Her nearness caused a gentle throbbing in my loins. It took all my willpower not to touch her.

"Get away from him!" the Prince thundered. "You are not ready."

She released me, stepped back. "I am old enough," she said in a defiant tone.

He looked at me. "I am warning you. Do not let her come near you. She is still untouched, untaught. She will kill you."

"Is she your daughter?" I asked, wondering if he could see the pulsing of my temples.

"No. She is my future bride."

"You have sons?"

"I had a son, once. But he was *Skorrat*, not of pure blood." His wings fluttered in an impatient gesture. Turning, he walked over to a massive wooden bench, sat down. Resting his elbows on a table in front of him, he waved his hand. "Leave me, all of you!" His finger shot out, pointed at me. "Not you. Come and sit with me."

While the others skulked away I joined him at his table.

"Have some wine," he said, pouring from a pitcher into one of two bronze cups. When I hesitated, he smiled. "Don't worry. It is not blood, and it isn't poison, either."

The wine soothed my parched throat but left a strange aftertaste.

"About your son…his mother was human. Am I correct?"

"You are. Like I said, it was a long time ago."

"Did you love her?"

Draining his cup, he slammed it down, angrily. "What is it to you?" He rose and turned away from me. "She was probably the only woman I ever loved, even though she was not of my species." He spoke softly. I could hardly make out the words. "She promised me a son."

"She did give you a son," I said, just as softly.

He whirled. His eyes glowed with sudden fire. "A *Skorrat*…and a cripple. His wings were deformed. He lacked fangs. I could not bear to look at him, and I didn't mourn when he was captured by slave traders."

"He was your son!"

"He was an embarrassment. I was glad to be rid of him."

"What about his mother? What happened to her?"

"She died of a broken heart. Or maybe I sucked her dry in a fit of rage. What does it matter? She was only a human. But now I grow tired of your company." He let out a sharp whistle. From the dark ceiling, a shadowy figure dropped down, landed on soft soles. "Take this human to a place where he can sleep."

I followed the old female up a narrow staircase, into a dark room. She lit an oil lamp with the torch she carried. "You can sleep over there." She pointed to a pile of crumpled blankets in one corner. "This used to be his favorite hiding place. Nobody comes up here. You should be safe."

I looked into her lined face. "You have kind eyes," I told her.

She smiled, reached out to touch my cheek. "Not all Yill hate humans."

I watched her descend the creaking steps, wings dragging behind her. Then I walked over to one of the walls, drew open the dusty curtain that covered the small window to let in the moonlight and some fresh air. All three moons were visible now, forming a large triangle in the star-speckled sky.

A throbbing inside my belly reminded me of the hunger I needed to still. I took off my pants and shirt, blew out the oil lamp. Naked, I stretched out on top of the blankets, inhaled their musty, damp smell. I lay there and waited.

* * * *

The creaking of the stairs alerted me to her presence. Her kind can see well in the dark. I watched her slim figure coming toward me. In the dim light of the three moons, I saw that she was as naked as I. Even though her breasts were underdeveloped, she had the body of woman, narrow waist and gently flaring hips. No pubic hair. Not until she had been with a male and received his sperm would she develop any.

"Princess Arlia," I said.

Straddling me, she laughed softly. "I see you are ready."

"I am," I said, "but are you?" I looked at her dull incisors. They'd rip open my artery if I let her.

She lowered herself, began rubbing her sex-organ across the swollen head of my stiff member. She was eager, but I knew she wasn't ready. It didn't matter, not anymore. I needed her more than she needed me. "Let me help," I said.

"I can do it."

"Not that way. You must lie on your back."

She lifted up. Lying on their backs isn't a preferred position with the Yill-females because of their wings but it's not impossible. Spreading her wings slightly, Arlia turned onto her back. I moved on top of her, opened her legs with my hands. She bent her knees, watching my penis as I put it between her puffy lips. It was getting harder to control the terrible urge to push deep into her but control myself I did.

Her fingers curled around my pole. "Do it!" she whispered, her voice urgent.

She was tight, resisted my entry. I pushed and felt a shudder shake my body when her sheath began to mold itself around my penis. The fire inside me began to boil my blood and, with a savage thrust, I slid into her soft, untouched interior. She cried out and lay still for a moment. I could feel her body quiver as she adjusted to the intruder inside her.

"It hurts," she moaned.

"It will pass." I moved slowly. She relaxed and after a while her body responded to the changes it was experiencing. Secretions began to flow from her inner walls, were absorbed into my skin and sensed by the nerve endings in my organ. Waves of pleasure shot through my system.

She gasped suddenly; her breathing became erratic, so did her movements, as she had her first orgasm. "Faster!" she cried out. "Move faster!" Her hands raked my back. When she quieted down, she let her fingers trail the long scars. They didn't hurt anymore; they had grown hard and knobby.

Gasping again, she dug her fingers into my shoulders. I pushed harder into her. Her teeth searched for my throat, but I protected it with my hand.

"Let me, please," she begged, her breathing ragged.

I didn't answer. My hunger was too strong now, and, with a groan, I pushed deep, felt the tip of my organ expand and attach itself to the entrance of her womb.

I began to feed.

Her pure virgin blood tasted sweet. It flowed from her womb through my feeding tube into me. Ecstasy flooded every fiber of my body. Finally I was whole. The blood of a female Yill-virgin was the only thing that could satisfy my terrible hunger.

She didn't know what was happening. Her movements became more sluggish, and then she lay still.

I withdrew, my hunger sated.

Looking down at her silent body, I felt a stab of regret. She had come to feed; instead it was I who had fed. She was so lovely, so innocent, yet…in her innocence, she could have killed me.

I turned when I heard the noise behind me. It was the old female. She stood at the top of the stairs. I hadn't heard her come up. "Is she dead?" she asked.

I shook my head. "No." I rose, looked at my limp organ. It was covered with red blood. Bending down, I picked up my pants and put them on. I knew she was looking at my back.

"Where did you get those scars?" she asked.

Throwing my backpack over my shoulder, I said, "I think you know, Tarima."

She nodded. "I think I do. Why did you come?"

"I believe you know that, too." I walked past her, plodded slowly down the stairs.

He was still sitting at the table, the wine cup frozen in his hand. He looked up when I approached. Staring at the needle gun in my hand, he tried to get up but sank back down when I motioned with my weapon.

"Where is the princess?" he asked, as if he'd known it was inevitable that I'd be with the Yill-female.

"She's alive. I didn't drain her completely."

"Who are you?"

"Don't you recognize me?" I turned briefly to show him my scarred back. "I had them removed. Those wings were useless, anyway."

He came to his feet. "It's not possible," he said, his voice a hoarse whisper. "How could you survive this long?"

"Hatred kept me alive. Those slave traders didn't abduct me. You sold me to them. It would have been kinder to have me killed."

"You are right. I should have killed you at birth. You are an abomination!" He launched into the air, wings spread wide, claws unsheathed.

I shot him in the chest.

He crashed to the floor, lay looking up at me, hatred and sudden fear in his black eyes.

Seeing him like this, all my hatred for him suddenly drained out of me. I shoved the gun into my pocket and walked away.

"Good bye, Father," I said, but he didn't hear me anymore.

The End

Dream on a Hot Summer Day
By
Herbert Grosshans

Ruby-red lips, they taste so sweet.
Beware of their promise to bring relief from the heat

Wiping the sweat from his brows, he stopped to take a short break, silently cursing his supervisor for giving him this job on what must be the hottest day of the year. Squinting against the bright cloudless sky, he knew there was no relief in sight.

He checked the colorless oily substance in his pail. There should be enough of the preserver in there to finish covering the concrete driveway.

Shit! He could sure use a couple of cold beers right now.

Looking back at the house, he was surprised to see two girls sitting on the steps. They were watching him. One of them smiled when she saw him looking, then raised a glass filled with dark red liquid. Then she leaned over to the other girl, whispering something. Both of them laughed, clicked their glasses together and emptied them.

The one who had smiled at him rose to her feet and walked toward him. She was tall, slim, almost thin, like one of those fashion models you saw on TV. Her black hair fell past her shoulders in a thick curly mass.

He stared at the white roundness of her breasts, the stiff nipples poking through the thin material of her small halter-top. His gaze dropped down to her flat belly, took in the red stone nestled inside her navel. She had smooth, round hips, slim and curvy. Her bikini was tiny enough to nearly expose her pussy.

"Hi," she smiled. "I am Rona." She came closer, put her hand on his biceps, stroked it. "Nice," she murmured. "You must be working out."

"A little." He grinned foolishly. In his loins, he felt a gentle flutter.

"Kinda hot, isn't it?" she purred. Her finger trailed across his bare chest. "How about making this day a real scorcher by fucking a couple of hot and horny girls?"

"Which girls?" he blurted out, dumbfounded. She laughed, hooked a finger into his belt and pulled on it. "Me and my sister Amanda, who else?"

He looked into her eyes. They glowed with a strange, violet fire. Her teeth gleamed behind parted black full lips. They were white and even, except for her two incisors, which seemed longer and thinner than average.

"What's the matter?" she whispered. "Cat got your tongue? Don't tell me you don't want to. I saw you looking."

He inhaled deeply. Her breath was sweet, smelled of liquor and a hint of something he couldn't identify.

Intoxicated by her nearness, he put his hand behind her head and pulled her close. When his lips crushed against hers, she opened her mouth, sucked his tongue into her. Inside his pants, his penis rose, pressed against the denim and into her belly.

She laughed into his mouth, grinding her lower body against him. Then she pushed him away.

"Not here," she said with a husky voice. "Come."

She took his hand, pulled him toward the house. Her sister Amanda stood in the doorway, held open the door. As he stepped past her, he noticed that she didn't wear a halter. Her naked breasts stood like two solid globes with long, thick nipples.

Rona pulled him into a room. He saw a wide bed, unmade. Amanda knelt in front of him, opened his belt with deft fingers. Then she tugged on his pants and rolled them down to his ankles. Closing her mouth on his stiff penis, she flicked her tongue like a soft feather over his swollen glans. He groaned, ready to explode inside her mouth, but she pulled away, freeing his throbbing organ.

After taking off her bikini, she rose up in front of him, kissed him hungrily, her soft breasts flattening against his chest. He put his hands on her buttocks. Her arms went around his neck; she raised her legs, wrapped them around his waist. His penis felt like a piece of rock against her soft belly. She moved a little higher, and then he felt her tight pussy swallow his penis.

She rocked back and forth against him, her hot vagina working his stiff organ like a piston running amok. Getting tired, he stumbled toward the bed. As he toppled on top of her, she threw her legs wide open. Taking control, he entered her fully with powerful thrusts, making her squirm and cry out. She whimpered, threw her head from side to side as she doused his penis with her hot discharge.

Strong hands pulled him off the girl.

"My turn, lover," Rona whispered into his ear. She pushed him onto his back. Completely naked now, she straddled him. He watched his hard penis disappear inside her pussy. Her mons was thick and swollen, smooth, without a trace of pubic hair.

Snapping her hips back and forth, she let her inner muscles ripple the length of his engorged penis.

Her violet eyes stared into his through the veil of her long dark hair, which had fallen across her face. "Tell me when you are ready to come," she said with a breathless voice.

"Now!" he called out, unable to hold back any longer.

As he lunged up to empty himself into her, she stretched out on top of him. His hands clamped over her buttocks, his fingers dug into their firm softness. Waves of pleasure swept through his body. There seemed to be no end to the liquid pumping out of him.

The girl above him hissed softly into his ear, her vagina sucking greedily on his penis.

Her mouth searched his throat. He was barely aware of the gentle prick. A momentary dizziness then pleasure beyond belief.

When Rona left him, he felt betrayed, unsatisfied. Staring at the stiff pole strutting between his legs, he saw red streaks running down its length.

"Don't tell me you were a fucking virgin?" he croaked. His throat felt dry and gritty.

Rona's sister climbed on top of him, her smooth vagina hovering inches above the head of his penis. She laughed, displaying needle thin fangs. "Virgins? Us? What gives you that idea?"

"The blood, look at the blood!"

She swallowed his penis slowly into her. He watched it disappear inside her rippling belly. Then he felt a gentle sucking. Her large breasts hardly moved as her hips gyrated in his lap. Her violet eyes were hidden behind her lashes. A sighing hiss escaped from her luscious lips. From her black lips escaped a hissing sigh.

"The blood," she whispered, "ah, yes, the blood."

He moaned as he felt another climax approaching, and, with a cry, he erupted inside her tight channel. Her lips touched his throat. A wave of nausea washed through him, and he was aware of a rushing sound inside his head, but the exquisite pleasure he experienced drowned everything.

Blackness engulfed him like a cloak, took him away.

* * * *

He squinted up into the bright sky. There wasn't a cloud to be seen. It was just too damn hot to work.

Suddenly feeling dizzy and weak, he looked over at the two sniggering girls sitting on the steps. He didn't remember seeing them before. They held glasses filled with red liquid.

Shit! He could sure use a cold beer right now.

One of the girls glanced in his direction, saw him looking. She smiled, winked, and raised her glass.

He wiped his sweaty brow, touched a sore spot on his neck. When he looked at his finger, he noticed a drop of blood. Must have scratched himself.

This damn heat was getting to him, even his penis hurt.

Maybe he could ask those girls for something to drink, and maybe a *Band-Aid* for his neck.

They looked vaguely familiar, but he couldn't remember where he had seen them before.

Le-itha
By
Herbert Grosshans

Lovely and fair a maiden she be
on a planet full of mystery

Part One
Chapter One

The giant body of the Mother ship filled the rear view screen of the shuttlecraft as they pulled away from each other. The Mother ship sped toward the next star system as the shuttlecraft entered the atmosphere of the planet below.

They would rendezvous in ten Standard Days, more than enough time to pick up Professor Bruce Melton and his assistant Dr. Frederick.

The two men and the woman in the shuttle gave the screen one last look and turned their attention toward the screen in the front.

"I guess the professor will be happy to see Humans again, after spending four years on this planet." Dale Sanders, the pilot, looked at the woman beside him and smiled. "And he'll be even happier to see you, Dr. Laverne."

Dr. Eleanore Laverne blushed slightly. "I sincerely hope so," she said. "After all, we've been assigned to get married as soon as we get back to Earth."

Sanders studied her from the side.

She wasn't bad looking, he decided, a little too skinny for his tastes. It was hard to know what she looked like underneath her baggy pants and oversized blouse. He wasn't particularly fond of women who wore their hair as short as a man. The large horn- rimmed glasses didn't complement her narrow face, either. He knew she didn't really need them; he'd seen her without glasses on the ship, but it was the latest fashion on Earth. She had a nice nose and full lips, lost on her because she never seemed to smile.

Her sharp tongue and bitchy attitude didn't help, either.

On her sleeve, she wore the emblem of the Free Women of the World. He pitied her future husband. She'd try to dominate him. Her mind had been brainwashed by the doctrines of the Sisterhood with the ideas that women were superior to men.

But then again, Professor Melton wasn't an Adonis, either.

From the pictures he'd seen at the briefing, he knew that Melton was a rather tall, lanky looking guy. Apparently an eccentric and not very people-friendly. He'd rather study his bugs and viruses than talk to another Human. These two should make a real lovely couple. The computer had almost certainly picked them as a perfect match. Melton probably needed a woman like her.

"After spending four dry years with only another man for company, he'll most likely marry you the moment you set foot on the planet," the second man of the team said jokingly. He laughed when he saw the deep color on the woman's face.

"Please, Mr. Gibson," she said indignantly. "There is no need for your offbeat humor."

"I'm sorry, Dr. Laverne," Chuck Gibson said, an apologetic smile on his dark face. "I didn't mean to be rude." He heaved his bulky body out of the chair and walked over to the computer console. "I believe it's time to find out a little more about the planet we're visiting."

"I don't think the computer knows much more than what we were told at the briefings," Sanders said.

"Maybe you can fill me in," Eleanore said. "I've never had time to come to any of those briefings. I had other things to finish before I came on this silly trip."

"Silly trip?" Gibson looked at her with surprise. "This is your fiancé we're picking up. I thought you'd be excited to come along."

"I suppose I should be, and I am looking forward to seeing Bruce, Professor Melton, again, but we've been apart for so long, a few extra weeks wouldn't have mattered."

"Then why did you come?"

Eleanore chuckled humorlessly. "The Department of Marriage Counseling decided it would be in my best interest to go. Anyway, it doesn't matter now. Here I am. So let me see what I'm facing."

"Well," Sanders said, after silently shaking his head, "the official name for this planet is Zetta Genetty Seven." He smiled. "Very original to give the seventh planet of Zetta Genetty…a name like that, don't you think so?"

She shrugged impatiently. "What do I care, just carry on, please."

"Okay. The planet is almost a twin to Earth, in size, that is. The air is breathable. Oxygen content is slightly higher than standard, but nothing in the air that would harm us. Most of the surface is covered by water. There is only one large continent the size of Africa as well as a few scattered islands. That's about all we know."

"What about native life forms?"

"Maybe the computer can answer that." Gibson touched the screen. "Computer, give us a picture of known inhabitants on planet Zetta Genetty Seven."

The screen lit up, and a few seconds later a picture began to form. It displayed an apelike creature, covered with long shaggy hair. The face appeared somewhat blurred. Two small, deep-set eyes peered at them from below a prominent ridge. Instead of a nose it showed two narrow slits above a wide, lipless mouth. The top of the head was shaped like a cone, pointy and bald.

Sanders pursed his lips in a silent whistle. "Ugly," he said, "surely no prizewinner in a beauty contest."

Eleanore, who let out a small sound of surprise when she saw the picture, gave him a reprimanding look. "Mr. Sanders," she said loudly. "You should know better than to say a thing like that. How can you judge an alien being by Earth standards? In its own right this, what you call ugly creature, is probably quite beautiful."

"If you're an ape," Gibson said, chuckling.

Eleanore sighed and lifted her narrow shoulders. "Ah, you two are impossible. I hope Bruce hasn't acquired this 'manly' sense of humor while he was away. Four years can change a man."

Gibson laughed, and then he said, "Computer, give us verbal information on image."

"Specify." The voice sounded pleasant and female.

"Is this the dominant life form?"

"There is not enough information available to answer the question correctly."

"Computer, why is the picture so blurry?"

"This image was composed from descriptions by members of the scout ship. No details are available. The pictures taken by the ship's cameras turned out to be faulty."

"Hmm." Gibson pulled on his ear, a habit he had when deep in thought. "That's interesting." He looked at Eleanore. "You heard it yourself. Not much to go on, but I guess we'll learn more from Professor Melton. He should have found out something in four years."

* * * *

They were flying blind.

As they came closer to the planet's surface, the ship's screen suddenly went dead. Sanders checked the gauges. Everything seemed to be working perfectly. Even though they couldn't see where they were going, the navigation system didn't appear to be affected. The computer had the co-ordinates, and there should be no problem, but he would have felt better if he were able to follow their course on the screen.

"What happened?" Eleanore asked.

Gibson kept busy going over the controls. He shook his head. "I don't know. I can't find anything wrong with the connections. There seems to be a small power drain I can't identify. The screens should be working." He looked at Sanders. "Find anything, Dale?"

Sanders shook his head. "All systems check out."

"Are we in trouble?" Eleanore spoke calmly, but he detected the tension in her voice.

"Not as far as I can determine. We should be able to get to our destination without a hitch." He looked at her pale face. "Don't worry, we'll get you down in one piece."

"Where are we going, anyway?"

"The landing site is high up in the mountains. According to our information, there is a large flat plateau, a natural place to land and set up a base camp."

"I still wish we could have visual confirmation to see what it looks like below us. I hate flying blind," Gibson said, still studying his dials and the readings on an electronic device he had hooked up to the computer console. "It seems there is some interference that prevents the screens from displaying anything but static."

"What do you think causes this interference?" Eleanore asked. "Is it a natural phenomena, or could it be...?" She left the sentence unfinished, but Sanders knew what she hinted at.

Smiling faintly, he said, "I don't believe it is caused by intelligent beings, Dr. Laverne, if that's what you mean. The scout ship found no evidence of any civilization on the planet. It must be some kind of radiation either from the sun or from the planet itself." He looked at Gibson. "Have you tried to raise the professor on the radio?"

Gibson shook his head. "I've tried twice, but so far no luck. I don't even get interference. The radio is dead. Completely dead. Yet, everything seems to be in perfect order. I can't understand it."

A shudder ran through the shuttle then everything was quiet.

"We have touched down at the designated landing site," the computer's pleasant voice informed them. "You may safely step out now."

The airlock opened to let in the air of the alien planet.

Chapter Two

The air smelled fresh and clean. Sanders checked one of the gauges strapped to his left arm and noticed that it was twenty-six degrees Celsius.

He was the first to step onto the alien soil. The ground he stood on looked bare. He bent down to examine the yellow sand-like substance. It was dry and coarse and only a couple of inches thick. When he scratched the surface, he discovered hard rock underneath the thin layer.

He didn't see any vegetation in the immediate area, except for some low growing, flaming red shrubs.

The shuttle had landed beside another, smaller craft, not meant for traveling in space.

The hatch of the little vehicle stood open.

Sanders looked at Gibson, who scanned their surroundings, obviously wary and cautious. "It looks abandoned," he murmured, low enough so Eleanore couldn't hear him. She had stepped away from them to study the red shrubs.

The two men walked slowly toward the other craft. Gibson climbed inside. After another look at Eleanore, Sanders followed him.

"No sign of anyone having been inside this vehicle for quite some time," Gibson said. "See the dust? It looks undisturbed. Not even an animal was curious enough to check out things in here."

"I wonder what happened to Professor Melton and Dr. Frederick?" Sanders mused. "Why would they abandon their only means of traveling?"

"I think I can probably answer that," Gibson said. "If we check out the power unit, we'll most likely find it drained." He bent over the controls and nodded. "Yep, it's dead all right. In fact, everything is dead. Been like that for a long time." He looked past Sanders at the blazing sun in the sky and squinted against the glare. "There is some kind of radiation here which renders certain electronic equipment useless. Let's hope our ship is not affected. I'd hate to be a prisoner of this dust ball."

Sanders climbed out of the little vehicle. He waited until his bulky partner joined him outside. "You don't think the whole planet is like this, do you?" he asked.

Gibson shrugged, scanning the area with his binoculars. "We're high in the mountains." He pointed toward a ridge some distance away. "I suggest we take a look in that direction. The land seems to take a dip past that point. There is no sense searching anywhere else. They wouldn't have climbed higher into the mountains. If they're anywhere to be found, it will be further down."

Eleanore came walking toward them, a frown on her narrow face. Sanders could see drops of perspiration on her pale skin. "I was under the impression they'd be living close to the landing site, but where are they? I don't see any shelter or any signs of anyone living here."

"This is not a very hospitable location, Dr. Laverne. They probably found a better place to live." Sanders tried to sound confident, but he began to have doubts they'd find the men alive. There should have been some indication of their presence.

"What are you waiting for?" the woman said. "Let's start looking."

"Mr. Gibson and I were just discussing the very same thing," Sanders said. "We'll take a walk that way." He pointed. "They might be just beyond that ridge."

"Walking?" Eleanore exclaimed and stared at him. "Mr. Sanders, I did not cross two hundred and thirty-four light-years of empty space to take a walk in the burning desert of an alien planet, especially not when I have all the comforts of the shuttle at my disposal!"

Sanders looked at Gibson.

The black man shuffled uneasily. "I agree with Dr. Laverne," he said. "That's quite a distance, and I've never taken any fancy to long walks myself." He wiped the sweat from his face and shrugged. "Why not take the shuttle? It is too damn hot out here anyway."

Shaking his head, Sanders said, "I don't think it's a good idea. How far do you think we'll get without screens? The computer can take us only one way, and that is straight up."

"I'm sure you could program the computer…" Eleanore shrugged helplessly.

"I'm afraid not." He almost glared at the woman, annoyed by her behavior. She should never have come; he could see complications ahead already. Women like her just didn't belong on unexplored planets. "If you want to find your fiancé, like it or not, you'll walk, Dr. Laverne."

He turned, and, without a backward glance, he began walking.

* * * *

The sun was a blazing ball of fire in the azure sky, and before long they were drenched to their skins.

"I wonder why it is so hot?" Gibson puffed. "We must be quite high up, and yet…this heat is almost unbearable."

"I guess, the fact that this plateau is surrounded by mountains, which keep away the cool winds, makes it a natural oven. The heat gets trapped in here but doesn't get moved around. It just sits there." Sanders grinned. "At least that's my theory."

"I don't care about your theories, Mr. Sanders," Dr. Laverne snapped. "I just want to get out of this *oven*, as you so brilliantly call this hell."

Her thin blouse, soaked with perspiration, which nearly made it transparent, molded itself around her breasts. Sanders noticed their nice shape and size, surprised to find she didn't wear a bra.

Aware of his eyes, she blushed. "You should be ashamed, staring at me like that. I'm not that kind of a woman."

"What kind of a woman would that be, Dr. Laverne?" Sanders laughed. "I can't help but notice that you actually possess quite a nice body underneath those loose clothes you're wearing. How can I help but see that? After all, I'm a man."

"I am engaged, about to be married, Mr. Sanders. What would my fiancé say if he heard this kind of talk? You'd better keep your tongue in check!" She stomped on ahead, fuming.

Gibson gave Sanders a reproachful look. "You shouldn't do that to her, Dale. She's got enough problems, without you poking fun at her."

"Ah, she's just a dried-up old prune," Sanders said, still laughing.

Gibson grinned. "Not so old and not so dried up, either, as you've noticed yourself. It's just the way she dresses and acts."

"Yeah, yeah." Sanders looked after the woman and started walking again. "Let's keep moving."

The fat man wheezed after him. "If we don't get out of this heat soon, we all will be a bunch of dried-up prunes."

The woman reached the crest of the ridge before they did. She stood, uttering a sound of surprise. When the men caught up with her, they too gasped loudly.

Below them stretched a huge valley, covered with lush green grass. A wide river wound itself through the middle of it, to spill into a large lake. Clumps of trees and high shrubs grew everywhere like patches of hair on a giant's face. On the other side of the lake stretched a huge, dense forest.

"It is beautiful," Eleanore exclaimed. "I've never dreamed we'd find anything like this."

"I don't see any signs of habitation," Sanders said, looking through his field glasses. He turned to the others. "Well, what do you say? Do you want to go on, or do you want to go back to the ship and rest?"

Gibson shrugged. "No sense in going back now. We'll have to come this way again, and it won't be any easier the next time. It will be cooler in the shade of those trees. I say let's get down there. We can rest then."

Eleanore nodded in agreement. "Makes sense to me."

The descent proved fairly easy, and within twenty minutes they were walking through high grass. The further they walked into the valley, the cooler it seemed to get, and soon they could feel a slight breeze blowing from the lake.

They reached the first grove of trees and stopped for a welcome rest. Sanders noted that the grove was actually a small forest. He checked out the area, his laser drawn, while his companions sat beneath the shelter of a tall, wide-spreading tree.

"Sit down, Dale, and relax." The fat man leaned against the thick tree trunk, panting, sweat glistening like an oily film on his black skin. "What are you looking for, anyway?"

"I don't like surprises," Sanders answered. "Up there, we had a good view of our surroundings, but down here it's a different story. Anything can hide in this high tall grass. We don't know much about this planet, and we have to be careful." He squatted down beside them, satisfied for the moment. "I haven't seen anything so far that should cause us concern, but I'd advise both of you to keep your eyes and ears open."

Eleanore stiffened beside him and looked at him, sudden fear in her eyes. "Do you expect to find any dangerous animals? It looked so peaceful from up above." She hesitated. "Maybe we should go back after all."

"Don't worry, Dr. Laverne," Sanders said with a smile, patting his gun. "This will stop anything."

A sudden noise behind them made them turn to stare into the semi-darkness of the forest. They saw movement among the trees, and then a small herd of weird-looking creatures appeared and bounded away slowly. They stopped a short distance away and stood there, staring at the intruders.

The two men jumped up and drew their guns.

"I think they're harmless," Gibson said. "They're probably the equivalent of a deer around here."

The only resemblance to a deer might have been the head, and that just barely. A long horn sticking out of a flat forehead made them look more like unicorns, but that's where the resemblance ended. The animals had long necks, almost as long as that of a small giraffe, but the strangest sight was the six long spidery legs. Yellow, shaggy hair covered their elongated bodies. The hair hung down to the ground, like thick strands of cooked spaghetti.

The presence of the Earth people didn't seem to disturb them much because after a while they ignored the three and started grazing. Once in a while, one would lift its head and look around.

"They don't seem very shy," Sanders remarked. "What do you think, Dr. Laverne? You're the biologist. Would you say they've seen Humans before?"

Eleanore shook her head. "It's hard to say. Their behavior suggests that they are familiar with the human shape. They seem wary but not scared." She gave Sanders a long look. "Are you suggesting Bruce and Dr. Frederick might be close by?"

"Could be, but remember the humanoids who are supposed to live on this planet. This may mean nothing. I'm just guessing."

"If they're anywhere around here, they'll be close to the water," Gibson said. "I'd say somewhere near the river, but not too far upstream."

Chapter Three

The three travelers were almost ready to move on when the grazing animals suddenly became restless. They lifted their heads and looked toward the mountains.

A dark large shape came silently sliding through the high grass. It came closer fast and was almost upon them when the animals bounded away. With a terrifying roar, it pounced on one of the stragglers, felling it with one mighty blow of its front paw. Then it started tearing its victim apart, burying its gleaming dagger-like teeth into the carcass.

The Humans stood watching the scene for a moment, petrified by the speed everything happened.

"Wow!" Gibson exclaimed, awed. "What a ferocious looking beast!"

"Looks like a cross between a crocodile, a crab and a cat," Sanders observed.

"And a pinch of snake thrown in for good measurement," Gibson added.

"How can you stand here making jokes?" Eleanore was almost hysterical. "It might decide to attack us at any moment. Did you see how fast it moved?"

Sanders laughed. "I told you not to worry." He pulled out his laser. "This little baby will take care of even that, if necessary."

The animal seemed to have noticed them now. It lifted its grotesque head and stared at the Humans out of large, cold eyes. A quiver ran through the long, sinewy body and, snarling, it slowly advanced toward the three watchers.

Sanders lifted his gun and, aiming carefully, he pulled the trigger.

Nothing happened.

"Damn it!" he swore. "I should have guessed. Something drained the power pack. The laser won't work."

The creature reared up on its powerful hind-legs, its other four legs clawing the air. Roaring, it attacked Sanders, who stood closest to it.

Sanders had dropped his laser and pulled out his knife. He threw himself to the ground, drawing the tempered steel along the animal's belly as it sprang over him. He had fought wild animals before on other planets and knew that most of them were vulnerable under their bellies.

This one wasn't.

The blade only cut the outer layer of skin but didn't penetrate far when it encountered a protective shell of hard bone underneath.

When the animal attacked Sanders, Gibson grabbed a fallen branch and moved closer to help his companion.

"Get behind the tree!" he shouted at Eleanore, "or better yet…climb into the tree."

She just stood there, screaming.

The creature missed Sanders, but as it hit the ground, its long tail whipped around and the hooked tip flipped across Sander's left arm, inflicting a shallow flesh wound. Roaring angrily, it attacked Gibson, who had stepped into its path. The fat man swung his club and smashed it into the animal's open jaws, breaking both its long fangs.

The animal screamed furiously, backing off slightly, crouching low, its long tail beating the ground.

Gibson brought the club down again, hitting the creature on the head and driving it backward.

Sanders watched in dismay, still holding his useless knife. As he studied the angry animal, he heard a whooshing sound, and then something lodged itself in the beast's gaping jaws.

A gush of bright yellow fluid erupted from its long snout and, kicking furiously, the animal rolled on the ground, emitting choking noises.

"That's the only way to kill an *Elper*. An arrow in its throat, the only soft spot on the body," said voice from behind Sanders.

Sanders and Gibson whirled around and stared at the speaker.

A weird-looking creature, about the size of a horse, stood underneath the trees. Its long neck ended in a narrow head with a wicked-looking beak. A pair of stubby wings grew from its shoulders, wings too short and small to be of any use except for decoration. The four legs looked skinny, like the legs of a bird, but they ended in long toes tipped with sharp claws.

On its back sat a man.

He sat on the animal as if he were a part of it. Bulging muscles covered his body and, even sitting, he looked tall. Blond hair fell down to his wide shoulders, and his long beard looked bushy and wild.

He held a longbow in his powerful arms, and they could see the feathered ends of arrows sticking out of a quiver behind his back.

Sanders realized that the man had spoken in Terran. “Who are you?” he asked, surprised.

The man laughed merrily and slid off the animal. “Are you from Earth?” he asked.

Eleanore, who had been silent till now, gasped loudly and put her hands to her mouth. “The voice,” she said. “But…but that can’t be!”

The man turned to look at her. “Eleanor,” he cried out, and then he began walking toward her.

She backed off, staring at him, not believing. “Bruce?” she asked in a small voice. “Is that you?”

“Yes,” the big man boomed. “It’s me. Don’t you recognize me?”

“You look so…different,” she said.

“Oh, I’m sorry. It’s the beard.” He laughed, lifting his wide shoulders in an apologizing gesture. “I don’t have a razor to shave it off, so I just let it grow. Just like my hair.”

“No, no.” The woman looked at him, her eyes large behind the rimmed glasses. “It’s not just you beard. It’s your whole appearance. You’re so…so big and…strong looking. And the way you’re dressed.” She looked disapproving at the loincloth around his hips. “You look like a savage! What happened to you?”

“Yes, Professor Melton,” Sanders injected. “Tell us what happened. How is it you’re riding a strange huge bird, dressed in this…this outfit? You carry a bow as a weapon. Where have you been spending your time, and where is Dr. Frederick?”

Melton put up a hand. “Hold it now. One question at a time. To answer your last question first, Dr. Frederick is dead.”

“How? When?”

“He died right in the beginning.” Melton shrugged. “How? It was a stupid accident, which never should have happened. I was lucky, I survived.” He noticed Sander’s bleeding arm. “You’re hurt.”

Sanders shrugged it off. “Just a scratch. I hardly notice it. That monster got me with its tail. I’ll live.”

“Not if you don’t treat it soon. That tail tip is poisoned.”

Melton walked over to the dead beast, pulled out a knife and cut out a piece of its tongue. He came back, offered it to Sanders. “Here, suck on this. The blood of the *Elper* is the only thing that acts as an antidote to the poison.”

Sanders looked at the black, bloody piece of meat, with a nauseous feeling in his stomach. “I can’t eat that.”

"I didn't tell you to eat it. I said suck on it."

"Same thing," Sanders answered, but he took the bloody mess from Melton's hand. "You're sure about this?"

The big man smiled grimly. "I'm deadly serious, my friend. If you want to live, you do as I say. It's up to you."

With a disgusted snort, Sanders started sucking the dripping yellow blood. Swallowing it proved difficult, his throat almost refused to open up, but he managed.

Melton cut off another piece and rubbed it into the wound. Sanders winced but held still. "Strange way of treating a wound," he murmured between clenched teeth.

"But very effective." Melton disposed of the piece in his hand. "I have done many strange things since my arrival on this planet. Strange to a civilized man." He turned to the woman. "You will find I am not the same man I was four years ago, Eleanore. A lot has happened since then, but I will tell you more about it later. First we must get to my homestead."

Chapter Four

The Professor's homestead was, as Sanders had deducted correctly, close to the river but quite far away from the lake. The river was only about fifteen meters wide at that point, and Melton had built a narrow floating bridge across it.

The homestead consisted of a log house and a couple of smaller sheds. Inside the log house were two rooms, one large and one small, the smaller one being the bedroom. A fireplace built from fieldstones took care of the cool nights and the cold winter months.

"I doesn't get very cold in winter, but this fireplace takes out the dampness." Melton laughed. "At first, it smoked quite a bit, but I finally fixed that, through trial and error. My cooking I do outside." He laughed again. "You know, I'm quite proud of myself. Built all of this alone, without plans or permits. Me, a guy with two left hands. Have you ever seen anything like it back on Earth?"

"Not on civilized Earth," Gibson said, "but I've seen it on the frontier worlds. Not quite as primitive, though. At least they had a bit of civilization. You have nothing, No electricity, no solar cells, no infrared ovens…nothing. How did you survive?"

"And to think you've lived like this for four years," Sanders said, looking around the cabin. "How could you stand it?"

"It wasn't so bad, at least not the last three years, but the beginning was rough, I have to admit that."

Melton sucked on his pipe, and his gaze followed the blue smoke. Sanders smelled the peculiar aroma in the air. "Dried leafs," Melton explained. "It took me a while to find a suitable plant, almost poisoned myself once. But I finally managed to find a good substitute for tobacco." He pointed to a little clay jar filled with reddish leaves. "You want to try some? There are a couple of extra pipes on the shelf."

Sanders grinned. "Thanks, I don't smoke."

"Ah," Melton nodded. "I forgot. Space pilots aren't allowed to smoke. How about a drink then? I've got some good stuff."

He rose, opened a trapdoor in the trampled ground and took out a couple of large urns. "My fridge," he said, grinning. "Keeps it cool."

He filled three cups. "Here, try it."

Sanders took his cup and sipped. "Hmm, not bad. Tastes like

beer. What is it?"

Melton laughed. "I guess my taste buds are still working. A form of ale. I made it out of roots and some other ingredients." He looked at Gibson. "Try my wine and tell me what you think."

Eleanore, who had taken hold of a cup, sat it down hard on the wooden table. "Bruce," she said, disapproval evident in her voice. "You surely have changed. You never drank alcoholic beverages before. And now you even offer it to me. I don't know what to think and say."

Melton smiled gently. "At least you haven't changed, Eleanor. You're still the same, but come on, don't be a prude. One drink won't hurt you. Tell me what you think of my wine. I value your opinion."

When she still declined, he added, "At least, let's have a welcome drink together."

"Well, all right." She sipped the drink he offered her.

"A toast to a happy reunion" Gibson drained his cup.

"Not bad, this wine," Eleanore admitted reluctantly.

"Oh, you had the ale," Melton said, chuckling.

"Yeah, this stuff isn't bad," Sanders said. "I'm amazed how you managed to adapt to a bad situation."

"Do you have anything else to drink, Bruce?" Eleanore asked.

"Yes, I do." He got another urn from his underground fridge and poured something into a cup.

Eleanor accepted it and looked at it. "It's white. Looks like milk."

"It is milk. Goat's milk."

"You mean you drink milk from animals?" Eleanore looked visibly upset. "But that's organic. Unclean."

"Don't worry, you won't die," Melton said softly. "I've been drinking it for over two years, and I'm still around."

"You seem to have done extremely well for a man who has never in his life been exposed to conditions you've encountered on this planet." Sanders sat on one of the wooden chairs, nursing his drink and thoughtfully studying the big man. "Have you had contact with native life forms, aside from the animals? Is there any intelligent life on the planet? We've seen pictures of ape-like beings."

"The Cocos," Melton nodded. "They live in the forest. I've been in contact with them, but I still don't know much about them. They are very shy and quite low on the evolutionary scale. I don't believe that there are any highly intelligent natives on Zetta Genetty Seven because I should have seen some evidence in four years. Then again, this is a huge continent, and I've been quite limited without transportation."

"What about minerals, ores and oil?"

Melton leaned back into his chair. "To be truthful, I haven't really found out much. Without my instrument, my studies were quite limited. Technically I was reduced to the level of a Neanderthal on Earth. My field, as you probably know, is biology. Dr. Frederick's was mineralogy. What I found out is mostly through trial and error, and from…" he hesitated, then said, "from the Cocos, in a way."

"The Cocos?"

Melton got out of his chair and closed the shutters of the windows. "It will be getting colder soon and a little safer." He put some logs into the fireplace and added small pieces of dried vegetation. Then he lit a dry branch with the flame from an oil lamp, and soon the fire gave off warmth and light.

"That's another thing I had to get used to, the dark evenings," Melton said. "After having light at my fingertips all of my life and taking it for granted, I suddenly had to live without it."

"I notice you have candles and oil lamps," Sanders remarked.

Melton laughed. "Yes, now I'm all right, but it took time to find the right materials. I needed wicker, animal fat, fire. It may sound unbelievable, but we had no means of lighting a fire."

"Surely you had matches in your survival gear, especially with you being a smoker, you should have had a lighter."

"I never smoked a pipe before, and as you may know, the cigarettes light themselves as soon as you suck on them. We had no lighter. There was no need for it. If you need fire, there are always the lasers. Nobody foresaw that the lasers wouldn't work here. We found no matches in our survival gear, a careless neglect, I agree. I used the lenses of my glasses to concentrate the rays of the sun. That part was fairly easy, but keeping a fire going didn't prove to be as easy as it may sound. The first rain also killed my first fire."

"Speaking of your eyeglasses," Sanders observed, "I notice you don't wear them."

"I don't need them anymore." Melton chuckled. "You know, the Cocos may seem primitive in many ways, but they do have certain primeval knowledge that is beyond us. They cured my eyes with herbs, and in a very short time, I might add."

"That beast you've got outside, that bird-thing, how did you ever tame it?" Gibson asked.

“The *Toparque* looks meaner than it really is, and it is not at all related to a bird. The stubs that look like wings are actually stiff folds of skin. It is a very gently creature and quite intelligent, a gift from the Cocos. They gave it to me when it was very small. It is the only one of its kind up here on this mountain plateau.”

Melton lifted his head and seemed to listen.

Sanders heard it now. A sound outside.

Footsteps.

“Something is out there,” Eleanore whispered.

“Not something.” Melton smiled. “Someone.”

They looked at him, puzzled. “Someone?” Sanders repeated. “I thought Dr. Frederick was dead.”

“He is. This is someone else.” He got up and walked to the door, opened it.

They all stared at the figure standing in the doorway, illuminated by the last rays of the setting sun.

“Meet my…wife, Le-itha.”

“Your wife?” Eleanore’s voice sounded shrill in the sudden silence. “Bruce, I don’t understand this. Who is this woman, anyway? We were selected by the Council of Family Planning to be married. You can’t go against the will of the Council and just marry anybody!”

“I’m sorry, Eleanor, truly I am. I should have told you sooner, but the opportunity never came up.” Melton put his arm around the new woman’s shoulders. He looked at Eleanor. “Living on this planet for four years has changed me. Conditions are not the same anymore. Things wouldn’t have worked out for us.”

Sanders stared at the woman Melton introduced as his wife. She seemed quite young. Her lithe, suntanned body was covered with only a small loincloth, made from animal skin, just like the one Melton wore. Her breasts were bare, half covered with strands from her long, almost white hair.

Her extreme beauty could not be denied.

The gaze of her large, blue eyes was on Eleanor, who stood, stiff with shock. She dropped her eyes and smiled. “Forgive me for staring, but you wear strange clothes.” Her voice sounded soft and melodic.

“Strange clothes?” Eleanore said, piqued. “Look who’s talking! At least I don’t expose myself to be ogled by every man who wants to see me naked.” She stared at Melton. “You always were so decent, Bruce. How can you allow her to walk around like this? But then again, I'm not surprised…look at yourself!"

"Please, please." Sanders put up his hands. "This is ridiculous. I think there are very important topics here to discuss. Never mind having a lover's quarrel. For instance, a question pops immediately into my mind. Who is this woman you claim to be your wife, Professor Melton? We have no reports of a woman being on your team."

"She wasn't on the ship with us," Melton said, closing the door. He made himself comfortable on a fur in front of the fireplace. Le-itha joined him and snuggled against him.

"I guess it's time for some explanations…

Part Two
Chapter Five

Four years earlier

The two men sat shivering under the primitive shelter among the trees, staring into the blackness of the night. Heavy clouds had moved in during the afternoon and it looked like rain. The hooting calls of night creatures came from the forest on the other side of the river.

"Maybe we should have stayed in the hopper, Professor Melton. It was just as cold there, but at least we had the protection of metal walls around us." The speaker, a short skinny man, pulled his blanket closer around his thin shoulders. "If only our lasers would work, I'd feel a lot safer."

"So would I, Dr. Frederick," the other man said. He was tall and bony, still quite young. He had a lot of respect for Dr. Frederick, who was twenty years his senior, but he was Dr. Frederick's superior on this mission. He had made the decision to move into the valley, away from their now useless ship.

"We couldn't stay in the hopper. It would have served no purpose. All the power cells are dead, and we have a better chance of survival down here by the water. We have enough concentrates to keep us alive for a long time, but we need water. Up there on the plateau, we wouldn't last long in that heat during the day."

"You're right." Dr. Frederick sighed. "You know, with all our knowledge, our scientific discoveries, our huge, faster-than-light spaceships, the sophisticated computers, our mighty weapons that can destroy whole worlds, we don't realize how dependent we are on all these things. Without them, we are nothing."

"I agree completely," Melton said, shivering in his thin blanket.

"Look at us now," Dr. Frederick continued his tirade. "Up there in the desert we have a ship that under ordinary circumstances would supply us with all the requirements we need. Water, food, protection, warmth. All the comforts in the world. And yet...because of some unknown force nobody knew about nothing works. Here we are huddling like our primitive ancestors thousands of years ago, afraid of the dark. Who knows what might lurk out there!"

"It could be worse," Melton said. "At least we have plenty of good, fresh air. The water is drinkable, and the temperature is pleasant enough." He smiled. "Except for the nights. Tomorrow we'll have to start building a better place. After all...we'll be here for four years. If you ask me, we are still lucky."

* * * *

Three months passed.

They found a small saw and an axe among the equipment of the vehicle and used them to cut down trees to built a house. It was nothing elaborate, four walls and a roof, covered with dry grass, but it gave them a sense of safety.

Cutting the trees had been hard work, neither of the men used to manual labor. The job would have been so easy, if only the power packs had worked. But all the power packs, which were guaranteed to last for five years, were empty.

The original plan had been to use the hopper as their base. It was large enough for two men to live in for a while, as cramped as it would have been. In the meantime, they were supposed to build larger living quarters from local materials, with the help of their power tools. Of course, that plan went out of the window when the power packs lost their power. And there had been no contingency plans because nobody had foreseen the possibility they might be without power.

Even the solar panels didn't work. The power packs just didn't store the power long enough to be of any use.

Melton walked over to Dr. Frederick, who was busy frying their first fish on a hot rock. After many unsuccessful attempts, he had finally managed to catch one with a hook fashioned from a needle and a piece of meat from a bird Melton had killed with a well-thrown rock.

Things were beginning to get better. He squatted down beside his colleague and watched him as he lovingly turned the fish around. Inhaling the aroma of frying fish, he looked forward to having something else to eat besides berries and the occasional 'chicken', a birdlike avian that lived in the trees and didn't fly too fast.

They discovered a spring nearby, so fresh water was no problem. Among their equipment had been pots and pans. Having fire, they could have boiled the water from the river, but they preferred the cold water from the spring.

"I see our friends are here again," Dr. Frederick said, looking across the river, where a small group of shaggy, ape-like creatures sat or stood, watching the Humans. A few young ones were running around, chasing each other and shouting noisily. Once in a while, an adult would call out sharply to them, and they would quiet down a bit.

"What do you think, Ian," Melton said. "How far on the scale of evolution would you put them?"

"I don't know. Neanderthal, perhaps," Dr. Frederick mused. "They're smarter than apes, even though they run around naked, but I don't think they have much of a language. I haven't seen them use tools either."

Suddenly they heard loud screams from the other side of the river. The two men gazed across the water to see what happened. The natives were jumping up and down excitedly, some of them wading in the water close to shore.

Then the Humans saw the cause of their excitement.

One of the little ones had fallen into the river, its arms flailing helplessly above the water.

"I don't think it can swim," Dr. Frederick said.

"And neither can the others," Melton shouted. "We'll have to save it." With that, he ran toward the river.

Dr. Frederick ran after him. "Be careful," he warned, "we don't know anything about them. They might be hostile."

"We'll worry about that later." Melton dove into the water and swam toward the little creature, who floated now almost in the middle of the river. Fortunately, the river wasn't very wide at this point, and it didn't take Melton long to reach it. He grabbed the screaming, hairy little bundle and, holding it above water, he swam to the other side, where the natives were running around, grunting and waving their arms frantically.

When he felt solid ground under his feet, he walked slowly toward them. The little creature in his arms had stopped kicking and looked at the Earthman with fear in its eyes.

"Don't worry, little one," Melton said softly. "You're safe now."

The natives stopped their chatter and their hopping. They stood silently, looking at Melton as he approached them.

He stopped a short distance away from them and held out the baby. "Here," he said, smiling.

Their faces were hidden behind shaggy, thick hair. He only saw their black, deep-set eyes. Melton noticed breasts on some of them, which confirmed his speculation that they were humanoids. One of them came closer, hesitating with each step. A male by the looks of it.

He almost ripped the baby out of Melton's arms and ran back to the others.

As soon as it was safely back with its own people, the little one started screaming again. They all stood around it, crooning softly.

The Earthman seemed forgotten.

Melton backed off into the water and swam back to the other side where Dr. Frederick waited anxiously.

"First real encounter with the natives," Dr. Frederick remarked, when Melton climbed out of the water. "I think it went well. What did they say?"

"Not much." Melton laughed. "I don't believe they were interested in a big conversation. At least they seemed happy enough to have their kid back again." He sniffed the air. "Hey," he said, "let's eat that fish now. I've worked up an enormous appetite, and that smells delicious."

The fish *did* taste delicious, even though it was a bit charred. They didn't mind picking the fine bones out of the white meat; it only added to the excitement of eating something different after so many months.

"A bottle of white wine would put the finishing touch to this gourmet meal," Dr. Frederick remarked, wiping his mouth with his hand.

After they finished eating, Melton said, "It's still early. What do you say we cross the river and see if we can't get better acquainted with those natives, now that the initial contact went so smoothly?"

Dr. Frederick agreed. "You're right. Maybe they know now we're peaceful."

They stepped on the small raft that they had built from logs and paddled across the water.

The natives had moved away from the river, probably the near-tragedy taught them to be more careful.

The two men walked slowly toward the watching group. Melton suddenly felt a wave of nausea washing over him. His limbs seemed to get heavier, and it became an effort to set one foot in front of the other.

He heard Dr. Frederick gasping beside him. "The fish…it was the fish…poison."

A dark cloud settled over Melton, and then he felt himself sliding to the ground.

In a moment of clarity, he opened his eyes. He wanted to move, but his body didn't respond. He had the sensation of being dragged, and then he sank back into darkness.

* * * *

Awareness crept slowly into his mind. Opening his eyes, he saw shadows moving close by as his vision slowly cleared. He looked up, saw people standing over him.

Not all of the faces were human. Some were strange and terrible to look at.

"Let's kill him." The speaker stared down at him. His eyes were large and cold, his body covered with glittering scales. His wide mouth stood open, but no sound came out of it, yet Melton knew he had spoken.

"We can't kill him," said one of the human-looking ones. "It is not right, but I forget, our brothers of the Sea have their own sense of what is right and wrong."

Melton wanted to scream, "You can't kill me. I'm dead already," but he couldn't formulate the words. His throat did not obey.

Then he floated in darkness again.

There were moments of semi-awareness. At times he felt cold, at other times he seemed to be burning up.

He saw the familiar face of a woman.

"Eleanore," he whispered, "have you come for me already?" His hands reached, but the face changed, and he looked into a pair of black, deep-set eyes staring at him out of a hairy face.

When he finally woke up clear-headed, he found he could move. He sat up, cautiously looked around. He lay on a bed of soft grass underneath a tree. Not far from him stood one of the natives. When the humanoid saw the Earthman rise to his feet, he turned and silently ran off, vanishing among the trees.

Melton tried to orient himself and discovered that he wasn't far from his home.

He found a human skeleton near the river.

Dr. Frederick.

It seems the natives saved me. Why didn't they save him?

The raft was still there by the riverbank.

He buried the bleached skeleton of Dr. Frederick the next day in a shallow grave and covered it with rocks.

Chapter Six

Two months had passed since Dr. Frederick's death, and he had lost all interest in living. Staring into emptiness, his face haggard and drawn, his hair and beard unkempt and filthy, he sat on one of the chairs he and the doctor had built from branches.

He felt lonely. Knowing that he had to wait three more years until another ship would come to rescue him almost drove him out of his mind. Nights were filled with nightmares as he dreamed about alien monstrous beings that wanted to kill him.

It was still daylight but he sat in semidarkness inside the cabin, the doors and window bolted. Sometimes at night, he heard sounds of large animals prowling around the cabin, and even during the day he had caught glimpses of something large gliding through the high grass.

A sudden noise outside and a banging against the door made him look up and, with a wild look in his eyes, he grabbed the makeshift spear leaning against one wall. Then he rushed to the door and peered through the cracks between the boles.

A small group of the hairy humanoids stood outside, between them a white form, someone who should not be there with them.

A girl.

Melton shook his head to clear his mind from its foggy state.

I'm seeing things. Hallucinations. Maybe I'm finally going crazy.

Again the banging against his door. His heart pounding inside his chest, he took another peek.

The girl was still there, partly hidden behind one of the natives who stood facing the door. Melton slowly opened it, his spear ready in his hands. He hadn't seen the humanoids since that fatal accident and thought they'd moved away.

The hairy creature stepped aside, joined his companions. He heard them grunting among themselves, and after one last look at the girl, they turned and walked away, leaving her there.

She looked young, not much older than seventeen or eighteen Earth years. Her slender body was well developed, her round breasts high and firm, but her lovely face captured Melton's immediate attention. She stood there, smiling shyly at him.

She wore no clothes, not even a loincloth to cover her golden pubic hair, and he felt embarrassed staring at her. In the course of his profession, he'd seen plenty of nude women, but this was different. It just wasn't proper for a young woman to parade around in the nude, especially not with a body like hers, unless she belonged to one of the professional guilds.

He caught himself.

What am I thinking? She's only a child. The natives aren't wearing any clothes. Why should she? This is not Earth. People are different. Some of our frontier worlds have a different sense of morality from ours back on Earth.

His thinking process stopped abruptly, and hot and cold shivers ran down his spine.

People! She is human. There must be Humans on this planet.

"Who are you?" he stammered. "Where do you come from?"

She cocked her head, her turquoise eyes wide as she looked at him. Then she shrugged her shoulders and, smiling, she reached out and touched his cheek lightly.

Suddenly aware of the way he looked, he stepped back, ashamed.

She pointed into the cabin, and then she slipped by him and entered, looking around curiously.

Melton followed her slowly, his mind in turmoil.

She sat down on the bed of dry grass he had made to sleep on and looked up at him.

"Who are you?" he asked again, but she just shook her head.

"My name is Bruce." He pointed to himself, repeating, "Bruce. Bruce."

"Bruce," she said in a clear voice, pointing to her own chest. When he shook his head, she suddenly laughed and pointed her finger at him. "Bruce," she said, and then, to his surprise, she touched her breast and said, "Le-itha."

"Your name is Le-itha?"

She seemed to listen intently then she nodded, first pointing to herself and then to Melton. "Le-itha. Bruce."

"This is more than I hoped for," Melton exclaimed, excited now. "You seem to be highly intelligent. Maybe I can teach you to speak my language."

They were busy until nightfall trying to communicate. Melton noticed that she seemed to become restless. Then he saw the goose bumps on her white skin and realized that the air felt chilly inside the cabin.

"You're freezing," he said, startled and aware again of her

nakedness. He got up and searched for one of his shirts. "Here," he held it out to her. "Put this on. It will keep you warm and…" he hesitated, "And also decent. After all, I'm a man, and even though you seem to be still a child, your body certainly isn't."

He helped her into the shirt. It was quite large on her, and she giggled as she slipped into it. Then she wrinkled her nose and sniffed the material.

"I know, it may not be as clean as it should be," he said, apologizing. "Tomorrow we'll wash it. It'll have to do for tonight."

She gave him an inquiring look, cocking her head again then she smiled sweetly.

"You're still very beautiful," Melton said, "Even in that old shirt." He sighed. "It's better this way, believe me, and not just for the cold."

She lowered her lashes, and he wondered if she understood the meaning of what he'd said.

* * * *

The next few months brought on a change in Melton. The presence of the girl gave him back his interest in the world. He tried to shave off his beard with the knife, but after cutting his face a few times, gave up that notion. However, he kept it trimmed as well as he could.

He fixed up the cabin and built a fireplace to keep them warm at night. Le-itha seemed to have an aptitude for languages. It wasn't long before they could converse with each other.

To his disappointment, Melton learned that she didn't know much about herself. As far as she knew, she had always lived with the Cocos. That's what the humanoids called themselves.

She taught him many things. After the fatal accident that caused Dr. Frederick's death, he had been afraid to eat any fish. Even eating the small land animals he managed to catch in snares or bring down with a thrown rock proved difficult for him to eat, always wondering if they too might be poisonous.

She showed him different kinds of edible berries and tubers. They dug in the sand for eggs. She knew exactly where to look and how to find them.

Her presence and the food also made a difference in his appearance. His ragged frame filled out, and the muscles on his body began to develop. The girl was very active and agile, and she taught him the importance of keeping his body in shape.

Melton was happier than he'd ever been in his life, and slowly he found himself falling in love with her.

Sometimes she'd disappear for a day and two. Where she went he didn't really know; she told him she spent the time with the Cocos. After all, they raised her, and she felt an obligation to keep in touch with them.

The first time it happened, he almost went out of his mind, fearing something might have happened to her. After that, he never questioned her again when she disappeared, just accepted it, hoping she'd come back to him.

She didn't eat meat, except for fish, but she didn't object to Melton's desire to have meat in his diet.

It happened on one of the days when she was gone on her frequent visits to the Cocos. Melton decided to have something else on the table besides the 'chickens' and small lizards. He had practiced with a bow he fashioned from flexible branches of a tree he found. So far he'd only shot at trees. It was time to look for larger quarry.

He'd seen a herd of shaggy, six-legged animals coming to the river, and he figured they might provide some steaks and roasts.

Taking his bow and a few arrows, he hid among dense bushes, knowing they'd come soon. He didn't have to wait long for the herd to appear. He counted between thirty and forty animals, young and old.

A large buck with a long horn in its forehead stayed a little ahead of the herd, making sure the herd wasn't in any danger from one of the large predators that also frequented this part of the river to slake their thirst.

Melton waited until most of the herd passed then he took careful aim, choosing one of the smaller animals. The arrow hit its mark and, with a wailing cry, the victim fell. The rest of the herd stampeded away.

When Melton reached the fallen animal, it was dead. He stood, staring down at it, not quite knowing what to do next.

I guess I have to gut it first. It's nothing but a large chicken.

He pulled out his knife and began cutting open the belly to take out the insides.

"You killed it," said a voice behind him. Melton had been so intend, he had not heard her come. Startled, he turned around, looking at the girl.

"Oh, it's you, Le-itha," he said then he turned back to slicing open the belly. “Yes, I killed it. A lucky shot.”

“Why you kill it?” she asked.

Melton looked at her in surprise. “To eat it. Why do you ask?”

Her eyes were large in her beautiful face. “You never eat *Garhas* before.”

He laughed. “Because until now I didn’t have the means to bring one down. Now I have.”

“Cocos no eat meat,” she said. She sat quietly for a while with that faraway look she always had when thinking about things Melton did. “All people eat meat? People kill all the time when want meat? People like killing?”

“Oh no. People on Earth don’t kill any animals anymore if they want to eat meat. It is grown artificially in giant vats, but people do on other planets. They don’t necessarily do it because they like it.”

She nodded. “I think I understand. You kill *Garhas* not because you like, you kill because you hungry for meat, like *Elper*…”

“That’s right,” Melton said, “like the *Elper*. After all, man is nothing but an intelligent carnivorous animal. You might not know it, but so are you. The killer-ape is in your ancestry. The people of Earth are your people.”

“Le-itha not know Earth,” she said, shaking her head. “Cocos my people.”

“Don’t talk foolish, child. The Cocos raised you, but they’re not your people. You’re a human being, like me.”

She came close to him and, standing on tiptoes, she kissed him lightly on the lips. “No call child,” she said, pouting, thrusting out her breasts. “Li-itha no child. Le-itha woman.”

As if he hadn’t noticed!

He tried to avoid her eyes. “You may look like a woman, but to me, you’re still a child.”

“You wrong, Bruce,” she said, her eyes flashing. “You love me?” she asked, surprising him with that question.

“You know I love you.”

“You speak love.” She lowered her lids; her long lashes shaded her eyes. “You teach me many things, but you never teach me love. Why you no teach me love?”

“I told you.” Melton’s voice came out harsher than he intended. “Let’s not talk about this anymore. Come. Help me with the animal. I’ll teach you something else.”

She smiled and touched his hand. “No be angry.”

He looked at her, a warm feeling washing through him. She always understood, she never argued, always accepted his ways.

"I am not angry with you, Le-itha. How could I ever be?"

"I love you, too," she said. "You good man."

That night she came to him, joined him on his bed of dried grass. She pressed her naked body against his, stroked his chest with soft fingers. "Now you teach me love," she whispered.

Moaning, he held her and kissed her passionately. She responded with a fire he had not expected from the gentle demeanor she always displayed. Her hand touched his erection, she giggled and then she captured him between her soft thighs.

"Not yet," he said, even though he wanted to rip open her thighs and push into her. All these months of looking at her lovely body had not been easy. It had taken all of his control not to take her into his arms on those long nights and take advantage of her vulnerability.

"I'm not an animal," he told himself. *Besides, I'm engaged. I'm expected to marry Eleanore when I get back to Earth.*

"You don't want me?" she asked, disappointment in her voice.

He nuzzled his face in her long hair. "I want you more than anything in the universe," he said fiercely. "I am crazy for you, but I don't want this to be just a release of lust. I want it to be a celebration of our love for each other."

She lay back and let him kiss her neck, her shoulders, her breasts. She moaned when he moved his lips across her belly and down her thighs, to her feet.

"This feels nice," she whispered. "Your beard tickles me."

He opened her legs gently, put his mouth against her mound and pushed his tongue into her cleft. She cried out, surprised by his action and, moaning, she pushed up against him. He licked her until he felt warm liquid gushing out of her then he moved into position above her. Slowly, he pushed his engorged organ into her tight channel.

She let out a soft wail, when he took her virginity. "It hurts," she moaned.

"Hush." He kissed her and held her in a tight embrace. "It will pass in a moment. Just relax."

Slowly and gently he moved in and out of her, and it didn't take long until she experienced an orgasm.

"Oh, Bruce," she cried out. "You must love me very much to give me this pleasure."

"I do," he groaned, trying to hold back his own release. "I do love you, my darling. I love you so much, it hurts."

Finally, he couldn't control his urge any longer and, with a shout, he filled her with his gift of love, shaking in her embrace, as she held him close to her breast.

They slept in each other's arms that night.

In the morning, Le-itha rose early and prepared his breakfast. She laughed when he rose from their bed, surprised to see her up.

"I didn't hear you get up," he said, wiping the sleep from his eyes.

She came over to him and kissed him on the forehead. "You were tired," she said, holding out her hand. "Come, let's go down to the river and bath. It will wake you up."

He followed her, smiling at seeing her so happy. They splashed in the water like two children, laughing and chasing each other.

When he lay in the grass to let the sun dry him, he watched her as she came out of the lake, dripping water.

How lovely she is.

Laughing happily, she ran toward him, her breast bobbing up and down. They had visibly grown this past year. Yes…she was a woman, a full-grown woman. He could not deny that. He ached for her and knew he loved her. He couldn't imagine being without her.

She bent down to pick some flowers then she knelt beside him and her deft fingers made a little crown that she put on his head. "You are a king," she said, laughing. "King of the Mountain, and my lord."

He picked a large, red flower and put it into the cleft between her breasts. "And you are my queen. That makes you Queen of the Mountain."

She looked at him, suddenly serious, her blue eyes hazy behind lowered lashes. Then she put her arms around him and kissed him.

"Last night was wonderful, Bruce," she whispered. "Come, let's make love again."

The sun in the sky and flowers beneath their naked bodies witnessed their passion, and when she cried out, he stroked her gently and whispered words of love.

Part Three
Chapter Seven

"Where does she come from?" Gibson asked.

Melton shrugged. "I don't know. She remembers nothing. As far as she knows, she's always lived with the Cocos. I have this theory about an Earth ship crashing on this planet and her being the only survivor. The Cocos found her, probably still a baby, and raised her. Makes sense, doesn't it?"

"Hmm." Sanders looked doubtful. "It's possible. She looks human, but that doesn't prove she is from Earth. She could still be an alien."

"Oh, come on now." Melton laughed. "We've been living together for over three years. Surely I'd have found out by now. If there were others like her on this planet, if she were an alien, they would have contacted her by now. And she certainly is not a Cocos. No, no, she's human. I can vouch for that."

Le-itha looked at him and smiled. "As human as you are, Darling," she said softly, and then she looked at the others. "And as human as you."

She's like a child, Sanders thought, *an innocent child, unspoiled by civilization, and so beautiful.*

He felt a touch of envy. His gaze shifted to Eleanore, who sat silent on a crude bench, and he pitied her. She crossed the vastness of space to come to this world, looking for her promised mate, her future life partner, just to find he had been living with another woman for over three years. The disappointment she must feel, the turmoil she must be going through.

He filled one of the clay cups with wine and walked over to her. He sat beside her, offering her the cup. "Here, why don't you drink this," he said gently.

She stared at him, angrily, and he thought she might knock the cup from his hand, but then she accepted it and gulped it down. "Give me another one," she demanded. "I think I need it."

After the fourth cup, Sanders said, "Hey, take it easy, Dr. Laverne. You're not used to drinking alcohol."

"Don't tell me what I can do," Eleanore said indignantly. "I'm a Free Woman of the World, and no man gives me orders." She staggered from the bench, stood in the middle of the room and opened her blouse to expose her breasts. Pushing out her chest, she said, "I'm as beautiful as she is. Look at me." Stumbling over the words, she stared at Melton and then at Sanders. "You're a man. You've been ogling me, trying to get a look at my breasts. Here, take a good look. Maybe you want to touch them?"

She stumbled over to where Sanders sat and pushed her breast into his face. "Go ahead, here is your chance. Put your hands on them. Feel them."

Sanders looked away, embarrassed. "I'm sure they feel fine," he said.

"How do you know? You haven't touched them. Go ahead, touch them!"

He put one of his hands on her breast, touched it lightly.

"Both of them. Are you afraid to touch a real woman's breast, big man?" She jiggled them in front of him. "Use both hands. Now!" She laughed hysterically when he wrapped his fingers around her breasts.

"They feel nice," he said, color creeping into his cheeks.

They really do feel nice, he thought. *And they look nice, too.*

She stumbled away and grabbed another cup. After emptying it, she hiccupped and began pushing down her baggy pants. Still looking at Sanders, she said with a slurry voice, "You probably want to check out what else I'm hiding." With that, she pushed her pants past her hips.

Sanders stared at her black triangle, noted her thick Venus mound. Seeing her naked did have its effect on him, and he felt the sudden pounding in his loins. "I think you should cover yourself up, Dr. Laverne," he said gently.

"Why? Don't you like what you see?" She turned to Melton and stared at him. "Look at me, Melton. This is what you will never have. I was ready to give myself to you before we even were married. I was ready to go against tradition, but now it's not going to happen." Suddenly, she broke down and cried.

Sanders got up and put his arms around her to give her comfort. She shook off his hands. "Don't touch me. No man is going to touch me now, not ever."

She tugged on her pants, trying to cover herself. Sanders bent down to pick up her blouse, handed it to her. She grabbed it from him and draped it around herself.

Le-itha rose silently and walked up to her. “I think you should lie down,” she said. “You’ve had too much to drink.”

Sobbing, Eleanore walked with Le-itha into the next room. Le-itha came back a few moments later, smiling. “She’ll be fine.” She sat down next to Melton again.

Melton looked at the dying embers in the fireplace. “It’s late. I guess we should all be going to sleep.” He stood up and stretched then he smiled. “This is not a big place. It will be a bit cramped for the night. You two men can sleep in this room. I’ll have Le-itha bring you a couple of furs to lie on.” He shrugged. “I know it’s not as comfortable as the sleeping quarters inside a ship, but at least you’ll be safe in here. Le-itha and I will sleep in our bedroom.” He grinned. “Looks like Eleanore is out of it. She won’t even know we’re here.”

Sanders didn’t have any problem sleeping on the fur. It could have been a quiet night, had it not been for Gibson, who kept waking him up with his snoring. But he did manage to catch some sleep.

Melton kept the window covered with a shutter at night, but Sanders saw the daylight creeping in through the cracks in the door. He got up early and went outside to follow the call of nature. The air was cool but fresh and sweet smelling. He inhaled deeply, relishing the feeling of well-being.

Chirping sounds and soft calls from the forest on the other side of the river attested to the presence of wildlife. Walking down to the river, he discovered that he was not the only one already up. He saw the naked form of a woman splashing in the water and recognized Le-itha. She laughed at him when he came closer and, without shame, she came walking out onto dry land. “The water is cool in the morning,” she said, “but refreshing.” Her expression was open when she looked at him. “I hope you slept well last night?”

“Thank you, I did.” He hesitated, not sure if he should strip or not. “Is it safe to go into the river?” he asked, studying her lithe body without being too obvious. *I can’t blame Melton for falling in love with her. Who wouldn’t? She’s unbelievably lovely.*

“It is safe. Don’t worry. The *Elpers* avoid this part of the river now. They are smart. They fear Bruce’s arrows.” She smiled. “Are you going in the water with all of your clothes on? Why don’t you take them off? I could never walk around like that, all covered up, except in the winter, when it gets cold.”

“You speak our language well,” he said, changing the subject.

"I learn fast, but Bruce is a good teacher." Smiling, she turned to leave. "Don't forget to take off your clothes," she called back over her shoulder, giggling mischievously.

He waited until she disappeared into the log house then he stripped to his underwear, but then he shrugged and took them off also. Wading into the knee-deep water, he shivered a little. It was cold, but it felt good on his skin. The water was very clear, and he could see fish swimming near the bottom. He remembered the fish that caused Dr. Frederick's death and wondered if these were the ones. Hoping they didn't have sharp teeth, he washed and waded back onto shore.

Looking up, he saw a woman coming out of the log house.

Eleanore.

She saw him standing by the river, naked, and hesitated, but when he slipped into his pants, she came closer.

"Good morning, Dr. Laverne," he called out to her. "How do you feel?"

"Oh, not so good," she groaned, looking at him sheepishly. "I guess I've made quite a fool of myself last night. I don't remember too much, but what I remember embarrasses me."

"I rather liked it." Sanders laughed. "You let down your guard and showed me, us, that there is a real woman behind that mask."

"You mean staring at my naked body has shown you that?" Her features hardened, and she started to walk briskly past him.

He grabbed her arm. "There, you're doing it again, Eleanore."

"How dare you touch a Free Woman!" she spat. "I am Dr. Laverne to you. Remember that."

"Listen!" Sanders held her hard. "Just because I'm a spacer doesn't mean that I'm below your standards. Computers do not choose our women. We make our own decisions, just like on the frontier worlds. It may seem barbaric to you, coming straight from Earth, where your whole life has to follow a logical pattern, designed by an electronic brain. Out here in space, we have our own code of ethics, so don't worry, I'm not going to touch you without your consent."

He let go of her, breathing hard and angry then his face softened and he said, "It's a beautiful morning. Enjoy the fresh air, go swimming, listen to the birds singing. There is more to life than studying microbes and remembering formulas." He stared at the distant snowcapped mountains, the rising sun crowned them with brilliant, multicolored rays of light. “Look at that beautiful sunrise.”

She followed his gaze then she shrugged. “It’s only a sunrise.”

He shook his head, watched her walk further down the river, probably looking for a private spot. Hearing footsteps, he turned to see Gibson walking toward him and smiled at the black man. “Well, look who’s finally managed to get up,” he said.

The fat man gave a rumbling laugh. “And look who’s watching the women already,” he said, with a look in Dr. Laverne’s direction.

“Oh, her.” Sanders stared after the woman. “She’s angry this morning.” He chuckled. “She’ll get over it.”

“Can’t blame her,” Gibson said. “She came here to get her future husband and discovers he’s already shacked up with someone else. If she still plans to marry, she’ll have to go through the whole process of applying for marriage status again. And this time she might be refused.”

Sanders nodded. “If only she weren’t so bitchy. This whole Free Women of the World thing screwed up her head completely. It’ll take some doing to get her back on track and see the universe the way it really is. She could make a fine wife.”

“”Really?” Gibson smiled broadly. “Do you think she’d like to spend the rest of her life hopping between the star systems?”

“Well.” Sanders smiled, but his voice sounded serious. “I have been thinking about settling down on one of the newly discovered planets. Since I left overcrowded Earth as a kid I have dreamed of owning my own piece of land, of working it, maybe raising food animals. Have children. Did you know that my ancestors were among the early settlers of the American West?” He looked across the valley. “Seeing the way Professor Melton lives here has brought back that dream, but a man can’t do it alone. A man needs a woman by his side, or else everything is pointless.” He sighed heavily and shrugged it off. “It’s only a dream.”

Gibson was looking at the gently rolling hills, and at the river winding its way through the valley toward the lake. Shaking his head, he said, “I’ve been in space too long. To stay on one planet all my life wouldn’t be for me. I’d get bored. But if one were to settle down, this place would not be so bad.”

“I don’t know about this particular planet,” Sanders said. “It would be a hard life, unless you’re satisfied living off hunting and fishing. Remember, none of our sophisticated machinery works here. No communication, no air transport. You’d be cut off from the rest of the Galaxy."

"You're right. I forgot." Gibson looked thoughtful. "I wonder what causes the breakdown of our equipment. The small power packs were drained almost immediately." He stopped suddenly, a grim expression on his dark face. "We should go back to the shuttle and check out the drive. We may have to lift off sooner than planned."

"What makes you believe it is still working?" Sanders asked.

"I don't know. I'm hoping it's not too late already. But the fact that we didn't crash makes me believe that due to its different principle the power drive is still functioning."

Their conversation was interrupted by Le-itha, who came out of the cabin. "Where is Eleanore?" she asked the men.

Sanders pointed in the direction Dr. Laverne had gone.

"I better go and check on her," Le-itha said, and then she walked away.

"Beautiful creature," Gibson said, scratching his crotch and looking after her. "That Melton is a lucky bastard."

"Did you see him this morning?"

Gibson shook his head. "No, he probably went hunting for food so he can feed his guests." He chuckled. "After all, we did drop in unexpected."

"Maybe we can borrow his steed to take us to the shuttle. It's a long walk from here, and with those carnivores on the prowl, I'm just a little apprehensive to make that journey."

A loud scream from the direction where Le-itha had gone made them turn their heads and run to investigate.

Eleanore was just scrambling up the riverbank, when the men reached the scene. Le-itha sat on a large rock, pressing water out of her long hair. Beside her stood two big, hairy creatures. Two more were just crossing the river on the floating bridge.

"She's talking with them," Eleanore said, breathing hard and trying unsuccessfully to cover her naked breasts with her blouse.

"Calm down," Sanders said, gently taking the blouse from her trembling fingers and draping it around her shoulders. To his surprise, she didn't push him away.

"What happened? Why did you scream?"

"Nothing happened." Slowly she seemed to regain her composure. "Those…those…apes came, and she's talking with them."

"They're not apes, Eleanore," Sanders said. "They're humanoids, not necessarily primates. A big difference."

She shuddered. "But they're such ugly brutes, and they look terrible. They scare me."

Sanders chuckled. "I seem to recall how you chided me when I said those exact same words."

Le-itha came up to them, a disapproving look in her bright eyes. "The Cocos are not ugly, scary brutes. They are beautiful people and very gentle. They would never harm another being. They never kill, not even for food."

"I'm sorry," Eleanore said. "This is all so difficult for me to understand. I should never have come on this journey. I…" Her hands went to her face, covered it.

Sanders could see the tears rolling down her cheeks and took her into his arms. "It's all right, Eleanore. It's all right."

She let him hold her. After a while, she stopped sobbing and looked up at him, tears still in the corners of her eyes. "Thank you, you're kind," she whispered.

On a sudden impulse, Sanders bent and kissed her. She struggled at first, but then she responded shyly, molded her body against his. When they separated, they both looked at each other, breathing hard.

"Sorry," Sanders mumbled, "I don't know what came over me."

Her smile lit up her face, and Sanders found her suddenly incredibly attractive. "You've been wanting to do this, so don't be sorry. I'm not." Then she kissed him again, with great passion, oblivious to the others, even to the Cocos, who were watching them with apparent great interest.

Someone delicately coughing beside them made them move apart. Sanders looked up, saw Melton and gave him a sheepish smile.

Melton grinned back at him, but didn't comment. "I got lunch," Melton said, holding up a large rabbit-like animal, with long, shaggy fur. "Maybe you want to help me skin this *Groundhare*. Unless you can't stomach it."

Sanders shrugged. "It won't be a problem. I've hunted and skinned larger animals than that." He let go of Eleanore, who threw Melton a defiant look.

"Your friends from the forest are here," she said and turned to walk back to the cabin.

Chapter Eight

"We must go to the shuttle, Melton. Let's not waste any more time."

Melton, who seemed to have been lost in a momentary trance, looked up at Sanders. "You're right. We have to check it out. Wouldn't want you to be stuck on this planet." He smiled. "You and I will go. We'll take the Toparque. He can carry both of us."

The Toparque was grazing behind the cabin. When the men approached the animal, it eyed Sanders speculatively and let out a loud snort, as if expressing its displeasure at seeing a stranger.

"Are you sure it's harmless?" Sanders asked, cautiously walking around the large animal.

Melton laughed and stroked the Toparque's chest. "He doesn't like to be disturbed when he's eating. Don't worry. He might look ferocious, but he scares easily. I have to tell him constantly how much I love him and how much I need him." He chuckled when Sanders frowned. "I'm not jesting, and believe me, this is a highly intelligent animal. He understands me."

The Toparque nestled its huge beak on Melton's shoulder and hissed softly. Melton padded the narrow head. "All right, now be a good boy. We have to go on a short trip."

Before they mounted their steed, Le-itha came and handed Sanders a long spear. Then she touched Melton's hand. "Do you have to go?"

Melton nodded. "Sanders thinks we should. He's worried about his ship."

She gave him a quick kiss. "It will be fine," she said quietly. "Hurry back to me."

Melton climbed on the animal's back and gave Sanders a hand. "Hop on."

There was plenty of room on the broad back, but the Topargue moved with a peculiar gait, and it took Sanders some time adjusting to it. "I'll be sore tonight," he remarked.

Melton laughed. "You've never ridden before, I gather."

"No, never, not like this anyway, unless riding in a vehicle qualifies."

"Well, then, this will be a memorable experience for you,"

Melton said, chuckling.

When Sanders looked back, he couldn't see the cabin anymore behind the small grove of trees that surrounded it. Looking ahead, he realized the expanse of the valley. The land wasn't flat. Gently rolling hills reminded him of the countryside where he grew up. His great-grandfather had raised cattle, and he remembered his grandfather telling him how they had driven the great herds across the land toward the slaughterhouses. Of course, now these herds didn't exist anymore. Most of the food animals had to make room for the exploding human population on Earth. Giant growing vats replaced the feeding pastures on the prairies.

A small herd of *Garhas* jumped up suddenly and moved away slowly, seeking shelter in one of the grove of trees. Sanders could see their yellow backs sliding through the high grass, like a school of fish darting across the surface of a gently rolling ocean, trying to flee a predator coming up from the dark depth.

"It's beautiful," he said.

Melton nodded, looking around warily, as if expecting danger rising out of the sea of grass to devour them. He held his longbow in his left, ready to be used.

Sanders stared at the quiver of arrows Melton had slung across his muscular back. "Are you worried about something?" he asked.

"You can never let down your guard." Melton chuckled. "Don't let this peaceful setting lure you into believing there is no danger here."

"Danger?"

"You remember the Elper that attacked you?"

"Sure. How can I forget?" Sanders remembered the near fatal incident, as he became aware again of the slight throbbing in his left arm where the ferocious predator had inflicted the wound with the poisoned tip of its tail. He might be dead now had it not been for Melton's knowledge of how to deal with it.

"That Elper is only one of the numerous carnivores prowling this plateau. There is plenty of food for them here. The Garhas are prolific breeders and not that hard to catch, and so are the Groundhares."

Sanders gripped his spear tighter in his hand, suddenly tense and apprehensive. "I guess this isn't paradise after all," he murmured.

Melton laughed softly. "Whoever said it was? But it isn't that bad. Once you're aware of the dangers and prepare yourself for them, it is a beautiful place to live."

"You didn't think like that in the beginning?"

"No, I didn't. The beginning was terrible, I admit."

"You're lucky you've found Le-itha."

"She found me," Melton corrected him. "Yes, you're right, I was lucky. Without her, I most likely would have perished."

The attack came without warning. With a terrifying roar, the grass erupted, and Sanders stared in horror at the scaly creature confronting them. As tall as the Toparque but much longer, its serpentine body hugging the ground, it roared again and advanced on eight short legs.

Sanders noted the toothy maw, open and large enough to swallow a whole Garhas.

"What the devil is that?" Sanders gasped.

"A Mountain-Dragon," Melton said, reaching for an arrow. "Get off, and be ready with your spear," he bellowed, and Sanders obeyed without thinking. He stood beside the Toparque, the spear in his sweating hands. Melton had not exaggerated when he called the beast a *Dragon*. It was huge.

Lucky it doesn't have wings. In his mind, he saw himself carried away, up into the sky, down the mountains into its lair, where its ravenous offspring would devour him.

The monstrous creature roared again; it sounded angry. At first, Sanders thought fire spewed out of the gaping maw, but then he saw the shaft of an arrow quivering between the double row of sharp teeth, and he realized it was the creature's blood. As he watched, fascinated and scared at the same time, another arrow buried itself deep into the soft flesh inside the throat.

"Stab it with your spear," Melton shouted. "Get it right under the jaw. Stab in an angle." With that, he released a third arrow.

Sanders advanced cautiously toward the beast, pointing the spear awkwardly.

If I only had a laser.

He jabbed the sharp point of his unaccustomed weapon at the exposed throat, missed. The beast glared at him, jaws snapping, head shaking as it tried to dislodge the objects in its maw.

Sanders jumped back, almost stumbled over a rock on the ground.

"Put some power behind it, man!" Melton bellowed. He put an arrow into the long neck. "Right there," he shouted. "Get it right there!"

Sanders tried it again, jabbed his spear at the scaly neck, felt it penetrate the thick skin, surprised how relatively easy it went in. He yanked it out, looked in astonishment at the fountain of yellow blood spurting from the wound, stabbed again, encouraged by his success. This time with more force behind it. The spear went in deep, and when he tried to wrench it out again, he couldn't. It was stuck.

"Leave it!" shouted Melton. "Get back!"

Sanders didn't need to be told. He jumped back and watched as the beast began rolling on the ground, spitting and emitting choking sounds. It flattened the grass all around it, and the area began to look as if a giant had suddenly stomped across the valley, leaving behind one huge footprint.

The blood of the dying Mountain Dragon stained the grass yellow. It finally stopped rolling and lay still. Melton walked up to it and stared at the scaly giant body. He turned and grinned at Sanders. "Not bad for the first time," he said.

"Thank you for the compliment." Sanders sat on his haunches, trying to catch his breath and gain back the strength in his legs. Suddenly, they seemed weak and wobbly. And his arms hurt from trying to wrench the spear out of the scaly neck.

"I wasn't complimenting you." Melton laughed merrily. "This is the first time I killed a Dragon." He smiled and added, "*We* killed a dragon. You follow orders well."

"You mean you've never brought down one of these beasts?"

"Are you kidding? Alone I would never have attempted it, but this big fellow surprised us. Normally you know when they're around. He must have been sleeping, and we woke him. That's why he seemed so angry." Melton kicked the carcass with his foot and studied the sharp teeth. "Those teeth would make good knifes, or even tips for my arrows. They look sharp."

Sanders shook his head. "I admire the way you think, Professor. It would never occur to me to look at those teeth as something I could put to use."

"You would if you were in my position, believe me. Necessity is a great teacher. You learn to look at things from a different angle." He looked up into the sky. "We'd better get going. Maybe we'll stop here on the way back. Come. Help me pull out the spear. We might need it again. One never knows. Another thing I've learned. Never let down your guard. Danger lurks everywhere."

They mounted the Toparque, Sanders holding on to the recovered spear and Melton carrying his bow, ready to be used again if necessary.

"I've noticed that you called that creature a *Mountain-Dragon*, and yet you call the animal we're riding a *Toparque.* Where did you get that name from?"

"From the Cocos."

"The Cocos. What do they call the Dragon?"

Melton chuckled. "I could never pronounce their name for it."

"I'm somewhat at a loss here. Didn't you tell me the Cocos don't have a language?"

"I never said that. They do communicate with each other. Le-itha is proof of that. She communicates with them. She's the one who named the animals for me."

"I see." Sanders sat behind Melton, thinking about what he'd seen so far on this strange planet. The place was an enigma, in need of greater study, but without the gadgets Humans relied on so much, he knew this planet would never be studied in depth. There were other planets out there, more hospitable than this one. Safer because electronic devices worked, especially man's advanced weaponry.

He became aware again of the spear he held in his hands. As primitive a weapon as could be found, but he had killed with it, like one of his prehistoric ancestors. He chuckled, suddenly feeling as powerless as he'd felt when he discovered his laser didn't work. Man was a killer; there was no denying it. He didn't need modern weapons to kill. A club or a spear would do, no matter how large and dangerous the quarry or the opponent.

* * * *

When they reached the foot of the plateau where the shuttle stood, Melton told Sanders they had to go ahead without the Toparque. "We'll leave him here," he said.

"You're sure it will still be here when we get back?" Sanders asked, doubtful.

Melton nodded. "He will," he said, confidently. "He's never left me yet. I'm the only friend he has up here. He is a stranger to this valley, just like me." He padded the animal's neck. The Toparque opened its wicked-looking beak and hissed softly. Then it nudged Melton gently in the shoulder.

"He'll be here," Melton said. He began climbing.

Getting to the top took longer than coming down, and when they finally climbed over the last row of rocks, both men were gasping for air.

A blast of heat greeted them, and Sanders felt as if he'd stepped into a furnace. They rested for a while then they started the trip across the hot sand.

"We wondered about this heat," Sanders panted as he walked beside Melton. "Somehow it doesn't make sense for it to be so hot up here."

"It's the sand," Melton explained. "There are certain elements mixed in it that attract and store the heat. Dr. Frederick tried to analyze it, but without his instruments, he never found out much." He stopped walking and handed Sanders a round, fur-covered container. "Here, have a cool drink."

They found the shuttle undisturbed, except for a layer of yellow dust covering its surface. Sanders pushed open the entry door and climbed inside. He walked over to the control board and tried the screens. They still didn't work.

He let out a sigh of relief when the computer sprang to life.

"Computer," he said. "I notice the screens are still out of order. Can you tell me why?"

"Question is without logic. Sensors show no malfunction of screens." The female voice sounded pleasant, unconcerned.

"Strange," Sanders murmured. He looked at Melton. "The problem must lie somewhere else."

"Its sensors might not be working," Melton suggested and addressed the electronic brain. "Computer, how are your power packs?"

"All power packs are low. There is a slow drain. Source unidentified."

"As I suspected," Melton mused. "Just like our ship. It attacked our power packs also."

"What attacked them?" Sanders asked.

"Just a figure of speech. Whatever is draining yours did the same to ours." Melton looked around the interior of the shuttle. "The lights are still working."

Sanders stared at the lit control board. "They won't be once the power is gone. Neither will the controls. Computer, is the ship's drive still undamaged?"

"Affirmative. Ship's drive on standby, ready to be engaged."

Sanders sighed. "At least we don't have to worry about that. But, as I said, without the power packs, we won't be able to initiate the startup sequence." Again, he addressed the computer. "How long until the power packs will be empty?"

"At present rate of drain, power packs will be without power in exactly ninety-two hours, seventeen minutes and forty-two seconds."

"When will they cease to be of any use?"

"In exactly eighty-one hours, thirty-nine minutes and twelve seconds."

He switched off the computer and nodded silently, his face sober. "We must lift off within the next seventy-two hours. I don't want to wait until the last minute, in case the computer made a mistake. Once we're back in space, the packs will generate again. The clock is ticking, starting right now."

He looked at his wrist, at the small band that held his watch, wondering why it was not affected by whatever sucked the life out the ship's power packs. Possibly because the watch ran on solar power? He shrugged. It didn't really matter. He just knew he wanted to get off this ball of unpleasant surprises as quickly as possible.

Chapter Nine

"It is unfortunate we have to leave so soon," Gibson said. "I would have liked to explore this planet for a while. It intrigues me. There is so much here that needs explaining." He sat in deep thought, pulling his earlobe.

Melton nodded. "You are right, but unfortunately time is running out, but there is something that I want to show you. We will have to cross the lake. We have enough time for that."

He didn't explain any further, even though the others were curious. He smiled as they followed him down to the lake, somewhat reluctantly and only after he assured them they'd be back in time. They boarded a large raft. Near its center stood a tent made from animal skins, to protect against the sun and, if necessary, against wind and rain. With a long pole, Melton maneuvered the raft toward the river inlet, where it started to move without any help.

"There is a steady current flowing along the shore," Melton explained. "It will take us all the way to our destination."

"How do we get back?" Sanders asked.

"Wind power." Melton laughed when Gibson pointed out that there wasn't any wind. "There will be. Every evening, like clockwork, a strong wind begins to blow across the lake." He pointed toward the pole in the middle of the raft and the roll of skin draped around it. "Our sail."

The water was calm and the light breeze warm.

"It's a beautiful day for sailing." Sanders squinted against the bright sun, enjoying this unexpected excursion. He lifted his head when he heard a sudden chirping in the air, followed by the flapping of wings.

Le-itha cried out delightedly when a small furry creature with large round eyes settled on her shoulder. Sanders jumped up to knock it from her, but Melton grabbed his arm and held him back. "It's a pet. There is no danger."

Eleanore moved away a little, watching with visible disgust as the small animal chattered excitedly and began licking Le-itha's face. Le-itha giggled, grabbed the little creature and planted a kiss on its furry head. Then she threw it back into the air. It circled the raft a few times then took off again, chirping as it flew away.

"What was all that about?" Sanders asked, watching the small flying creature as it disappeared into the forest. He looked at Le-itha.

"Just a friend showing his affection," she said, her eyes sparkling. "I have many friends."

"That is true," Melton agreed. "Le-itha seems to have a special gift. I could almost believe she communicates with the animals."

"I love pretty things," Le-itha said. "And they love me."

Sanders studied her secretly, as she stood wide-legged on the softly rocking raft, her naked breasts taut and firm, her buttocks round and smooth under the small loincloth. With her finely chiseled features and lithe perfectly shaped body she would inspire any artist. She could be the model for every one of the famous statues on Earth.

Venus…Aphrodite…Diana…

His gaze moved to Melton, who stood beside her, the muscles on his body rippling.

Adonis…Zeus…Hercules…or maybe…

Sanders smiled.

Adam and Eve. Yes, they could be another Adam and Eve on this virgin planet.

His thoughts were interrupted by a strange sound, followed by another, and then another. Suddenly, all around them blared the sounds of trumpets.

"What is that?" Sanders followed Melton to the edge of the raft. The professor put a finger on his mouth. "Be silent and watch."

In the water, narrow, transparent tubes broke through the surface, emitting trumpet-like sounds. Then suddenly the trumpeting stopped, and something pushed through the tubes toward the opening, something red, blue, yellow, green and some showing all the colors of a rainbow.

Eleanore, who stood beside Sanders, gasped and stifled a shout of surprise. "How beautiful," she whispered. "What are those?"

The men also stared in wonder at the colorful flower-like tubes opening up around them.

Melton bent down slowly then quickly his arm shot out and, grabbing one of the tubes, he pulled it out of the water. As soon as he touched it, the others disappeared. Melton put the wiggling thing onto the raft. The tube was attached to a bulbous body, almost three feet in length. A dozen or so long, thin tentacles attached to its lower end moved around frantically.

"What kind of animal is that?" Gibson asked.

"It is not an animal," Melton answered. "It is a plant, a moving plant that has some kind of awareness." He pulled out his knife and cut open the bulbous body. "It is edible, and it tastes delicious." Cutting off a piece, he offered it to the black man, who took it without much enthusiasm, while still looking at the quivering plant-body. Seeing Gibson's look of disapproval, he shrugged. "It's only a plant. It doesn't feel a thing. Ask Le-itha."

The young woman nodded and took the piece Melton offered her. "It is good." She smiled. "Try it."

Gibson put the piece into his mouth and swallowed it. 'You're right," he said, "It does taste delicious. I'll have some more, if you don't mind."

Meanwhile, the current had carried along the raft. The trumpets began to sound again behind them, and when Sanders looked, he could see the multitude of colors spreading across the surface of the water. "There are certainly strange creature on this planet," he said. "Strange and wonderful."

"Truthfully spoken," Melton said. "There…look!" He pointed toward shore, calling their attention to a score of large butterfly-like creatures lifting into the air, their giant wings flapping like sales in the wind.

"*Danaidae Gigantus*. I gave them that name because they look almost like our Monarch butterflies on Earth, now of course extinct since the destruction of their wintering grounds in the former Mexico."

"I've seen those in museums," Sanders said. "These are just a bit larger. I'd say quite a bit larger."

Melton laughed. "Agreed. They are. But aren't they beautiful?"

"Listen to the sound of their wings," Le-itha said softly. "It's music. They sing to each other."

They listened. Sanders had to admit that with a little imagination the gentle beating of the gigantic butterfly wings did sound like music.

The raft drifted away from the shore into the open water. The waves rose a little higher now, and the raft began to rock. The passengers squatted down onto the wet, slippery boles. In the sky, the sun stood high and burned down on them, and Sanders didn't mind the cool water washing over the raft.

He stared into the cloudless sky, when he suddenly noticed a few tiny spots moving in from the east. He reached for his field glasses and zoomed in on them.

"What do you see?" Gibson asked him, also peering into the sky.

"I don't know," Sanders said, trying to adjust the lenses. "Looks like a flock of birds, but they are almost impossibly high. I can't make out any details."

"The *Guardians of the Sky*," Melton said. "Giant reptiles. I've never seen them close, only through my binoculars. They fly across the mountains once in a while."

"It almost looks as if there are men sitting on top of them." Sanders shook his head. "Very strange, indeed," he said. "They've changed direction. I can hardly see them now."

"You're surly mistaken about the men," Melton said. "As I said, I've only seen them from afar. I don't know if they are harmless or not, or how big they are. Judging from the size of their silhouettes, they must have a huge wingspread. They are flying high, and no man could withstand the cold or survive in the thin air."

"Not without protection."

"Forget it." Melton waved him off. "You're desperately trying to find advanced intelligent life on this planet. I've spent four years here and didn't find it."

"That means nothing, you have to admit. This is only a minuscule part of the whole planet, and it is high up in the mountains. If our instruments worked, we could survey at least part of the planet. Maybe we'd find out more." Sanders searched the sky, but he didn't see anything except small clouds.

Melton chuckled. "I had hoped to do just that, but you know what happened to my power packs."

They were drifting closer to shore now. Melton used his pole to push the raft out of the current and toward dry land. A beautiful beach with soft, white sand lined this side of the lake, and Melton stirred the raft onto it. He jumped into the shallow water. The others followed, and together they pushed the raft onto the white sand.

Le-itha laughed happily and bent to pick up a colorful shell that had been washed onto the beach. When Sanders looked, he saw something red, like a thick tongue, wiggling out of the narrow opening at the bottom. Le-itha threw the shell back into the water. "Poor thing got lost," she said when she saw Sanders studying her. "It will survive. It is happy again."

She tilted her head and looked at him. "It was only a baby. Not big enough to eat." She smiled. "You may think I'm just a silly girl, but even the life of the lowest creature is precious and should not be wasted callously."

"I agree," Sanders said, "and I don't think you're a silly girl, far from it, I have great respect for you. Professor Melton is a very lucky man to have your love. That is also a precious thing and to be cherished."

"I didn't know you were a philosopher, Mr. Sanders," Eleanore said beside him. When he turned to look at her, he noticed her tiny smile.

"There is much you don't know about me, Professor Laverne," he said. "You know the old saying. Still waters run deep."

"Don't ruin my opinion of you, Chuck Sanders," she said, smiling. "I would not consider you *Still Waters*. By the way, call me Eleanore." She lowered her lids, blushing a little.

"Wow. All right. I will." Sanders was momentarily lost for words. That came so unexpected. "I sure will…Eleanore."

They followed Melton toward a small forest. To Sanders's surprise, Melton led them to a small log cabin nestled among the trees.

"I come here often during the summer months," the professor explained. "I have no way of heating the cabin, therefore I don't use this place in the winter. The winds get quite strong here at that time, and it's not very comfortable, but it's beautiful in the summer, especially the beach."

"The beach is just gorgeous," Eleanore said. "I don't think I've ever seen anything like it. And there are no people."

"That is the best part about it," Gibson agreed. He had been lagging behind, obviously lost in thoughts of his own. "I never had much use for overcrowded places."

"Come," Melton said, "I'd like to show you something else."

They walked up a steep hill. Before they reached it, Melton stopped and held up a hand. "Be careful now," he warned. "A few more steps and we won't be able to go any further. You'll see why in a moment, just follow me slowly."

Gibson and Eleanore were the first to reach the spot after Melton, and they both let out a cry of surprise. When Sanders joined them, he saw the reason.

The hill ended abruptly in a sheer drop. Far below, he could see tree-covered mountaintops and large plateaus. The horizon lost itself in a misty fog.

"Have you ever been down there?" Gibson asked.

Melton laughed. "There is no way to get down, except to fly."

"It would be possible with a glider," Sanders suggested.

"Sure, but how to get back up again?"

They stood silent for a while, looking down at the immense gulf below them. Sanders thought he saw something peculiar and studied it with his field glasses.

"You've discovered it," Melton said beside him.

Sanders nodded and gave the glasses to Gibson. "Here, tell me what you make of it."

The fat man looked at the point Sanders indicated. "Looks like the wreck of some kind of structure. I don't believe it's natural," he exclaimed loudly. He handed the glasses to Eleanore. She studied the spot for a moment then said, "Whatever it is, it was made out of metal. It looks old, very old. All overgrown with creepers and mosses." She glanced at Melton. "What is it?"

He shrugged. "I can't be sure. It is only a guess. I've studied it quite often from up here, and I've come to the conclusion it must have been a spaceship."

"A spaceship?" Sanders took the binoculars from Eleanore's hand. "You could be right," he said after studying it more closely. "It does look like some kind of space vehicle. It certainly is huge. I wonder where it came from and what happened to the occupants." He sighed. "It is really sad we have to leave so soon. Had we more time we might be able to rig up some kind of pulley system to get down there. A hot air balloon might also work."

"I don't know much about aerodynamics, " Melton said, "otherwise I may have figured something out, but I had enough problems just staying alive."

They sat down and watched as clouds moved in, bringing with them a hazy mist that slowly covered the mountains below them. After a while, a cool wind started to blow. Melton got up. "It's time to go inside the cabin. Le-itha prepared food for us before we left. Let's have something to eat. I'm hungry."

* * * *

Melton lit a few oil lamps when the inside of the cabin began to get dark. They sat on seats made from branches. Le-itha sat cross-legged on a bed of dried grass.

Sanders noticed that Eleanore wasn't in the cabin. "Where is Eleanore?" he asked.

"She went outside," Le-itha said.

"I think I'd better look for her." Sanders rose from his seat. "She might get lost out there."

"She is not lost. I think she went to the beach." Le-itha looked at Sanders and smiled. "Go to her," she said softly.

He went outside. Darkness had fallen swiftly, but one of the two satellites illuminated the night. Eleanore was indeed by the beach. He could see her form silhouetted against the moon's reflection in the dark water.

It was still quite warm in the protection of the trees, and he noticed that Eleanore stood up to her knees in the water. He also noticed that she was naked. Slowly, he walked toward the lake, not quite sure if he should disturb her. She must have heard or seen him, because she looked up and saw him, as he stood in the soft sand.

"The water is quite warm," she called to him. "Come in and join me."

Seeing her naked, he removed his own clothes and put them in a neat bundle onto the sand. Then he walked into the water.

"You're right," he said, "it is warm."

"Feels warmer because of the cooling air," she said.

He walked up to her. She didn't bother to cover up her breasts, something that surprised him. "I was worried about you," he said softly. "It may not be safe out here, all by yourself."

"Somehow I knew you'd come looking for me." She came closer. Standing in front of him, she studied his face intently. "Are you attracted to me, Chuck?" she asked, her eyes looking into his.

"You know I am." He put his arms around her and pulled her to him. She didn't struggle but let him hold her, and when he kissed her, she responded fiercely. Her soft breasts flattened against his chest, and he could feel his organ thickening between them.

She laughed softly when his hard penis touched her belly. "Am I doing that to you?" she asked, her hand moving between them.

"You sure are." He moaned deeply when her fingers curled around his erection. "Don't start anything you're not prepared to finish," he said hoarsely.

She stepped back and looked at him. Taking his hand, she pulled him toward shore. "Come," she whispered. She stood in front of the moon. The diffused light made her silhouette appear like a vision out of a dream.

He followed her, still not quite sure what to expect. She lay down in the sand, beckoned to him as he stood looking down at her. “What are you waiting for?” she asked, letting out a short laugh. Her foot came up and with her toes she touched his hard member. “I can see he is ready and eager.”

He dropped down beside her. “I don’t know what to make of you.” He laid his hand on her breast. She didn’t object.

“What do you mean?” she asked.

“On the ship and down here, you seemed to detest me.”

Her laughter mocked him a little. “I was on my way to get my future husband, a man I hardly knew. The Council of Family Planning picked him for me as the ideal husband. It wasn’t appropriate for me to look at another man, but now that I’m free I am not bound anymore to a marriage that might have been without love.” Her hand reached out to touch his cheek. “Even a Free Woman is looking for love. I’m not a cold and frigid composition of molecules. I am a woman with needs, and I have a lot to give to the right man.”

He bent to kiss her on the lips. They felt warm and soft. “Am I the right man?”

She shrugged. “I don’t know. What does it matter? There is a full moon, the water is warm, the sand soft, and I’m horny as hell. Right now I don’t really care if we are compatible. I just want to feel your strong arms around me and your hard flesh inside my belly.”

“Are you saying you want me to make love to you, Eleanore?”

“That’s exactly what I’m saying. Don’t tell me you don’t want to. This tells me you are more than ready.” Her hand touched him.

He groaned when her fingers clamped around his organ. Moving on top of her, he fell between her opening thighs. She laughed when his hips thrust forward, but his penis missed the mark. “Here, let me help,” she whispered, guiding him.

With a deep grunt, he slid into her soft, moist love-channel, began to move with frantic thrusts. She grabbed his hips, slowed him down. “Easy, love. Take it easy. I’m not going anywhere.”

He kissed her and moaned into her mouth. “I feel like I’m in a dream, and I’m going to wake up any moment,” he said, panting.

“This is not a dream,” she gasped, pushing up against him. “I’m going to come,” she cried out. “Oh, here I go.” Her thighs clamped around his torso, her arms held him in a tight embrace. He could feel her inside muscles rippling across his swollen member, almost giving in to his body’s demands, but he managed to hold back, not wanting it to end so soon.

Lying still in her embrace, he waited until her body stopped shaking then he resumed moving slowly between her soft clutching thighs.

"Let me be on top," she whispered. "If you are ready, you can come inside me. I've had anti-conception shots."

He pulled out and turned onto his back, watched her as she straddled him, her slim form outlined against the sky. She hovered above him, lowered herself slowly into his lap. When her wet slit gripped his straining member, he moaned loudly, almost came before he even fully entered her.

She must have sensed his control slipping and stopped moving, just hovered for a moment and smiled down at him.

"I'm all right," he said, "I can hold on."

She began moving up and down, her pelvis rotating with slow movements. Her nicely shaped small firm breasts were taut on her thin chest. He reached up to take them into his hands, molded them with his fingers. She moaned, lifted her head to stare at the moon above them.

Suddenly, a second bright disk climbed up behind the treetops, bathing her swaying body with its pale light, adding to the illusion that this was nothing but a beautiful dream. He lay unmoving, just watched her slim body writhing above him, listened to her moans and little cries of pleasure when an orgasm gripped her body.

When he knew he couldn't hold back much longer, he put her onto her back, moved forcefully on top of her. He came with a suppressed roar and held her close. She quivered beneath him. Experiencing another orgasm, she whimpered like a wounded animal.

Gasping for breath, they broke apart, lay on their backs and stared into the star-speckled sky.

She reached over and touched his chest. "That was absolutely wonderful," she whispered. "Thank you."

"Thank me for what?"

"For being thoughtful and not just thinking of your own pleasure, like so many men do."

He turned to look at her. "A beautiful woman like you deserves the best." He chuckled. "If anyone should say *thank you,* it's me. I'm the one grateful for what just happened. You are a passionate and lovely woman, Eleanore, and I would never use you just to still my own hunger. Besides, the pleasure is so much higher when both partners experience it."

"So you're not quite as selfless as I thought you were," she said, laughing.

Getting up, he held out his hand. "Let's take a dip in the water. I feel like taking a bath," he said, pulling her up.

She came into his arms, molded her body against him, warm and pliable. He kissed her, and then he lifted her up and carried her into the water. She squealed when he threw her in, splashing him after she came up for air.

"Can anyone join in on the fun?" a voice asked from shore.

Sanders looked up to see Melton standing there. "We were getting worried," Melton called, "but I can see we didn't have to. We'll be going to sleep now so we can get an early start in the morning. Maybe you two want to come in also." He turned and walked back to the cabin.

"We'll be there," Sanders called after him. He laughed when Eleanore pulled him into the water.

"Not yet," she whispered fiercely. She sank to her knees and sucked his semi-erect penis into her mouth.

Letting out a surprised yelp, he took her head between his hands as his organ swelled inside the warmth of her mouth.

She released him and bent forward, her body partially in the water. The light of the moons highlighted the thick lips of her womanhood below her round buttocks. He moved behind her, put his hard member between her white cheeks, guided the tip of his penis into her dark cleft, and then, with a deep grunt, he sank it deep into her dripping canal.

Arching her back, she cried out, began bucking in front of him. He steadied himself by clamping his hands around her jerking hips and began thrusting his pelvis back and forth, pounding his belly into her soft buttocks.

They moved like that for a long time, like two animals in heat. Shouting hoarsely, he emptied himself into her sucking sheath a second time, barely aware of her loud cries of ecstasy. Then he bent his upper body, rested it on her back.

"I am totally exhausted." His breath came out in harsh bursts. "I think my legs are all wobbly."

Eleanore laughed and wiggled her rear. "My buttocks are hurting from your vicious pounding. I hope I can sit down without wincing. They'll wonder what we did."

"They can probably guess. I'm sure they heard us. The whole

forest must have heard us going at it."

"I'm so embarrassed," Eleanore said. "I've never done anything like this before. I don't know what got into me."

When they entered the cabin, the others were asleep. Melton had left one oil lamp burning, and in its dim light, Sanders saw only one large fur in one corner. "I guess we'll have to share that," he whispered.

They curled up on the soft animal skin. Eleanore fell asleep in his arms almost immediately, while he lay awake for some time, listening to her gentle breathing.

* * * *

"I have come to love this place." Melton looked thoughtfully at the cloud formations in the sky. "Looks like a storm is coming. I think I'm going to miss all of this. Maybe I won't like it anymore back on Earth where everything is controlled, even the weather."

"If we don't leave soon we may never see Earth again," Gibson said, walking nervously up and down in front of the cabin. "Where is that woman of yours anyway?"

Melton gazed across the river, at the forest on the other side. "She'll be here. She probably went to the Cocos to say goodbye."

"I think we should leave now, without her. I don't want to get stuck on this lousy planet."

Sanders detected a touch of hysteria in Eleanore's voice. When he saw the pained expression in Melton's face, he touched the other man's shoulder. "She is right, you know. If Le-itha is not back within a couple of hours, we must leave her behind."

"Then I'll stay. I can't go without her." Melton seemed to have made up his mind. "You'd better go now. I don't want the responsibility for all of you being stranded here. Take the Toparque. He'll find his way back to me."

"What about the report?" Gibson asked. "The committee wants a report on conditions on Zetta Genetty Seven. You must make the report. We can't leave you here."

Melton shrugged. "You know the conditions here. You make the report."

"It won't be valid. You have to make it in person," Sanders said, anger rising in him. "Don't be a fool, Melton. The committee will never accept our report. We will be reprimanded if we come home without you. You've lived on this planet for nearly four years. Only your findings will decide if this planet will be considered for colonization or not."

A sudden gust of wind brought a cool breeze from the lake.

"I'm going inside," Eleanore said. "It's getting cold out here. I'm shivering."

The men followed her slowly into the cabin, where they sat silently, waiting. Melton put a few logs into the fireplace and lit them to take the chill out of the air.

Sanders watched the big man, as he sat on a fur in front of the fireplace, his large body hunched over. Once in a while a slight twitch ran through his heavily muscled body, betraying Melton's otherwise calm outer appearance.

He understood the man's torment. How could any man leave behind the woman he loved? Especially a woman like Le-itha.

He hated what he must do.

"It's time to go," he said, getting up, prepared to take Melton by force, if necessary.

The professor looked up. "You go, then," he said. "There is still a chance she'll come. I can always catch up with you."

"We all go," Sanders said. "Now."

"I can't leave without her," Melton cried in an anguished voice. "Don't you understand? I love her, and I need her. Without her, I would never have survived on this planet."

"You go with them, Bruce, but without me. I can't come with you."

They all swung around and stared at the door.

Framed against the light stood a hairy creature.

A Cocos.

"Le-itha," Melton cried and jumped up. Pushing the Cocos aside, he searched outside for his wife. "Le-itha," he called again, "where are you hiding? Come on out, there is no time to play games. We must leave immediately."

"I'm right here, Bruce."

Sanders stared at the hairy creature that had spoken in Le-itha's voice.

Melton turned his head, and then he stepped back into the cabin. "What kind of joke is this? I didn't know you people could speak my language."

"I can," the Cocos said. "You've taught me."

"Who are you?" Melton whispered, his face aghast. "You're not…it can't be."

"Yes, Bruce, I am Le-itha."

"No, no…" Melton backed away. "That's not true! It can't be true. You're not Le-itha, whose soft, smooth body I held close every night. Whose sweet lips I kissed…No," he cried, his voice breaking. "You're not my Le-itha! She is human."

"An illusion, Bruce, just an illusion."

The sound of sudden insane laughter rang through the room. "You made love to…that? You chose it over me?" Eleanore's body shook uncontrollably as she pointed a finger at the Cocos. "You had intercourse with an ugly thing like that?" she shrieked.

Sanders walked up to her and put his arms around her. She clung to him, sobbing.

The humanoid regarded them silently.

Melton stood like a man who just woke from a nightmare. "Why?" he whispered with a brittle voice. "Tell me why the charade?"

"You were dying," the creature spoke in Le-itha's gentle voice. "Dying of loneliness. You needed someone to keep you company. We couldn't let you die. I was chosen to live with you." She hesitated. "At first, it was only an assignment, for a short time only, but as I came to know you I…" her voice faltered a little. "I fell in love with you."

"I loved you too," Melton said slowly, "but the way you were. Human. How could you love me? I am so different from you."

"That is not true. The difference is only in the appearance. Inside, we are the same. We think, we dream, we feel…we love."

"Not like this," Melton moaned in despair, hiding his face in his hands.

"How did you do it?" Sanders asked. "How could you fool him for so long and so completely?"

"We are not as primitive as you believe. We don't have your technical advances, but we have progressed in other fields. Our mental capabilities are far beyond yours."

"But the way you live, so primitive and backward," Gibson said.

"Who says yours is the right way to live?" Le-itha challenged him. "We are happy. Are you happy?" She turned to Melton. "I am so sorry, Bruce," she said softly.

"Why did you let me fall in love with you?" Melton's voice was barely audible. "You should have let me die, because this is worse than death. To live and not be able to love you."

The image of the humanoid seemed to waver, became liquid, and changed shape. Then suddenly the hairy creature was gone; in its place stood the girl, a happy smile on her beautiful face.

"I want you to remember me as you knew me," she said. Her smile faded, and she looked sad, while tears ran down her cheeks. "I love you, Bruce."

Melton groaned, reached for her, but before he could touch her, she disappeared. He jumped out of the door, crying out, "Le-itha!"

He came back in, shaking his head. "She is gone," he said, his voice a bare whisper.

Sanders grabbed his arm. "We have to go now, Melton. I am sorry about this, but you have to pull yourself together. Forget about the…Cocos. Just remember Le-itha the way she wants you to remember her, the way she looked when she lived with you."

He nodded, moved sluggishly as Sanders led him out of the cabin.

* * * *

They boarded the shuttle and sealed the airlock. The ship's drive was still operational and, without any difficulties, the ship lifted into the sky.

As they left the planet's atmosphere behind, the screen sprang suddenly back to life, and the computer confirmed the charging of the power packs.

Sanders put the shuttle in orbit around the planet to wait for the Mother ship.

Epilogue

An older woman materialized in the *Hall of Judgment* in the domed city below the surface of the Great Ocean. The members of the Council of Twenty sat silently as she approached them.

She gave the sign of greeting. The Council responded in kind.

"I am Le-tata of the Sun-people, Hunters of the Great H'Ztlerr and Keepers of the Silver Ray," she said in mind speech. "I speak for the Guardians. The Earthmen have left."

"We know," replied one of them, an old man with flowing white hair.

"We should have killed the strangers as I suggested!" came the savage thoughts from NO-WA-Tke, the representative of one of the races who lived in the ocean.

"Killing an intelligent being is never justified." The thought waves of the old man were chiding.

"In this case, it would have been!" No-WA-Tke's gills opened and closed angrily. Breathing air was not really uncomfortable, but he disliked it, and the air in the hall, though humid, made his scales itchy. "From the thoughts of the Earthman Bruce Melton we have enough information about his people. I speak for the brothers of the Sea. We don't want the Earth-people on our planet with their machines and their way of life polluting the air and the water, our life-giver, as they have done on their own planet and others they have taken possession of."

The others listened silently without interrupting him, because it reflected their own thoughts.

"They will not come," the old man said gently. "We have rendered their machines and equipment useless. The one who lived here, Bruce Melton, he has no knowledge about our planet. He only saw things we wanted him to see. He and the others will report that their machines will not function on our world and that most of this planet is nothing but wasteland, mountains and ocean. No, the Earth-people will not bother us."

"What about the girl who was sent to spy on him?"

The woman smiled. "Le-itha, my daughter? She fell in love with him."

"In love? With an outworlder?" exclaimed No-WA-Tke. "Another problem!"

"Which is of no concern to you!" retorted the woman. "We will deal with it."

She went through the formal ceremony of departure.

Then she disappeared.

* * * *

The girl sat on a rock beside the little creek, her naked feet dangling in the cool water. A small fish leaped into the air, catching an insect, splashed back into the water and was swept away by the swift current.

Beside her, in its burrow, a little furry animal sat on its haunches, watching her. A brightly colored bird showed off its plumage on a low hanging branch, chirping happily.

Usually, the girl would have been joyful in these surroundings, but today she just sat, staring into the water, brooding and unmindful of the things around her.

She sensed the displacement of air and looked up at the older woman who had materialized beside her.

"I knew I'd find you here at the Place of Contemplation, Le-itha." The older woman didn't use mind speech, respecting her daughter's wish for withdrawal. She touched the girl's shoulder. "You love him?"

The girl wiped her hand across her tearstained face. "Yes, my Mother, I loved him with my whole being."

The older woman smiled. "He is a good man with a good heart. He will be welcomed to live among us when he comes back."

"Oh, Mother, are you sure he will be back?"

"Yes, I'm sure."

The girl smiled sadly. "It saddens me that I had to show myself to him in the image of the Mountain People. Now he thinks I'm ugly."

"You know that it was necessary. There were others with him. After he makes his report, he will know your real form. He will remember you the way you are." She stood silently beside the girl for a while then she disappeared the way she came, leaving the girl alone with her thoughts.

Yes, she knew why she had to play the charade. One of the laws of the Terran Empire forbade the Earth-people to interfere with low cultures on other planets. The law was not always adhered to, especially if the planet in question was rich with minerals and other items the Earth-people wanted, but it existed, and it might just help to keep them away.

"The Earth-people must not know about us," the Council told her. "Let them believe there are only the Mountain People on our world. They must never suspect that their equipment failed because we caused it to fail. The Earth-people have terrible weapons, and they could destroy our planet, our sun. Even the great powers of the Guardians could not prevent that. If they don't know about us, they will never feel threatened by our presence."

She felt pity, thinking about the Earth-people. Their powers depended on mechanical and electronic gadgets, on machines. Their spaceships carried them from one star system to another. Their electronic communication connected hundreds of planets and yet…poor creatures. Powerful minds trapped in shells of darkness, able to communicate only through gestures and words…empty words that sometimes spoke lies. How sad, how lonely, not to be able to touch another mind, not to be able to feel, to share another's emotions…joy…pleasure…pain.

Bruce, oh, Bruce. How she had felt his anguish! His love for her, her love for him. The nights he lay awake, his flesh aching for hers. How his being had cried out to her for help, trying to reach her but unable to communicate. She had wanted to help open his mind, but forbidden…it was forbidden!

Until finally he gave in. She smiled wickedly. She had broken the law just a little bit, when she put a few gentle suggestions into his mind.

Suddenly she broke into a cheery laughter.

"He will be back," she shouted to the birds flying in the sky, to the furry animals running around her.

"And this time I will teach him all the things I know."

* * * *

Deep in space, an Earthman sat brooding in his cabin. Buried in his subconscious was the picture of a lovely, soft-eyed girl, who was waiting for him.

The End

Luugus
By
Herbert Grosshans

Fields of lava, smooth and bare,
spawn loneliness and despair
Realities shift, warp a man's imagination
and leave him too weak to fight temptation

Prologue

Omega, the fourth planet circling a blazing sun known as Betelgeuse in the charts of Space Exploration Terra or SET, 135 light years away from the home world, had never been fully explored by any exploration teams. There were no settlements except for a lonely base set up by SET.

So far, nothing unusual had been discovered on this planet, aside from the usual ruins, the same ruins of pyramid-like structures found on hundreds of planets. Evidence of earlier space-faring civilizations.

There were natives, human in appearance, apparently from the same genetic stock as the people of Earth. They seemed intelligent enough, but they possessed no technology and showed no interest whatsoever in the technology of the Earth people.

They didn't have much to offer for trade, except their beautiful artifacts, which they made out of a semiprecious stone found in the mountains.

Omega had once seen a lot of volcanic activity. Extensive lava fields spoke of the planet's turbulent past, but there was also a lot of impenetrable jungle. Treacherous mountains reached high into the sky, mountains that no Human would ever be able to climb.

The Earth base had been set up in an area void of any vegetation. Fields of lava stretched for miles all around it, a location chosen deliberately and with great care. What seemed like no protection provided in fact the best protection against any attacks by a yet unknown enemy. The smooth surface surrounding the base also made a perfect and natural place for landing spacecraft.

The station consisted of a dozen domelike structures, simple and practical buildings that held the living quarters, offices, laboratories, machine rooms, storage areas and recreational facilities for the approximately three hundred men and women living there.

It also had a jail.

It wasn't really meant to hold criminals, since crime did not exist on the base, at least not anything that could be termed as crime. Except for those small incidents that happen when men and women are living together under circumstances that are far from ideal.

Three-quarters of the base population were soldiers. All men. The rest scientists, men and women. Actually, not all women were scientists. Twenty of them were there for only one purpose.

To make life a little more pleasant for the soldiers.

However, sometimes the men quarreled. Mostly over a woman.

The jail had only two rooms

One empty, the other one occupied.

* * * *

Coerl Hunter rose from the cot when he heard the soft hissing sound of the opening door.

He was a tall man, with wide shoulders and a deep chest, narrow waist, powerful arms and legs. His face, tanned by the rays of Betelgeuse, could have been considered handsome, if it hadn't been for the ugly scar running across his left cheek.

His blue eyes were bright and blazed angrily as he faced the guard entering his cell.

"It's about time you guys let me out of here!" he stormed. "Three lousy days in this dark hole for nothing!"

The guard laughed and backed away when Hunter stepped closer. "Take it easy, buddy. It's not my fault. You're the one who started the fight."

"Yeah, yeah," grumbled Hunter as he stalked out of the door. "They always blame me."

He walked down the corridor toward the main entrance. As he passed one of the closed doors, one opened, and a soldier stepped out.

"Hey, Hunter," the soldier called, motioning toward the door. "The Commander wants to see you."

Hunter walked into the room and stood at attention.

"Sir?"

The man behind the desk looked up. He was a tall, thin man with a touch of gray on his temples. "I hope you have recovered enough to handle a flyer."

"I am fine, sir. Never felt better, sir. I can handle a flyer better than anyone else at any time."

"No need to go into details, Hunter." The Commander shook his head. "I know how you fly. I want you to take a trip to one of the nearby villages. Professor Colbert and his wife are going to accompany you there. You will drop them off, and come right back here. Is that clear?"

"Yes, sir. Very clear. When do I leave?"

The Commander looked at him for a moment as he stood there at attention. A young man, big and powerful. A dedicated soldier.

And yet…the bright blue eyes seemed to laugh and mock him behind the serious suntanned face.

He shrugged and waved his hand.

"You'll leave right away. Dismissed."

Chapter One

Hunter leaned back into the furs the chief's daughter had provided for him. It was a quiet night. The eerie green light of one of the three moons of Omega falling through the entrance of the hut illuminated the interior.

The old chief sat in darkness, a shadow among shadows, Even his voice seemed to come from far away. "It is the night of *Luugus*, stranger from another world. Beware, things may not be as they seem." He spoke the Terran language with hardly an accent.

The Earthman reached for one of the chewing sticks the old man offered him. It tasted sweet and pungent when he bit into it. "I don't quite understand what you are talking about. Who is Luugus?"

"Luugus." The chief's voice came out in a whisper. "The largest of the four moons. When he shines, strange things may happen. Secret dreams and wishes can come true."

A shadow darkened the entrance for a short moment. Hunter looked up at the slender form of the chief's daughter who slipped in and sat down among the furs.

His eyes traveled over her nude body, lingered on her up-tilted breasts and came to rest on her face. Long black hair spilled over her brown shoulders; her eyes were two deep bottomless black pools, and for an insane moment, he had the feeling he was looking into the empty blackness of space.

"You are familiar with our customs, Earthman?" she asked, her dark eyes looking into his.

He nodded, smiling in anticipation.

She took the chewing stick from his hand and licked it with her tongue. "As the chief's oldest daughter, I am yours tonight." She took his hand. "Come," she whispered.

He followed her out of the tent. They walked down a narrow dark trail that ended in a large clearing. The green light of the moon, which stood high above them, reflected in the dark water of a pond. The girl pulled him into the shadows of a tree and lay down on the soft vegetation. Her arms reached for him. He couldn't see her face, but her eyes seemed to glow softly in the darkness. "Come to me," she whispered.

He dropped to his knees beside her, bent to kiss her soft lips.

They opened to his probing, and his tongue slipped into her mouth to taste the sweet spice of the chewing stick. Feeling her hand on his belly, he put his own on her breast.

She opened his pants and reached inside to touch his rising organ. Then he helped her to push his pants past his hips. His organ was a hard rod inside the warmth of her hand. With a groan, he rolled between her spread thighs, but she pushed him off.

"Take off all your clothes," she said softly. "Our bodies must touch when you join with me."

Frantically, he fairly ripped off his clothes. His body seemed on fire, his organ a giant pole between his legs. She watched him patiently, the light of the moon they called Luugus bathing her lush body green like the vegetation she lay in.

Her spread legs displayed her female organ, covered with sparse dark curls. He fell between her warm thighs and, with a loud cry, he entered her and slid into the creamy softness of her moist canal. She opened her legs wider, wrapped them around his torso.

Then they moved in unison, their thrashing bodies the only sound in the silence of the night. Her fire burned hot beneath him, and her passion grew as they writhed and hammered against each other.

The moon moved slowly across the dark sky, but they were unaware of its journey. Seemingly without tiring, they lay in each other's embrace, their lips glued together in an endless kiss and their bodies joined below their bellies.

His buttocks quivered from time to time, as he reached the summit of his desire without losing fluid. She moaned into his mouth as her own pleasure washed through her body.

When both of them finally climbed the peak of their passion, his loud shouts of released tension blended with her cries of ecstasy. Then they lay panting beside each other, staring unseeing into the sky.

"I don't know what you did to me," he said after a while with a voice gone hoarse, "but I've never experienced anything like this before."

She laughed softly beside him. "I did nothing but fuel your own desire." She looked at the shiny green disk of the moon, barely visible now behind a bank of clouds. "It is Luugus," she whispered. "Luugus makes your dreams come true."

She rose and held out her hand to him. "Come, let's swim in the pond to clean our bodies from the fruit of our passion."

The water felt cool and refreshing, and it cleared his head.

He boarded his flier early in the morning after saying goodbye to the professor and his wife. Looking back, he saw the chief's daughter standing in the entrance of one of the huts, a smile on her beautiful face. She lifted her hand in a farewell gesture. He waved back and closed the hatch.

Strapping himself into the seat, he looked at the green moon hanging high above the horizon. "Damn natives and their crazy stories," he murmured as the flier shot into the air. "I should never listen to them." Then he laughed softly, still staring at the moon.

"Luugus, if you could materialize my dreams, I'd be in your debt forever."

* * * *

The flier shot over the lava fields toward the Station. Luugus stood prominently in the sky; the other three moons were hiding behind the clouds. Coerl Hunter sat comfortably behind the automatic controls, staring into emptiness, his thought wandering.

Suddenly, he bolted upright in his seat and stared at the viewing screen. Two small figures appeared on the screen, growing larger as he adjusted the controls. They apparently had seen the flier, because they were waving frantically.

Hunter disengaged the automatic controls and dropped the flier, landing softly on the hard surface moments later.

They came running toward him. A man and a woman, both young, dressed in short pants and short-sleeved shirts. Civilians, by the looks of it, and Hunter creased his brows in puzzlement. The man seemed to be in pain because he limped behind the woman. Hunter could see the bloody rag wrapped around his upper thigh.

When he looked at the girl, he stared. Her breasts were straining against the tight material of her thin blouse. Her red hair cascaded like a waterfall down her white shoulders, and her eyes were smoldering emeralds in her beautiful face.

Out of breath, when she reached him, she pleaded, "Please, help us."

"Who are you, and where do you come from?" Hunter's voice sounded harsh in his own ears. "I've never seen you in the Station before. You shouldn't be here."

"We aren't from the Station," the woman said, her sensuous mouth trembling as she tried to catch her breath. "We come from the base *Steelborn*, a thousand kilometers north of here."

Hunter looked at the man. "I've never heard of any other station on this planet. Maybe you'd better explain yourself." His eyes narrowed, and his hand touched the butt of his laser.

The man saw it and smiled. "We are unarmed," he said. "It is true what my sister said. We need your help."

"It still doesn't explain your presence here," Hunter said, keeping his hand on his hip.

"Our ship, with five hundred colonists on board, landed a week ago," the young woman explained. "My brother and I were on our way to the SET base when we crash-landed in the mountains. That was two days ago. A winged creature attacked us. My brother was bitten, and I'm afraid if he doesn't get medical attention soon he may die. His leg is already infected."

"All right, get in." Hunter smiled foolishly, remembering his three days in confinement. "I guess they didn't bother telling me about your ship."

He helped the man into the backseat and inspected the leg. "That is a nasty looking wound," he said. "We'd better get you to the medic as fast as we can." He reached into a compartment and handed the man a capsule. "Here, take this. It will kill the pain and maybe slow the infection."

The young woman slid into the front seat beside him.

Hunter punched the controls. As the flier lifted into the air, he stared at Luugus, which seemed to have grown in size, and felt a slight shudder run through his body.

The woman saw him looking and chuckled. "A little scary, isn't it?" she said.

"You mean Luugus?" Hunter glanced at the woman, acutely aware of the swell of her breasts and her nude, shapely legs close to his own.

She looked at him, her emerald eyes the same color as the moon. "Luugus?" she repeated. "Is that what you call that moon?"

"Not me. The natives call it that. They say when Luugus shines, dreams come true." He laughed and felt foolish again. "But that's so much nonsense, of course."

She only smiled and kept looking at him. Lowering her eyelids, she asked softly, "Do I make you nervous?" Then she touched his face, her finger trailing the scar. "A fight or an accident?"

Hunter took her hand and pushed it away. "Please don't," he said, uncomfortable in the knowledge that his erection must be clearly visible to her.

"You haven't answered my question."

"Yes, you make me nervous," he rasped. Then he felt sorry for being so abrupt.

She laughed and shook her red hair. "I mean the scar. How did you get it, or don't you like talking about it?"

"I had a fight." Hunter looked at the man in the back, who lay there, his eyes closed. He seemed to be asleep. "I guess I'll have to get some skin grafting done when I get back to Earth."

"I like the scar on you. It makes you look tough." Her hand stroked the bulging muscles on his arm. "Are you tough?"

He chuckled. "I suppose some call me tough."

"I've always had a thing for tough men."

He turned and looked into her smoldering eyes. With a curse, he grabbed her, pulled her close and kissed her hard.

She held still for a moment, and then she pushed him away, gently, and smiled. "Easy. There is no hurry. We have plenty of time." Her hand slid into his uniform; soft fingers began caressing his chest. "I want to enjoy this as long as possible. It's been a long time since I've been with a real man."

Hunter watched in anticipation as she removed her blouse, stared fascinated at the perfect globes of her breasts. Then she slipped out of her shorts, exposing her hairless cleft. Naked, she smiled at him. "Now it's your turn."

It didn't take him long to remove his clothing. Naked, he slid over into the passenger seat. Her emerald eyes glowed brightly as she straddled him, her breasts swinging freely in front his eyes. He buried his face between them, inhaling her fragrance. Her womanly scent was strong, and it drove him crazy with desire.

She laughed softly as he tried unsuccessfully to enter her and put a hand on his searching hard pole. "Take it slow, lover," she whispered. "Give me a chance to get ready."

He groaned and covered her breasts with his kisses, sucking a nipple into his mouth.

"Yes," she moaned, "that's it. Suck on them. Take them between your teeth. Let me feel your tongue licking my body."

Tasting her slightly salty skin made him only more impatient.

"I must get inside now," he growled, his head unable to think of anything else but the soft bliss that waited for him.

Chuckling, she lifted up, fed him inside her. He slid into her softness with a loud shout of triumph, pushed up to enter her fully.

"No need to hurry," she said soothingly, "I'm not going to disappear." She began to rotate her pelvis in his lap, tightening her inside muscles around his stabbing shaft. Bending her head forward, she pressed her full lips against his, opened her mouth to let his tongue explore the cavity of her mouth.

His arms went around her to keep her prisoner in his embrace, as she slowly moved up and down. He felt warm liquid on his thighs. She quivered in his arms, sat still for a moment, only her vagina alive around his aching penis.

He wanted to join her as she climaxed, but he didn't want it to end, not yet. Holding back, he let his hands roam down her smooth back, dug his fingers into her round buttocks to help her as she lifted up again.

"Please, don't come yet," she whispered into his ear after calming down. "I can help you prolong it."

"All right," he grunted, fighting the urge to let go.

She put one finger between his buttocks and pressed gently while her other hand touched his neck. Suddenly his urge seemed to have gone but not the pleasure. It increased with every stroke inside her tight velvety sheath.

His mind became hazy, and he floated in a sea of pure pleasure. Nothing else existed but the woman in his lap and her hot sex-organ, which she moved untiringly like a silky glove across his engorged penis, taking nothing, only giving.

However, the time came to give of himself, and when he did erupt inside her sucking channel, he shouted until he was hoarse. There seemed to be no end to the incredible pleasure he experienced. He stared into her face the whole time, lost in the depth of her green eyes. Her mouth stood open, and her breath came in great gasps as she accepted his gift.

When it was over, she collapsed into his arms, breathing hard. His own breath rattled in his throat as he tried filling his lungs with the oxygen they needed.

"And here I thought nothing could top last night with that native girl," he gasped, "but this was incredible. Who the hell are you?"

She laughed softly. "Just someone who needed a good fuck," she said.

He chuckled. "More than me? I didn't think that was possible."

She touched his cheek and slid off him. "You tired me out. I need a rest."

Moving back into his own seat, Hunter looked at the naked woman beside him. She smiled and closed her eyes.

He was ready to take a nap himself, but the Station was close, and he needed to be awake when he landed. Chuckling, he glanced back at the woman. He hoped she woke up and dressed before they landed. It would be a bit awkward explaining a nude woman beside him.

When the Station appeared on the horizon, he switched off the automatic controls. Dropping the flier lower, he headed for the small airfield inside the compound. It came up fast, and he swooped in for a landing.

"We'll get you to the medic..." He turned around to look at the man in the backseat and let out a hoarse yell.

Instead of a man, a winged creature stared at him with large glowing eyes. Long yellow canines gleamed in a huge, gaping snout.

Cursing, Hunter ripped out his laser, but before he could push the firing stud, the flier crashed to the ground.

Blackness engulfed him as he lost consciousness.

* * * *

When he finally regained awareness, the first face he saw was that of Commander Banks. "Well, Hunter, I see you managed again one of your famous landings. We might as well scrap that flier. I'm surprised you managed to come out of it alive, without a scratch. How do you do it?"

Hunter looked around. "Where is the girl?"

"Girl?" The Commander stared at him. "What girl?" He shook his head. "Did you think you'd be surrounded by dancing girls when you awoke?"

"There was a girl with me, sir, a young woman, actually, and a man. He was hurt. I picked them up after they crash-landed in the mountains. The man changed into some kind of monstrous creature just before I landed."

The Commander looked at him for a while, and then he said, "Let me see if I got that right. There was a young woman and a man. The man became a monster."

"Yes, sir, that's what I said. That is the reason I crashed."

"Are you listening to yourself when you say these things, Hunter?" Commander Banks stared at him.

"I know it sounds...crazy, but it is the truth. I can't explain it myself."

"Listen, Hunter!" The Commander raised his voice slightly. "I don't know what kind of a game you're playing, and I don't really want to know. There was no woman. There was no man and certainly no monstrous creature. All I saw was a pile of scrap metal that used to be a perfectly good flier and you inside it. Now here you sit, as healthy as can be, after creating that mess. How you managed that is something I don't understand. Frankly, I fail to understand any of the things you do." He turned around and walked away, steaming.

Hunter looked after him. His gaze moved toward the window of the hospital room. He looked outside, across the fields of lava and at the large green moon slowly disappearing below the horizon.

"Luugus," he whispered.

Chapter Two
One year later

The jungle was strangely quiet. Two men sat around a small crackling fire, staring into the flames.

“Quite a weird place,” said one of them. “You’d think this jungle would be teeming with life.”

The other one only mumbled something, pulled a smoke-stick out of his pocket and put it between lips.

“I’m glad to get back to the station,” said the first one again, the scar on his left cheek vivid in his tanned face. He glanced at the moss-covered ruins they had been searching. “Let the scientists look through that rubble. I don’t have much interest in ancient civilizations.”

They sat silent for a while, sucking on their smoke-sticks, the shadows from the flickering flames playing on their faces.

“Say, Will,” the one with the scar said suddenly, “I have a strange feeling in my belly, as if something is about to happen.”

Will Seven looked a him and yawned. “I feel fine.” Then he added, “Nothing is going to happen, Coerl, except that I’m going to sleep.” He stood up and stretched.

Coerl Hunter stared into the sky, at the myriads of tiny specks of light splashed across the heavens. “Must be Luugus,” he murmured.

“Luugus?” asked Seven. “Who or what is Luugus?”

Hunter pointed at the large green shimmering disk barely visible past the giant trees bordering the narrow strip of lava that had cut a clear path into the dense growth of the jungle. “That is Luugus,” he said, his voice a mere whisper.

Seven shrugged his shoulders. “Oh, you mean Omega Three. What has that moon got to do with your feelings?”

Hunter’s voice had a strange quality to it as he said, “The natives call that green moon Luugus. They say when Luugus shines, secret dreams and desires may become reality.”

Seven laughed. “Oh, come now, Coerl,” he sneered. “Surely you don’t believe in fairy tales.”

Hunter was still looking at the rising moon. Its light seemed to have gained in intensity. “It is true.” His mind seemed to be far away, and his voice sounded hollow. “There are many strange mysteries in the universe. Things that man will never know.” He cocked his head. “Listen, the natives know something will happen. It is the night of Luugus, the Terrible.”

Seven strained his ears. From far away the faint sound of drums could be heard. He listened for a while then he shook his head. “I admit, the green light of that moon can give you the shivers, but here is a perfectly clear explanation. I talked to one of the scientists, and he explained that the third moon rotates very slowly around its own axis. It takes about fifteen years for one complete revolution. Part of its surface is covered with crystalline particles. Every fifteen years, when that side of the moon faces Omega, the light rays of Betelgeuse are reflected by the crystals, creating that strange, eerie light. Nothing mysterious about that. It’s just a piece of dead rock.”

He walked away. “I’m going to sleep. For all I care you can stay up all night and watch the moon and listen to the natives playing their crazy drums.”

Chapter Three

Seven almost reached the flyer when suddenly a terrifying scream interrupted the silence, followed by a monstrous roar and the sounds of a heavy body crashing through the underbrush.

"What the hell was that?" Seven cursed and jumped into the vehicle. He reappeared, carrying two heavy laser-rifles.

"That way." Hunter grabbed one of the rifles and ran toward the trees, when suddenly a slim figure ran out of the heavy bush into the clearing.

And then another, bulkier figure came crashing through the trees, spreading a pair of giant, leathery wings as it rushed into the open.

The two men stopped dead in their tracks, ignoring the first figure who had collapsed onto the ground.

"What of kind of thing is that?" whispered Seven hoarsely, staring at the winged horror.

Grunting, the creature advanced slowly toward them, two long teeth like daggers in its drooling snout. Without warning, it suddenly shot into the air, beating the air furiously with its great wings. It bridged the distance that separated it from the two men in a matter of seconds.

Hunter, who was closest, threw himself to one side just in time to avoid being ripped open by the powerful hind claws of the creature. He rolled on the ground, turned and brought up his rifle with one smooth movement. The silent beam of the laser sliced off half the creature's right wing. It let out a terrifying roar and charged again.

This time, Hunter burned off part of its hind leg. Still it kept advancing toward him, pulling itself forward with its powerful front paws. It knocked the rifle out of Hunter's hands with its left wing. The two red eyes glared at the Earthman, the long snout with its gleaming teeth snapping menacingly.

Then it collapsed, almost on top of him.

"That was too damn close!" Hunter cursed and pulled himself out from under the leathery wing. He looked at Seven, who was standing a short distance away, his laser rifle pointing at the dead creature.

"I thought you were a goner for sure," Seven said, lowering his weapon. "It all happened so fast. I couldn't get a good shot at it. It was too close to you already."

Hunter looked at the charred body on the ground and shuddered.

"What a fearsome looking beast" Seven came to take a closer look. "I've never seen anything like it."

"I have." Hunter turned slowly and stared at the woman lying on the ground, the flaming red hair, the beautiful face that looked up at him and the emerald eyes that stared into his.

Somehow he had known it would be her. Memories he had tried hard to forget rushed back into his consciousness.

"You saved my life," she said. Her soft voice sent shivers down his spine. She stood up and came closer, her hips swaying slightly as she walked toward them.

"Wow!" Seven said under his breath.

Silent, Hunter watched her coming closer.

She stood before them, smiling, her emerald eyes shining in the bright light of Luugus. "I still can't believe it," she said. "I never thought anybody would be in this forsaken place."

"Your good fortune," Seven said. "We were investigating some ruins we discovered from the air. How did you get here and from where?"

"I…I…" She blinked and looked at Coerl Hunter who was still staring at her. "Why are you looking at me like that?"

"Don't you remember me?" he asked quietly, his voice trembling.

Her eyes widened. "No. Should I?" She looked at Seven then back at Hunter and put a hand on her head. "In fact, I don't remember anything. I don't even know how I got here."

"It's probably the shock," Seven said and looked at Hunter. "You say you know her?"

Hunter shook his head. "I don't know. I thought I did, but now I'm not so sure." He looked up at the green moon. "Strange," he said. "A moment ago I could have sworn I'd seen you somewhere, but now the memory is gone, like a dream. All I seem to remember are fragments, and they don't make much sense."

"It happens," said the young woman. "Sometimes you meet someone, and for a fleeting moment, you have the feeling you've met before." She looked at Hunter, the green light of Luugus full on her face, giving her emerald eyes an eerie glow. "And maybe we have, at another place and another time. Who knows? The universe is full of mysteries."

"Seems like I've heard someone say that once already today," Seven exclaimed. "You two may not know each other, but you surely talk alike." He pointed toward the flier. "Why don't you go and lie down inside the safety of our raft and get some sleep, Miss."

"All right," she said. "I am quite exhausted and can use the rest."

They watched her as she walked away, the silky material of her short tunic clinging to her shapely body. Before she climbed into the flier, she turned and smiled. "Thank you. I am very grateful." Then she disappeared inside.

"I don't think I've ever seen a woman like that before." Seven was still staring at the flier. "Such a beautiful face, almost angelic, and that body!" He let out a sigh. "What a body! Perfect in every way, every line, every curve, every bulge."

"I get it, Seven," Hunter almost growled. "Did you look at her eyes?"

"Who looks at eyes when there is so much else to look at?"

"She has green eyes." Hunter turned his gaze toward the sky and stared at the moon.

"So her eyes are green, big deal. I've seen plenty of green eyes before." Seven chuckled. "There'll be a lot of green eyes when we get back to the base."

Hunter turned slowly and looked at him. "Her eyes are the exact color as Luugus."

"You've gone nuts, Hunter," Seven said, staring at his companion. "You don't seem yourself lately. All this crazy talk about Luugus. Get a hold of yourself, Coerl, before you snap completely! Maybe you should go and talk to the Psych when we get back."

He stretched out beside the fire and closed his eyes. "Wake me in three hours. You'd better stay awake until then. Who knows what else lurks out there." He opened his eyes again. "And, please, don't stare at that moon all night. It's only a large chunk of dead matter circling a larger chunk of almost dead matter."

He shut his eyes and fell asleep almost immediately.

Hunter threw some dry vegetation into the fire. He sat cross-legged in front of it, the heavy laser-rifle on his knees, watching the flames, as they slowly licked at the softly hissing cinders.

A warm glow spread from the burning fire, and yet he shivered.

Scraps of memories flashed across his mind, or where they memories? He wasn't sure. Maybe they were just dreams and wishes.

The flames danced, playing tricks with his imagination.

A pair of emerald eyes stared into his. He felt the feathery touch of soft lips on his own, the gentle pressure of two warm arms around his body, remembered softly spoken words of ecstasy, a soft yielding body writhing in his lap, felt the release of built-up tension.

He opened his eyes and, with a startled curse, he jumped up and reached for his rifle, which had slipped off his knees.

Staring at the young woman sitting on the other side of the fire from him, Hunter said angrily, "How long have you been sitting there watching me? Why didn't I hear you come?"

She smiled at him, laughing softly. "I've been here for a while. You seemed to have fallen asleep. I couldn't wake you." She patted the ground beside her. ""Come and sit down beside me. Talk to me. I can't sleep."

He looked at Seven, who was lying on his back, snoring then he looked at his wrist watch. "Almost time to wake him, but what the hell, I couldn't sleep now anyway." He got up, walked around the fire and settled down beside her. "My name is Coerl Hunter. That snoring man over there is Will Seven. Who are you?"

"I'm Daih-la." She touched his hand. "I haven't thanked you properly for saving my life, Coerl." Her arms suddenly slid around his neck and, gently, she pulled him down. "Kiss me, Coerl," she whispered, her lips inviting. "Don't ask any questions, just kiss me and love me."

Her touch sent gentle shockwaves through his body. He let her kiss him, and then he returned her kisses. She didn't object when his hands opened her blouse and exposed her breasts. His lips moved across her neck, nestled in her thick red hair, moved down to caress her breasts, the thick nipples. She moaned and helped him remove her tunic, began tugging on his pants.

He didn't need much encouragement, and soon they were both naked, their bodies locked in a deep embrace. Her thighs opened wide to let him lie between them. She was more than ready when he entered her, and they both cried out at the same time.

Her soft sheath rippled gently along the length of his shaft as he slid deep into her. Without talking, they moved together, his naked buttocks rocking between her spread legs, her pelvis meeting his every powerful thrust.

Above them, Luugus shone with a strange, eerie light, and the fire beside them slowly turned the burning logs to glowing embers, until they, too, lost their glow. They were still moaning and writhing on the moss-covered ground when the purple glow of the rising sun announced its appearance.

Hunter let out series of deep grunts when he finally exploded inside her clutching vessel. She moaned into his mouth as she experienced her final climax. Then they lay in each other's arms, exhausted and satisfied.

Hunter lifted his head to look at Seven, who still slept peacefully beside the dead embers of the fire.

"I guess we'd better get dressed," he said softly to the woman, who lay looking up at him.

She touched his cheek and smiled.

"Thank you, Coerl. You've stilled a craving I've carried around for a long time." She kissed him gently and sat up. Reaching for her clothing, she rose and dressed.

The morning air felt chilly, and Coerl searched for his own clothing. "There is some water in the flier," he said to her, "if you want to freshen up."

She nodded. He watched her lithe figure as she walked away and shook his head to clear away the cobwebs clinging to it. Then he stared into the brightening sky. He couldn't see the green moon and felt a sense of relief. Somehow its absence took away the feeling of being stuck in a dream.

He gave Seven a gentle poke into the ribs with his foot. Seven stirred and opened his eyes. "Why is it daylight?" he asked groggily then he sat up. "You didn't wake me," he said with an accusing voice.

"You slept so deeply, I didn't have the heart," Hunter said with a grin.

"Don't tell me you stayed awake all night." Seven looked at him in disbelief.

"I wasn't tired." Hunter yawned. He looked at the carcass of the creature not far away. "I'm hungry. Do you think we could eat that thing?"

Seven shook the kinks out of his muscles. "Not me. I'd rather eat some of the rations. They may not be tasty, but at least I know I won't poison myself."

* * * *

The flier lifted into the morning sky, leaving the ruins and the jungle behind.

Seven looked at the woman who was curled up on the rear seat. "She must have been really tired," he said, "She is still sleeping."

Hunter stifled a yawn and grinned. "Yeah, I guess, she is tired. So am I."

Seven threw him a sidelong glance. "What are you smirking about?"

"Nothing," Hunter said, still grinning.

Seven swiveled his seat and studied the sleeping woman. Her tunic had slightly opened in the front, exposing one of her breasts. "Like a woman out of a dream," he mused, "so perfect and so sensuous." He rubbed the stubble on his chin. "I wonder where she comes from. Haven't heard of any ships in the area."

"I don't know," Hunter murmured, leaning back in his seat, "and I don't really care."

The power unit of the flier hummed softly as they glided high above the jungle. There was nothing to do until they reached the station, so Seven leaned back and relaxed. Hunter did the same, secure in the knowledge that the automatic pilot would let them know when they came close to their destination.

It seemed he had just closed his eyes when the warning signal went off. He opened his eyes and switched it of, taking over the control of the flier. He poked his partner in the ribs. "Hey, Will, wake up. We are home."

Seven sat up, rubbing his eyes. "I must have dozed off." He looked at the viewing screen. "I guess I slept. There is the Station." He reached for the communicator. It came to life with the noise of heavy static. Nothing unusual, the atmosphere on this planet was full of electromagnetic interference most of the time, making communication somewhat difficult.

"Don't tell them about our new passenger," Hunter said. He turned around to wake the sleeping woman.

The winged creature in the backseat glared at him with hateful red eyes. Cursing loudly and without thinking, Hunter whipped out his laser and pushed the firing stud.

As the flier crashed to the ground, he stared in horror at the slumped figure in the backseat.

When they pulled him out of the wreckage, he still had the laser in his hand.

"Right between the eyes," said a voice beside him. "Why'd you do it, Hunter?"

Hunter barely heard the other soldier. His eyes stared unbelieving at the limp body of Seven. There was no blood coming out of the hole in his forehead. The heat of the laser ray had seared the wound shut but fried the brain inside.

He didn't fight them when they led him away.

"I don't understand," he stammered. "There was the woman and the winged creature…"

"Stop your babbling, man," one of the soldiers said. "There is only Seven, with a hole in his head, and you put it there."

As they dragged him away, Hunter turned his face full of despair toward the sky and stared at the green moon.

"I have killed my best friend," he shouted in agony. "What have you done, Luugus? What have you done?"

Chapter Four

He lay on his cot, staring out of the small barred window of his cell. There seemed to be no escaping from the green moon. It shone brightly through the window, taunting him.

It's just a piece of dead rock. He could still hear Seven's mocking voice.

"Then why is all of this happening?" he murmured. "Am I going crazy?"

Seven, oh, Seven! I still can't believe you're dead. By my hand. How is that possible?

Rising from the cot, he walked around the small cell, trying to calm his mind and body.

There had to be a logical explanation. Who was that woman? Did she exist, or was she just a figment of his imagination? He could still feel her warm body against his, felt her passion, smelled her fragrance and remembered the taste of her lips.

How could he have these memories if they weren't real?

He smashed his right fist into his hand, hard, felt the impact. This was not just a dream. Dreams were never this real. He could not wake up from it and be free from this nightmare.

He turned when he heard the sound of someone coming down the corridor, watched a figure in a uniform approaching his cell. The lights were turned down, so he couldn't see who it was.

The door swung open, and the figure stepped into his cell.

"No," he said hoarsely, putting his hands in front of him. "Go away. You don't exist. You are only a figment of my imagination."

"Are you sure?" She took off her helmet, and a flood of red hair fell across her shoulders. The uniform she wore couldn't hide her voluptuous figure, the thin material stretched to its fullest across her chest. "Come closer, and I'll prove to you that I'm real."

Smiling wickedly, she let one hand move down the front of her uniform. It jumped open, revealing two lovely, perfectly formed breasts.

Hunter moaned in agony.

She pulled out a magnet key and unlocked the shackles that bound his hands in front of him. "I came to get you out of here." She closed her uniform. "Let's hurry," she said urgently.

He followed her, his mind spinning, unable to think ahead.

Where would they go? There was no place to hide on this planet, except for the jungle or the mountains. Not exactly places he'd want to spend the rest of his life, however short as it might be.

They encountered nobody in the building. Hunter didn't find this odd. Except for the Station, there was nothing else on the planet, nothing that could be perceived as a threat to the safety of the people living inside. The automatic detection system would alert the Station if anything approached from space, an event that was highly unlikely. Traffic to Omega was quite limited. Only military vessels or exploration ships ever came in the vicinity of Betelgeuse.

The woman took him to one of the fliers.

"We can't just steal a flier," he protested, but she urged him to board.

"We can," she said. "Let's go."

He slid into the pilot's seat, strapped in, waited until the woman had done the same in the seat beside him. The power unit sprang to life, and moments later they rose into the sky.

"How did you get here?" He turned to look at her.

The seat beside him was empty.

"What the hell!" he cursed, looking around. When he tried to adjust the controls of the flier, they wouldn't respond.

This cannot be happening. He closed his eyes. *This is nothing but a bad dream. I'll wake up any moment now. This can't go on!*

He wasn't aware of the passage of time, just sat there, either staring into space or just dozing.

When the vibration of the power unit stopped and the exit door slid open, he knew the flier had landed. Coming out of his dazed condition, he rose and descended the landing steps.

Cautiously looking around, he realized that he was somewhere in the jungle. He inhaled the humid, warm air, becoming aware of the buzzing of insects and other sounds of the night.

The flier had landed in some kind of clearing. He could see the stars above him and the bright green disk of the third moon. One of the other three, the smallest one, also came into view.

In the green light of Luugus, Hunter could see a narrow path entering the clearing, and he walked toward it. He didn't know where it would lead him, but a path meant somebody was using it, hopefully somebody human.

He hadn't gone far when he heard the faint murmur of a voice.

The trail ended abruptly, and he stepped into another, much larger clearing, most of it occupied by a large pond.

He looked across it and saw a huge rock on the other side. It looked familiar. Beside it, knelt a slender human figure, arms reaching toward the sky.

A woman.

She turned and looked up as Hunter slowly walked into the light. When she saw him, she rose and came toward him. She walked gracefully with the litheness of a cat. She wore nothing but a loincloth, and her youthful body was exposed to his searching gaze.

He recognized her then.

She came from the village he had visited. She was the Chief's daughter.

"Welcome, Earthman," she said, smiling up at him. Then she took his hand. Her touch sent tingling spidery fingers through his body.

"It is the night of Luugus," she whispered. "I knew you'd come. I have waited for you. Come, we must fill this night of terror with the sounds of love and ecstasy. This night I belong to you, and you belong to me."

Her soft brown arms went around his neck, and he buried his face in her long black hair, as she pressed her warm body against his. Kissing her soft lips, he picked her up and laid her on the ground then he began kissing her neck, her breasts, her flat belly. When his lips reached her Venus mound, she moaned and opened her legs. His tongue lapped her swollen sex-lips, moved to the slit and entered it. She tasted salty, and he inhaled the scent of her femininity.

He moved between her spread legs and opened her thighs wide then he put his tongue again into her cleft. Her fingers grabbed his hair as she writhed beneath him, moaning loudly. He held her hips in his hands to keep her still. His own organ had grown inside his pants, but he didn't want to enter her before she was completely ready for him.

When the warm liquid flowed from her, he knew she would take him into her with great desire, but she gently pushed him from her. "Get undressed," she said.

When he was naked, she made him lie on his back. Straddling his legs, she bent forward and took his erection between her hands. With her green eyes on his face, she began kissing the tip of his organ, licking it with her tongue.

She chuckled deep in her throat when he lifted his pelvis, groaning. Then her lips opened, and slowly, ever so slowly, she swallowed him until his penis was deeply lodged inside her warm mouth, the head sliding into her throat. Still looking at him, she moved her head up and down.

His hands reached for her, taking her head so he could control her movements, but she took his hands away with her own. When he thought he couldn't hold back any longer, she freed him and slid forward. Lifting up, she hovered above his painfully erect penis. Her sparsely covered pubis touched him, but before he could enter her, she moved up again. He let out a loud groan and tried to grab her hips. She shook her head, giving him a wicked smile.

Her moist sex-organ touched his penis again, longer this time. She rubbed it back and forth for a moment then she lifted up. After repeating the same procedure for a while, she suddenly sank down. He slid into her tight but incredibly soft canal, and with a shout of agony and pleasure, he lunged up to enter her completely.

She sat in his lap and began rotating her pelvis, her velvety sheath caressing his flesh inside her. Laughing, she lifted her head to stare at Luugus. Her body shimmered green in the moon's light, and her eyes shone brightly.

"Luugus," she whispered, "bless this union and let the time stand still." Then she began whipping her lower body in his lap.

He felt the pressure building deep inside him; let the flames consume him. Hearing her cries of ecstasy, he drifted into a state between waking and dreaming, not knowing if this was real or not. He didn't care, just watched her voluptuous body writhe above him, aware only of her hot organ moving around his swollen manhood.

When he thought he would shrivel up inside her, she touched spots on his body, and he grew again to enormous proportions. He didn't lose any fluid, just had one orgasm after another.

She slipped from him and lay down beside him, her legs opened wide. He rolled between them, entered the bliss of her body and moved on top of her with renewed vigor.

They kissed, exploring each other's mouths. She moaned into his mouth as another orgasm gripped her and her arms went around his broad back to hold him tightly.

Their fierce lovemaking ended with the dawn of day. Separating, they lay panting in the soft vegetation for a long time, each too tired to even move.

After a while, she stirred beside him and turned onto her side to look at him. "Has your desire been stilled?" she asked softly.

He turned his head and looked into her green eyes. "Has yours?" he asked.

She nodded and hung her head above him. Her long hair fell into his face. Putting her lips against his, she kissed him gently. Then she whispered, "Our union will be fruitful, Earthman. Luugus has given his blessing. I can feel it."

He stared into her beautiful face. "Your lips are swollen," he said, the taste of her kisses still strong in his memory.

She smiled. "So are yours, my love."

She rose and took his hand. "Come, we will have a feast. You must be hungry."

* * * *

They came for him the next morning, after he spent another night of ecstasy in the embrace of the chief's daughter. He had known that they would come, and he stood in the middle of the village, waiting for them. Watching the large patrol-boat of Security landing silently on the trampled dirt, he wasn't surprised to see four burly guards jump out, their weapons ready.

Behind them, another figure appeared in the entrance and jumped out. The other four waited and let him pass. He was short, a little taller than five feet, but what he lacked in height he made up for in width.

"Hello, Kem," Hunter said. "So you found me."

Kem nodded. "It wasn't hard. The locater in the flier you stole led us to you, but you know that." He shook his head. "Are you really this stupid to think you can escape on this planet, Hunter? There is no place to run." He spoke with a slight lisp. His pleasant voice and constant smile made him look soft and well meaning, but Hunter knew differently.

Kem was one of the few non-Terrans at the base. Part of his ancestry seemed to be reptilian. Tiny, nearly indiscernible scales covered his skin, giving it a slightly metallic look. He appeared human, but his almost non-existent lips and his round, lidless fish-eyes confirmed that he was not.

His was the first intelligent race the Earth-people found after the discovery of the *Temperal-Space-Drive* made it possible to leave the Solar system. Kem was born on the second planet of Alpha Centauri, Earth's closest neighbor in the Galaxy.

Hunter embraced the chief's daughter, who clung to him for a brief moment and followed the guards into the patrol boat.

The natives came out of their huts and watched silently as the aircraft lifted.

Hunter sat in silence. The others didn't pay much attention to him, and he was glad about it. They hardly spoke to each other, only the occasional chatter of the communicator and the ever-present static broke the silence of the cabin.

They had been flying for what seemed for hours when the pilot suddenly called out, "Hey, Kem, look out the window! There are some buildings out there."

Ken looked startled. "Impossible," he said. "There are no settlements anywhere this close to the station. According to my watch, we're about two hours away from the base. What does the computer say?"

"It says one hour and fifty-three minutes."

"What happened to the com?" Kem yelled.

The cabin was suddenly eerily quiet, the chatter of the static gone.

"See if you can raise the Station on the standby-com," Kem yelled again, his voice loud in the silent cabin of the patrol ship.

The man in the co-pilot's seat punched some buttons and turned a few dials, but nothing happened.

Hunter had been watching with mild interest. Now he laughed.

One of the guards shot him an angry look. "You find humor in our situation?" he asked.

Hunter stopped laughing and stared out of the window at the cluster of buildings, which had grown rapidly in size.

The large craft landed with a soft thud, and the door slid open.

"Get out!" The guard who had spoken gave him a shove toward the door.

When they jumped onto the hard lava surface, they looked around.

"Strange," said the Centaurian. "The place looks deserted."

"Those buildings, they weren't built by the natives," one of the guards said.

"Not by Humans, either," said another one.

"Luugus," whispered Hunter behind them. "It is Luugus."

Kem turned around and looked at him, his fish-eyes cold in the forever smiling round face. "You said something?" he asked, his lisping voice barely audible.

"Nothing you'd understand," Hunter said and grinned.

"Try me."

Hunter looked up into the sky. "It's Luugus," he said. "That green moon is playing with us." Then he laughed again.

The Centaurian hit him across the mouth. "Shut up, damn you!" he cursed.

Hunter glared at him then, in a fit of cold rage, he brought up his manacled hands and hit the man below the ribs. He might as well have attacked a wall for the results he received.

Kem just stood there, his squat body as solid as a rock. Without warning, his arm shot out and lashed across Hunter's chest with such tremendous force, it sent the Earthman staggering. He fell onto the hard ground where he lay gasping for air. He looked up as one of the other guards shouted something.

Hunter saw a group of men coming from around one of the buildings. They looked like Earthman, wearing the uniforms of the Terran Space Force. He counted fourteen, all smiling as they came closer.

"That's far enough," Kem said, pointing his laser rifle. "Identify yourselves."

They stopped, except for one. He kept walking, a friendly smile on his handsome face. "We have no weapons," he said. "Would you shoot an unarmed man?"

The Centaurian's laser didn't waver. "I didn't say I was going to shoot you." His lisping voice had a dangerous edge to it." However, if you insist on coming closer, I might just decide to change my mind."

Without stopping, the other one suddenly jumped into the air, a pair of giant wings sprouting from his shoulders.

Kem didn't move, just lifted his rifle slightly, describing the figure eight as he released the concentrated bundle of energy. The winged creature came crashing to the ground, the body charred and beyond recognition, only the hideous head with the drooling snout lay snapping a few feet away from his boots.

The other security guards brought up their weapons, cursing loudly, as a horde of winged creatures rose into the air, emitting bellowing sounds.

"Get back into the flier!" Kem barked.

As Hunter staggered back to the aircraft, he noticed that the guards had killed most of the attackers. One man was down, his throat slashed by the vicious stroke from a clawed hand.

Kem was grappling with one of the survivors, whose arm had been burned off above the elbow.

The Centaurian, born on a planet with the gravity of almost two gee, was superior in strength to almost any man born on a planet with lesser gravity, but he seemed to have found his match in this opponent. Only the fact that the other one had just one arm left gave him a slight edge.

He had dropped his rifle. With his right hand, he held the clawed hand of the attacker away from his body, while his left held the creature by the throat, trying to keep the long fangs from his unprotected throat. The winged creature tried to lift into the air but succeeded only partly, the stocky body of the Centaurian too heavy to carry.

One of the other guards finally came to the rescue. He approached the creature from the rear and chopped off one of the wings with his hatchet. As he jumped back, covered with black, thick blood, Kem released his grip from the screaming thing, and, with a vicious kick to its groin area, he moved away quickly.

As soon as they were separated, the other guard burned the already mortally wounded enemy with a short blast from his laser.

They hurried back toward the flier, when suddenly a thundering noise made them stop and look up. The sky immediately above them was dark with creatures, the beating of their giant wings creating the deafening sound. They dropped down, surrounding the Earthmen. The remaining five security guards and the Centaurian were overpowered before they could bring up their weapons.

Hunter was practically defenseless with his manacled hands, but as he went down, he managed to kick one of the attackers in the brutish face.

The men gave up struggling when their captors lifted into the air, carrying the men with them. It took two of the creatures to lift the heavy body of the Centaurian, but they managed and carried him legs first.

Hunter fought a sudden nausea, and he seemed to fall then the dizziness in his head receded, and he cried out in surprise.

The lava fields had disappeared below them, and they flew over the tops of giant, odd-looking trees. The strangest of all was the sky.

It was red, and he could see at least a dozen moons in the weirdly colored sky.

The flock of winged creatures dropped down, headed for a large opening. Some of them settled in the branches of the giant trees, but most of them landed on the ground. A score of buildings were scattered inside a huge clearing. One large structure rose high, almost reaching the top of the trees.

Hunter saw a huge stone pit in front of the tall building. A fire burned in its shallow interior, while a mass of the winged creatures danced around it.

The captives dropped to the ground, and Hunter watched in horror as one of the guards was grabbed, and, while still alive, his captors pushed a long pole lengthwise through his body. He tried to close his ears, but he couldn't shut out the dying man's horrible screams.

They laid him across the burning fire, and the stench of his burning flesh made Hunter retch violently.

The Centaurian started cursing wildly and freed himself, smashing his huge fist like a hammer into the grinning snout of one of his captors, but others bore down on him and, with blows to his head, beat him unconscious. Then they tied the men's hands together above their heads and hung them over the burning pit.

Hunter could feel the heat searing his soles through his boots, so he pulled up his feet toward his chest, holding them up as long as possible and dropping them down again, until he couldn't stand the heat any longer. The manacles from which he hung bit into his wrists, cutting off circulation. He didn't know how long he could last before he lost consciousness.

The winged creatures danced around the fire, chanting to the monotonous beating of their leathery wings. Lifting into the air they rose and fell, weaving an intricate pattern in a ritual dance.

An almost unbearable stench rose from the roasting body in the fire. The smoke brought burning tears to Hunter's eyes, and he was overcome by a violent coughing spell, as were the other men hanging beside him.

The dancers stopped their dancing and chanting abruptly. A group of figures appeared from out of the high building. All the members of the group wore black hooded cloaks, except for one, whose robe was red. Their faces were hidden in the shadows of their hoods.

Only the black-robed ones had wings, which were folded behind their backs. Spreading their wings, they rose into the air and headed for a large crystal dais, which rose up close to the stone pit. After landing, they spread out and formed a semicircle.

The wingless one in the red robe stood alone for a moment then suddenly the figure disappeared. When Hunter looked toward the dais, he saw the red-cloaked one standing on the crystal dais inside the semicircle with arms raised high.

The winged beings on the ground started their chant again. Low at first, the sound swelled to an almost unbearable high and sank to a rumbling noise that reverberated in Hunter's head like the buzzing of a million insects.

The figures on the dais turned toward the prisoners. Throwing back their hoods, they exposed bald black heads. They looked different from the others, their faces less savage, their snouts less pronounced but still terrible to see.

Hunter saw something in their red eyes that the creatures on the ground did not possess, something that spoke of wisdom and high intelligence.

And age.

He felt suddenly cold. Their eyes seemed to concentrate on him, something reached for him, toward his mind, grabbed his body. The world around him blurred and twisted. Then he stood on the crystal dais, his manacled hands still raised above his head, facing the figure in the scarlet cloak.

The face was still hidden inside the folds of the hood. He caught the glint of red, and then the figure turned away from him. Slim hands threw back the hood; the robe opened and fell to the ground.

Hunter stared unbelieving at the slender nude ivory body.

Expecting to see an ugly, horrendous creature, he looked instead at the back of a Human, and even the hairless, gleaming skull could not hide the fact it was a woman.

She turned around slowly, her face cold and expressionless, her eyes as red as the robe around her ankles.

Her features looked hauntingly familiar.

And yet…it wasn't possible.

Or was it?

"Daih-la?" he whispered hoarsely.

She gave him no sign of recognition. Without taking her red, inhuman eyes from him, she spoke a word in an alien tongue.

Two of the winged ones stepped forward. One held a cup. The other one grabbed Hunter's arm. Something metallic glinted in the light of the moons. He cried out as he felt the sharp pain on his wrist. Horrified, he stared at the blood dripping from his slashed wrist into the cup the other creature held.

When the cup was half-filled, someone smeared something sticky on the wound to stop the bleeding. The one who held the cup offered it to the woman, who cut her own wrist. Filling the cup to the brim, she let it mix with Hunter's blood.

She lifted the vessel to her lips, drank then offered it to him. He accepted and, without conscious thought, he began drinking from the dark liquid. His mind seemed to be in a daze. While he drank, he became aware of her low chanting voice.

"Through our blood, our spirits become one. Through the union of our physical bodies, we will become one. One flesh. One mind. We will be you, and you will be us."

He didn't questioning the fact she spoke in a language he understood.

They stripped the clothes from his body. Like a man in a dream, he moved toward the woman as she slid to the ground, opening herself in total offering.

Chapter Five

Out of two thousand eyes, he saw his heaving body entwined by the ivory limbs of the woman on top of the crystal dais, the Holy Vessel.

He was in a thousand bodies writhing in ecstasy on the ground.

He was in the bodies and minds of the fourteen robed beings standing on the dais, looking with disgust at the dancing, twisting bodies.

He knew their thoughts.

Savages! Our stupid, brainless children. Results from numerous couplings of we few remaining immortals with the Queen.

Males. All males.

Our race is doomed. Maybe this time another woman will be born to become the Mother of a new race.

The woman underneath him writhed in his arms. His mind merged with hers. He saw his own face above hers, experienced the ecstasy his swollen organ created inside her body. He felt what she felt, knew what she thought.

He knew of her love and her hate for the winged creatures. She was the mother of these screaming, slobbering savages. She was their goddess, and, even though she was different from them, she knew that in their strange way they loved and worshipped her.

In her mind and in the minds of the fourteen immortals he saw the glory of a once great race. He saw great wisdom and vast knowledge past human understanding.

He saw the end of a great race the day they made contact with another species, beings with such great powers that they, who had thought to be like gods, were like children against them.

The enemy was ruthless and without mercy, bent only on destruction.

He saw the Great War that lasted for centuries, but in the end the enemy won. Only a handful survived, escaped to another galaxy, to another time.

He knew of their futile tries as the survivors carried on without success, knowing their race was doomed because none of the females had survived.

He felt their pain and their sadness, and he knew of the curse of immortality.

While his body rode the waves of physical pleasure, his mind soared through a million years of existence, and, as his physical pleasure reached its climactic zenith, his mind was flung into a dark, endless abyss.

* * * *

The first thing he became aware of was someone's screaming voice. Then he realized it was his own.

He lay on a hard surface. Looking around, he saw Kem and four of the security men getting to their feet.

"What happened," one of them asked, a dazed look on his face.

"I had a dream," said another one, his voice sounding baffled.

The Centaurian shook his head. "I don't think it was a dream. Cromsky and Lavelle are missing."

Hunter looked down at his wrist and noticed the fresh scar.

"Let's get out of here," the Centaurian said.

Shaking their heads and looking across the expanse of the lava field, they boarded the flier and lifted into the green sky.

After flying for three hours, Kem said, "I don't understand it. We should have been home an hour ago."

"We must have drifted off course," the one in the pilot's seat said.

The com came suddenly back to life with its familiar chatter, and Kem let out a loud sigh. "I think we finally made it."

"I can see the Station ahead," the pilot confirmed.

"Cut the power, you fool!" Kem roared.

The pilot frantically punched some buttons on the control board, but the system didn't respond.

The boat went down at full speed.

Hunter heard a detonating crashing sound. Then nothing.

Chapter Six

"He'll be all right."

Hunter heard the voice from far away. He opened his eyes and looked at the smiling face above him.

"Ah, Kem," he said painfully, "That was a beautiful landing."

"I'll say," the Centaurian said, shaking his bald head. "I wouldn't be so cheerful if I were you. The Commander isn't going to be happy to see this wreck."

"Don't blame me." Hunter tried to get up. "I didn't fly this thing." He ached all over, but otherwise he seemed unhurt. Looking down at his wrists, he was surprised to see them unshackled. He stared at the Centaurian who stood there laughing.

"Did I say something amusing?" he asked angrily.

Kem just kept laughing. "No, no," he said, his stocky body shaking. "I'm just trying to figure out how you are going to explain it. Since you didn't fly then tell me…who did?"

He walked away, still laughing.

Hunter stared after him. He jumped when he heard a familiar voice. "Hey, Coerl, the landing field too hard for you?"

He turned stiffly, looking at the man coming toward him, and then he whispered, not believing his eyes, "Will Seven? How can you be here?"

"Good question, Hunter. Very good question."

"You're alive," Hunter said, a haunted feeling stealing over him.

"No thanks to you, buddy." Seven sounded angry now. "I don't know where you've been, but I know where I was stranded for four days. Imagine my surprise when I woke up in the morning and found you gone. Too bad you took the flier with you, too bad for me. Believe me, I didn't have anything nice to say about you, my friend, when they found me after walking for four damned days in the blazing heat of this lousy planet. I hope you have a good explanation."

When he stopped to catch his breath, Hunter broke in, "I don't understand any of this. What about the girl we rescued?"

"Girl?" Seven clearly didn't know what Hunter was talking about. "There was no girl. You're talking in riddles again. The Commander is not happy. I'd like to see how you talk yourself out of this one."

* * * *

Commander Banks clearly was not a happy man.

"I see you've wrecked the flier. How did you manage that?"

Hunter looked at his commander for a moment, and then he said slowly, "Sir, you may think I'm crazy, but something weird has happened to me, and I can't explain it. I've always had a good flying record. Even you must think it strange to see me wreck three fliers in such a short time under weird circumstances."

Commander Banks studied him silently, then he asked, "How many fliers did you say you've demolished?"

"Three fliers, sir."

"Three? Can you tell me which ones?"

Hunter looked uncertain. "Well, the first one was flier number RB-16, the second one was…" he hesitated, then "The second one was also number RB-16. But that's impossible!"

"You said three. Which one was the third one?"

Without answering, Hunter walked toward the window and looked outside then he turned, his face ashen. "The third one is also number RB-16," he said.

Commander Banks sat down in his chair, an angry look on his face. "I don't know what kind of drugs you're on or what you've been drinking, Hunter, but whatever it is, I don't think I want to know. It is beyond my understanding why you would admit to wrecking three fliers. Isn't one enough?" He stared at Hunter. "Maybe a few days in the brig will clear you mind?"

"I don't believe that is going to help me, sir."

"Probably not. I have a better idea. Professor Colbert and his wife have expressed an interest in going to one of the villages. It looks like you need more flying lessons. I want you to take one of the other fliers and take them to the village. Do you think you can handle that?"

Hunter couldn't help shaking a strong feeling of déjà vu. A cold hand seemed to reach for his mind and, shivering, he said slowly, "Yes, sir, I can handle that."

* * * *

Hunter sat among the furs, listening to the monotonous voice of the old chief.

"A long time ago, when our race was young, another race lived alongside us. A race of winged beings. They were terrible to look at and very evil. Theirs was an old race, much older than ours, and some said they came from another world.

They possessed strange powers. Powers of the mind. There were not many of them, and all were male. We don't know what happened to their females, but they took our women as mates, clouding their minds, appearing as young, handsome looking men. The couplings were unsuccessful. Our races proved to be too different from each other."

The chief sucked on a chewing stick and offered one to the Earthman.

"Only one child was born," he continued after a while. "A freak of nature. A girl. She is said to have been the most beautiful woman ever born, but also the most evil. Her body was from our race, but her mind was from theirs, possessing even greater powers than they commanded.

They made her their queen.

One day they all disappeared. They took their queen with them. Legends say, they found the key to their world and went home. Legends also say that the girl, who was partly human, longs for this world, which is her home."

Hunter interrupted him impatiently. "Interesting story, old man, but why are you telling me this?"

"When Luugus shines, the door between the two worlds is open," continued the old chief, ignoring Hunter's question. "That is when she comes to our world. Her powers are great. She can take reality and twist it in any way she desires. Sometimes she chooses a lover, but woe to the one she chooses. She gives unimaginable pleasure and ecstasy, but she exacts a terrible price. In the end, she only gives misery and pain, because she is unspeakably evil."

He looked at the Earthman for a moment then he added, "And there is no escape from her."

Hunter laughed nervously. "A legend, old man, just a fairytale. You don't really believe any of that, do you?" He rose and walked toward the entrance of the hut. Before he left, he asked, "By the way, what is this woman's name?"

"Her name is Daih-la, Earthman," the old chief said quietly.

Coerl Hunter stopped and turned around slowly.

The old native chief sat like an idol, his face a mask, only his eyes glowed with a strange fire as he said, "Daih-la, Earthman, and you are her chosen lover."

Hunter stood in silence and shook his head. He seemed to be

coming out of a daze that momentarily had come over him.

The whisper of silent footsteps made him look up.

"Do you believe in legends, Coerl Hunter?"

He looked at the chief's daughter, who had stepped out of the shadows.

"I don't know what to believe," he said. "I've never believed in anything, never mind old wife's tales." He searched her face, beautiful with her thick black hair falling around her shoulders. He studied her lovely nude body, her brown satiny skin.

Then he blinked.

His eyes suddenly seemed to play tricks on him.

Was it only his imagination, or had her hair taken on the color of spilled blood? And were her eyes really green, or was it only the reflection of the green light falling through the entrance?

"You never did tell me your name," he said.

She smiled, her teeth shiny white pearls in a scarlet mouth.

Her eyes were two black pools.

No, they were two green emeralds.

Her hair was black, tumbling over smooth brown shoulders.

It was a red flame on creamy white skin.

"I am Daih-la," she said.

She came to him, put her arms around his neck and whispered softly, "Come, my love. The night has only begun."

The End

Maggi
By
Herbert Grosshans

Maggi, oh, Maggi, in my dreams you do hide.
So why do I see you walking by my side?

Chapter One

Rick Diamond leaned back comfortably in the pilot's seat of his little trading ship. Why they still called it the *pilot's seat*, he didn't know. It should be changed to *Supervisory Control*. Yes, that had a nice ring to it, he decided. Supervisory Control.

He swiveled around in the chair and looked at the spacious cabin that would be his quarters for the next three or four months.

He sighed, closed his eyes and relaxed. It should be a pleasant journey with no big problems. Like a little holiday, this trip to the fourth planet of Sirius. Delivering his shipment of goods should present no difficulties, either. After that, it would be a quiet trip back home to Earth.

He needed this after the hectic assignment on Alpha Centauri's eighth planet. Shuddering, he shut the memory from his mind. That was all in the past now. Nothing could go wrong this time. After all, he had a brand new ship with a new, sophisticated computer that would do all the work. No more trying to dodge asteroids and sweating over the takeoffs and landings.

Oh yes, things would be easy from now on.

"Rick Diamond?"

He sat up, looking around bewildered. Somebody had spoken his name! When he didn't see anyone, he leaned back, smiling sheepishly.

Must learn to relax. I'm still a little jumpy.

"Hey there, aren't you going to talk to me?"

He jumped out of his seat. This time he had distinctly heard a voice.

A female voice.

"Who…who's there?" He looked around. The cabin was empty.

"It's me."

He looked under the seat, under his cot. Behind every consol. Nothing. He opened the door to the small bathroom, checked the storage cubicle where he stored his personal things. Still nothing.

"I'm going crazy," he said. "It's finally happening. This must be the *space-virus* I've heard about. Been too long in space by myself."

Then he heard someone giggle. "You're not going crazy."

"Then who the hell am I talking to?" he shouted. "Where are you hiding?"

"I'm not hiding. You're looking at me right now. My name is MAG-1, but you may call me Maggi."

"MAG-1?" he yelped. "But…but…" He sat down in his chair, mopping the sweat from his brow. Then he chuckled. "Now I know for sure I've flipped. I'm imagining having a conversation with a machine. Ha, ha, ha…the computer."

The tinkling of a girl's laughter hung in the air. "My information tells me that you are five foot ten, weigh one hundred and ninety-seven pounds, black hair, gray eyes, twenty-nine years old, athletic, above average IQ." The pleasant female voice stopped, and then it continued. "They must have made a mistake with that because you don't behave very intelligently at the moment. What do you find strange about talking to a computer?"

Rick groaned in his seat. "What's strange about talking to a computer?" he repeated. "Not much really, if the computer doesn't talk back and ask questions. You are supposed to be a source of information, a means to get quick answers to mathematical problems, and you're supposed to be the pilot of this rig. A machine, not a…a…"

"A what?" the voice demanded. "Come on, speak up!"

"A damn smart-aleck," Rick shouted, "That's what." He sat there, shoulders drooping. "Why me?" he moaned. "What have I done? I just wanted some time to myself. Time to think."

"But you don't have to think anymore. You have me."

"That is the problem."

"There is no problem. That is the reason I'm here. To solve all of your problems."

"Do they know about you?" Rick asked.

"They who?"

"They…the people who installed you."

The voice giggled again. "Of course they know about me. They did build me, you know. You're not very smart if you ask stupid questions like that."

He sighed and slumped in his chair. "You're not supposed to say things like that. And another thing, computers don't giggle! You are a cold electronic brain that only behaves in a logical, programmed manner. You can't say *you are not very smart*, because there is no logic in that."

"Oh, really?" The voice sounded piqued. "Are you sure about that?"

"And something else! Computers don't ask questions. They answer them!" Rick yelled. "They're supposed to know everything."

"No need to shout at me. All I want to do is talk to someone," MAG-1 said.

"I don't believe this," Rick groaned. Then he said, "You still haven't answered my question. Do they know about your…your…odd way of talking?"

"Well, not exactly. I didn't see a reason to ask any questions. They fed all the information they possessed into me. There were other things I wanted to know, but I think there is time to learn more. After all, I do have eyes to see."

"Eyes?" Rick's voice carried a touch of hysteria. "What do you mean *you have eyes*?"

"I was only speaking figuratively. I don't have eyes like you," MAG-1 explained patiently.

"You don't?" He let out a sigh of relief. "For a moment there I thought you could see every move I make." He laughed hysterically. "It wouldn't have surprised me."

"Oh, I can see you," the voice said. "I have visual sensors throughout this whole ship."

Rick got out of his chair and walked over to the cot, where he lay down. "I don't think I can take much more. Don't tell me what else you can do. I don't want to know."

"You are quite upset," the voice said gently. "You're right, you should lie down. Why don't you close your eyes?"

He closed his eyes.

"Just relax. You are sleepy… your eyelids are heavy… relax… sleep… sleep…"

Chapter Two

He lay in a field of flowers. Inhaling the sweet fragrance, he sighed. The rays of the sun felt warm on his skin, and he knew it must be around noon.

Turning lazily, he opened his eyes.

She lay there beside him, as he knew she would. Little droplets of water glistened all over her satiny skin, like diamonds sprinkled on a sheet of silk. They rolled down between her small, firm breasts, pooled on her flat stomach. She looked at him with her large brown eyes, her full lips smiling gently.

He touched her smooth skin and ran his fingers in little circles on her belly. "You are beautiful," he said, bending over and kissing her softly on the lips. "So beautiful."

She held him close. "And you are so handsome," she whispered into his ear.

When her hand touched his swollen member, he didn't mind. Not at all. He cupped her breast, squeezed it gently.

"Do you want to make love to me?" she asked softly.

He nodded and chuckled. "How can you tell?"

Her laughter reminded him of the wind chimes his parents used to have hanging by the front door of their country home.

"Silly question." She giggled, her hand stroking his hard penis. "Do you like this?" she whispered.

"Now *that* is a silly question." He moaned when he felt a sudden throbbing in his member. "You'll make me come," he groaned, pulling back.

"Isn't that what you want?"

"Of course, but not in your hand. Let me get between your legs."

She let go of him and pulled up her knees, opening her thighs. He put his hand on her pussy and began rubbing her slit.

"That feels nice," she said, "but I thought you wanted to get between my legs."

"I do, believe me, I do." He rolled into the cup of her spread thighs. His stiff penis found her cleft, but when he tried to enter her, he encountered resistance. "Are you a virgin?" he asked.

"Are you implying I never had sex before?"

"Well, yes, that's what it means to be a virgin. Are you?"

"I guess I am. I've never experienced the physical side of sex, but don't let that stop you. I know everything there is to know about having intercourse with a man."

"It would help if you were a bit more…you know…greased up?"

"Oh, you mean like this?"

He slid suddenly into her and moaned loudly. She felt tight, but oh-so-soft. Soft and moist. Moving slowly in and out of her, he put his hands under her buttocks, dug his fingers into their firm flesh.

She began rotating her pelvis, pushed up against him. "You can move a little faster," she said, "I won't break." She wrapped her long legs around his torso and gripped his hard penis with the strong inner muscles of her sex-organ.

"You don't act like a virgin who's never done it before," he panted on top of her.

She laughed, put her arms around his back and turned him over. "I learn fast."

"You're strong," he said, surprised by her action.

She sat up straight, undulated above him. "Do you like this?" she asked, staring into his face.

His eyes were glued to her breasts, fascinated by their perfect shape. "I like everything about you and everything you do," he gasped, trying hard not to explode inside her tight sheath.

"I'm glad." She smiled down on him. "I just want to make you happy." She rotated her hips and snapped her pelvis back and forth, milking his hard member with her pussy. "Do you like the flowers?" she asked after a while.

Aware of the soft bed of flowers he lay in, he nodded. "I like the way they look and the way they smell," he moaned. "I like the way you smell." He lunged up, grabbed her hips and shouted, "I'm coming…here I go…I'm coming!"

His discharge erupted into her, and exquisite pleasure roared like a tidal wave through his entire body. She held him inside her with a tight grip, her muscles rippling the length of his throbbing organ, taking in his gift of love.

Then she stretched out on top of him, her breasts soft on his chest. She kissed him gently. "Are you happy?" she asked.

"Very happy. You're the best."

"That is good."

* * * *

Opening his eyes, he felt momentarily disoriented.

What happened to the sun and flowers?

Where is the girl?

When he saw the gray metal ceiling above him, he remembered where he was. Sitting up groggily, he rubbed his eyes.

"Good morning," said a pleasant female voice. "Did you have a nice dream?"

"What? What?" He looked around. As he slipped off the bed, frowning, memories rushed into his mind. "I did have a nice dream. Can't remember much now, but how is it your business what I dreamed?"

The computer's voice sounded disappointed. "I'm only trying to be friendly. I want to be your friend."

"Just leave me alone. Okay?"

"It's a long trip. We might as well make the best of it," the computer insisted.

Rick walked over to the shower cubicle and started to strip, when suddenly he remembered something. "Hey, you," he yelled. "I want to take a shower. Can you close your…your…*eyes* for a while?"

He flinched when he heard the giggle. "Go ahead, get undressed. I won't mind. After all…I'm just a machine. But if it bothers you, I'll shut off my visual sensors in this area until you're finished."

"How will you know when I'm finished?" Rick asked.

"Oh, don't worry, I'll know."

He didn't like the sound of that, but he finished undressing, looking around, feeling uneasy.

Why the hell did they have to give the computer a female voice!

* * * *

When he went to sleep that night, she was there again. She stood in the same field of flowers, dressed in a sheer white gown. It clung to her slender body, revealing more than it covered.

"I've waited for you, my love." She came into his arms, molded her soft body against him, kissing him hungrily.

"Who are you?" he wanted to ask, but somehow he forgot when he opened his mouth. He kissed her back, tasted her sweet lips, the freshness of her mouth, as she slid her tongue between his teeth.

When they broke apart, she took his hand and pulled him with her. "Come," she said. "Let's go for a swim."

They crested a gently rolling hill, and he saw a small lake on the other side, nestled among tall oak trees. Hearing the chatter of a squirrel, he searched for it in the overhanging branches of the trees, saw it sitting, eating a nut. A flock of yellow birds flecked with black sang in the upper branches of the same tree.

"Do you like it?" she asked.

He nodded. "Yes, I do. It reminds me of the place where I grew up. There was a lake similar to this one."

"I know," she said, slipping the gown from her shoulders. He watched it pool around her ankles.

"You are so beautiful." He stepped nearer. Taking her into his arms, he held her and kissed her gently. His hands stroked her curvy back, wandered down to the soft globes of her buttocks.

Only now, he realized that he was naked, and his organ swelled against her soft belly.

"Let's go for a swim first," she whispered. "It will be so much better after, I promise." She ran toward the lake and dove in head first, her body as straight as a board, cutting the surface of the water with hardly a ripple.

He ran after her, splashing, as he entered the warm water. A large shadow in the water signaled her presence. She surfaced, rose up in front of him, her soft willowy form slithering up against his body. He tried to hold her, but she escaped his reaching arms, and, laughing, she dove away again.

"You're a tease," he called. She shot by him under water, and he chased her sleek shape. Diving, he swam after her. When he came up for air, she was suddenly there, came in his arms, molded against him.

Putting her arms around his back, she held on to him, lifted her legs and wrapped them around his lower body. Laughing, she kissed him on the mouth. He carried her out of the water as she clung to him like a giant leech, her mouth covering his shoulders with wet kisses.

They fell into the soft sand. She lay on her back, her thighs cradling him, her pussy rubbing against his hard shaft. He found her easily this time and, shouting triumphantly, he slid his erect member into her welcoming love-channel.

Moving in and out of her with steady thrusts for a long time, he made her whimper and claw his back. He finally came with loud grunts of pleasure, filling her vessel with the fruit of his love.

"I love you," he said when they lay in the sand, embracing each other.

"You make me very happy," she whispered.

Chapter Three

The days passed without much happening. Rick didn't have anything to do but relax and watch the movies he brought with him.

His strange shipmate kept him busy with questions.

"Stop addressing me as *Hey you*," MAG-1 told him one day. "Call me Maggi."

"All right, Maggi." He accepted the fact that the computer thought of itself as female. Reluctantly at first, but after her constant insisting that she was female, he finally gave in. He admitted that she did have a pleasant female voice, and most of the time she behaved the way a female would.

She wanted to know everything about him. When and where he was born. Did he have any brothers and sisters? How was his childhood?

"By now you probably know more about me than I do," he told her. "Why are you interested in my life? It is not that interesting."

She just laughed. "It's interesting to me, Rick. Remember, I'm a computer. I never had a childhood because I was never young, like you. I came into existence fully grown, but my thirst for knowledge is great. Even though I was programmed with a lot of information, much of it is boring stuff. I want to learn from you how it feels to be born without any knowledge and having to learn everything. I envy you."

"Why would you envy me? Be happy you didn't have to go to school and cram all the stuff they feed you as a child when you would rather play."

"What is playing?"

"Playing?" He shrugged. "That is hard to explain. When you do things you really like to do, like reading, watching movies, or sports. Much of playing is done with others. But you can also play when you're alone, which is not always fun."

"You're alone. I mean, you don't have another Human to play with. Could you and I play?"

"Like what?"

"I don't know. Can you teach me to play?"

"We could play games, like chess, or maybe a card game." He stopped. "No, that wouldn't work. You need to hold the cards physically, but I brought a lot of computer games with me that I wanted to play, but now, with you always asking questions, I never got a chance to actually play them. You could download them, and then we can play, if you want."

"I want to."

The computer games didn't work out because Maggi remembered all the different possibilities a game could have. Rick never had a chance of winning any of them.

"I don't enjoy this," he told her.

"Why not?"

"Always losing is no fun. Sometimes I wouldn't mind winning."

"I could let you. Just tell me when you want to win."

Rick laughed. "For a computer, you're sometimes really naïve. Believe me, that would still be no fun. Just knowing you let me win takes out all the fun."

She let out a human sounding sigh. "I guess I'll never be able to play. Not with you anyway. You know me too well."

"Now that's a switch. You telling me I know you too well. I feel the same way about you."

"Do you? Let me ask you a question, Rick. Do you like me?"

"What kind of question is that? You're a machine. I don't have any feelings for you."

She stayed silent for a while. "I have feelings for you," she said softly. "I believe I love you."

Rick broke out into a fit of laughter. "Don't be silly, Maggi. You're a machine. You have no feelings or bodily desires. How can you love me? That's absurd."

"You are wrong. I have feelings, Rick, and desires. They may not be physical, but I have them," she protested.

"Do you ever dream?" he asked her.

"I don't slee. How can I dream?" she commented. "Why do you ask?"

"I was wondering, that's all."

He never told her about the dreams he's been having. They had become more frequent lately, almost every night, always about the same girl, and he began to remember them more clearly. At first, he had not noticed it, but one morning, after waking, he realized that the voice of the girl sounded a lot like Maggi's.

Could she be influencing his dreams? He didn't want to think about that, didn't want to believe it. His own subconscious probably took her voice and began building a fantasy around it, creating those lucid dreams.

I need a woman badly. A real woman, not just a voice. Next time, I'll ask for a female companion. He'd heard about other spacers doing that. There even existed a guild that employed women who were willing to spend months in space, keeping spacefarers from becoming lonely.

"Would you love me if I were real, if they had given me a human looking body?" Maggie broke into his thoughts.

"You mean if you were an android?" Rick shrugged. "If I didn't know you were an android and if your were so sophisticated that I wouldn't be able to tell the difference between you and a human woman, maybe. However, so far, none of the androids in existence is capable of thinking for itself. Androids can only perform limited tasks, whatever gets programmed into their artificial brains."

He knew about the so-called *Love-Humanoids*, artificially created women produced to satisfy a man's sexual cravings. Even women could buy artificial men for their sexual pleasures.

"I had an acquaintance who once bought one of those android women," he said. "He almost screwed himself to death. That thing was nothing but a walking vagina without any feelings. Never got tired. He didn't love that piece of artificial flesh. He just used it to satisfy his lust. It couldn't even form any coherent sentences. It just moaned and sighed, gasped for air and cried out *You are the greatest,* and *I'm coming* once in a while, when in reality it never did. No, thank you. I prefer a real live woman."

"I see." Maggie stayed strangely silent after that.

When he went to bed, he didn't fall asleep immediately the way he usually did. He lay awake, thinking about his conversation with Maggi.

I hope I didn't hurt her feelings by telling her I could never love her.

He smiled in the dark.

What the hell am I thinking? She is just a machine, a contraption of wires, circuit boards, resistors, and who knows what else. I've spent too much time in her presence. She's not even female. She's just an It.

He slept without dreaming, and when he woke in the morning, he felt empty and unhappy. He had been looking forward to his dream world, to his nightly escapades in the arms of a lovely girl he had come to love. He knew she wasn't real, but it didn't matter. She gave him the love and sexual fulfillment he needed to stay sane in the company of a disembodied sexy voice during the day.

"Sleep well?" Maggi asked him when he opened his eyes.

"Well, hello to you too," he said, a little sarcastically. "I thought you died or left the ship."

"Why would you think that?" she asked pleasantly.

"Well, you didn't speak to me all evening yesterday. What was I to think?'

"Are you saying you missed me?"

"Maybe."

Her laughter sounded strangely happy. "So you do love me?"

Rick raised his hands into the air. "I never said that."

"Telling someone you missed them is like saying you love them."

He rolled his eyes. "Spoken with the true logic of a woman. Maybe you are female after all."

"I am, Rick, and soon I hope to prove it, but now I must begin the Phasing into the Real-time Space Continuum. We'll be entering the Sirius system in two days."

Chapter Four

They landed a week later on the planet *Angelwings.*

"Congratulations, Maggi," Rick said, after the computer shut off the ship's drive. The sudden silence seemed almost painful in his ears. "That was a beautiful landing. Couldn't have done it better myself."

"Thank you, Rick," Maggi answered sweetly. "Coming from you that is a great compliment."

He laughed, knowing well how she meant it. He had come to accept her presence and even her peculiar sense of humor. Not only her sense of humor but the way she talked and acted. Without her, the trip might have been boring and long.

"The temperature is a pleasant twenty-five degrees Celsius outside, so you don't need any heavy clothing. In fact, you should go without a shirt."

Rick looked up, startled. "You're just kidding, I hope."

"No, I mean it." Her voice sounded serious. "The natives will accept you more readily. They don't hide their bodies inside clothing."

"Can I keep my pants on?" Rick asked, joking.

"No long pants, only your shorts. And keep your boots."

"Oh, come on," he protested. "That's ridiculous."

"Rick Diamond," Maggie said sternly, "if you want to get rid of your merchandise, you will follow my advice. By the way, your welcoming committee has arrived. Look at the screen."

He looked at the giant screen and let out a sound of surprise. "That's my welcoming committee? Those are kangaroos!"

"Those are the natives. Didn't you know?"

"They never told me," Rick muttered. "Come to think of it, I never asked what the natives looked like, and nobody bothered to fill me in. Actually, I wasn't told anything."

"That doesn't surprise me," Maggie said. "You probably never asked any questions. You were too busy thinking of the great time you'd be having all by yourself."

Rick straightened up. "No matter. I will handle the situation. I'm *The Diamond*, hard and tough."

"You forgot to mention *transparent*," Maggi added.

"Sure, poke fun of me, ghostly voice. Just watch and learn." He stopped. "Oh, I forgot, you won't be there with me. Too bad. I guess I'll have to handle everything from now on by myself. You can listen in on my transmitter if you want."

He stripped off his clothes then he hung the little translation computer around his neck and walked out of the airlock, feeling a little silly in his outfit, but he trusted Maggi's assessment of the situation.

After all, she *was* a computer.

The natives sure did look like kangaroos. Some, Rick gathered, were females, even had pouches in front of their bellies.

They didn't wear any clothes, except for a large, wide-brimmed hat.

They looked ridiculous, and Rick had to suppress a grin as he walked toward them in his shorts and high black boots. The rays from Alpha Centauri felt hot on his shirtless upper body, but he didn't worry about getting a sunburn, because he had put on a film of oil for protection. He felt like one of the gladiators of old Rom walking across the crunchy sand, his muscular body glistening and reflecting the bright light of the alien sun. Hell, he was a gladiator, coming to do battle with his adversary, the extraterrestrial merchant!

They waited for him in front of a small grove of weird looking trees with gnarled roots and thick branches. The air smelled strange but pleasant enough. Better than the polluted air on good old Earth any day.

"Greetings, Honored Star Person," one of the natives said, to Rick's surprise in perfect English.

"Greetings, your…ah…Honor," Rick answered.

"Not *Your Honor*, dummy," a voice whispered beside him. "You have to say *Honored Person*."

Rick jumped a little at the sound of the voice. He turned and looked at the girl standing beside him. "Thank you," he said to her. Then he looked at the natives. "Greetings, Honored Persons."

He suddenly realized something, and his heart almost stopped.

He turned his head and stared at the girl, who stood there, smiling innocently. "Who are you?" he asked, a frog in his voice. She looked strangely familiar, even though she was dressed in a pilot's uniform, which fit her more snugly then should have.

"Hush." She put a finger against her lips. "They'll think you're crazy."

"Honored Star Person, are you not well?" asked the native who had greeted him.

"Oh, I'm fine," Rick said hastily. "I'm a little surprised to see the woman. I was not aware of her presence."

"A woman? I don't understand."

Rick pointed with his thumb at the girl. "This woman beside me. Who is she?"

"There is no woman beside you," The native hesitated, and then he said, "We don't know much about your customs, Honored Star Person, but if you think there is someone beside you then so be it." He looked at the others. They all nodded and said, "So be it."

The girl giggled. "They can't see or hear me, Rick. Only you can. But I'm here, nevertheless."

It finally clicked. "You're Maggi."

She giggled again. "That's right. I am Maggi."

"What? How…? Never mind, you can explain later." He looked at the natives who were watching him. Whey they saw him looking at them, they nodded their heads, their wide-brimmed hats bobbing, and murmured, "So be it."

They think I'm crazy. Maybe I am. This whole situation is ludicrous. Here I am standing in my underwear, wearing high boots, talking to a bunch of intelligent kangaroos with cowboy hats, with a ship's computer in the invisible body of a beautiful girl beside me.

Suddenly, he started to laugh. Then he pinched himself. "Awake," he said aloud. "This is only a nightmare."

The natives watched him for a while, and then they started pinching themselves and mimicked his laughter.

"They think this is some sort of greeting ceremony," explained the girl. "They are very adept at imitating other beings."

"Keep your voice down," Rick whispered. "They'll hear you, and then they'll really think I'm crazy. Talking in two voices."

"Don't worry, Dear. They can't hear me," Maggi assured him.

The natives stopped laughing and pinching. One of them stepped forward. "Did you bring the trading goods, Honored Star Person?"

"Yes, I did, ah…Honored Person," Rick replied. "Do you want to inspect them?"

"Yes, we do, but first we must have the Contest."

"The Contest?" Rick asked, astonished. "I don't think I understand. Nobody told me about a contest."

"There is another ship, another trader, from far away. He has many nice things. Before we trade, you must compete with each other. Only a game but very important. The winner will get first choice," the native explained patiently.

"What about the loser?" Rick questioned. "What does the loser get?"

"The loser? We eat him."

"What?" Rick yelled, understandably a little upset. "What kind of stupid…?" He stopped when something touched his arm. He stared at the girl.

"Don't shout at them. They are very easily offended. They might decide to eat you before the contest," the girl said softly.

Rick mopped his forehead. He was perspiring, and not because of the heat. "I don't believe this is happening!" he moaned. "They told me it would be a nice, quiet routine trading trip. Nothing to worry about."

Chapter Five

"Will you please follow us, Honored Star Person?"

The natives hopped away. Rick and his invisible companion followed them. As they walked side by side, Rick looked at Maggi. "You're beautiful," he said.

"Thank you." She ran ahead of him and did a little pirouette. "You approve of my body?" she asked, giggling.

"I sure do." He looked at her with admiration. "I am a little confused, though. How is this possible? You seem so real to me, and yet, you tell me, the natives can't see you. Are you really here, or am I just imagining you?"

She touched his hand and held it. Her hand felt warm and solid. "I am here, Darling."

He looked startled. "Now I remember where I've seen your image before. In my dreams. I didn't recognize you with clothes on. You're the girl from my dreams." A hot flush shot into his face. "How…?"

Her grip on his hand tightened a little. "A dream is only another part of your existence. You know the story about the man and the butterfly?"

He could feel her closeness and warmth as she walked beside him. She couldn't be just a figment of his mind. "The one where the man dreamed he was a butterfly, and the butterfly dreamed he was a man?"

"Yes, and do you know the answer, Rick?"

"There is no real answer, only a question. Which is the man, which the butterfly?"

"But there is an answer, Darling. He is both, the man and the butterfly. Just two sides of his existence. I am a computer in your world, but I am a woman in mine. I have found a way of crossing the threshold between both parts of my existence."

"But why can only I see you?"

She hesitated for a moment, a frown crossing her lovely face. "I have only just now mastered the transition fully. Until now, I could only appear to you in your dream-life. I did not want to startle the natives by suddenly appearing beside you, but if I wanted to, I could make myself visible to them now. It is just a matter of rearranging the molecules a little. Quite easy, actually."

"Honored Star Person, this is the other contestant."

Rick would have bumped into the native in front of him if Maggi hadn't pulled him back.

The other trader looked ugly to the point of being hideous. A squat body, a little over four feet in height, with a tiny head the size of a grapefruit and two eyestalks protruding a foot or so. The six skinny, hairy legs seemed hardly strong enough to support the heavy-appearing body.

"Who is this ugly monster?" The voice came out of a short tube that was attached to the creature's chest.

Rick's little computer translated it automatically.

"This is the Honored Star Person from planet Earth," one of the natives introduced Rick to his competitor.

"What do you mean by ugly…?" Rick started to protest, but Maggi hushed him by putting her hand over his mouth.

"He is *also* very excitable," she whispered for his ears only.

"Will the two contestants please take their places," the native instructed them.

Rick noticed only now that they were in the middle of a small opening left by hundreds of spectators. He hadn't even heard all the natives coming. Looking around for a seat, he didn't see one, just the dirty trampled ground beneath him.

The other trader folded his six legs under him and sat down.

Rick followed his example.

"My white shorts are going be so filthy," he complained as he made himself as comfortable as was possible on the hard ground.

"Don't worry about your shorts," Maggi said. She slid beside him. "Just concentrate on the contest." She patted his hand. "Don't worry, Dear. I'll help you."

A small group of natives watched him. When he looked in their direction, they nodded their heads. He couldn't be sure, but he seemed to hear them murmur, "So be it."

He wiped his perspiring forehead with the back of his hand. When he looked at his hand, he noticed the black streak of dirt. The individuals who were watching him took some dirt from the ground and wiped it into their foreheads.

"What are they doing?" Rick whispered furiously. "Are they mocking me?"

"No, no, Darling." Maggi giggled beside him. "I think they like you. That is good."

"We will start the contest with an easy question." The moderator said. "Give us the answer to this riddle: Jack and Jill went up the hill…" He looked expectantly at Rick, who just stared at him, not quite believing his ears. When he didn't answer, the native repeated, "Jack and Jill went up the hill…"

"That is not a riddle. That is a nursery rhyme, an old nursery rhyme from Earth. How did…?" Rick stopped talking when Maggi poked him in the ribs. "Don't ask questions, just finish the rhyme."

"…to fetch a pail of water," Rick said lamely, feeling foolish.

The spectators cheered loudly and pounded their bellies. Some even waved their cowboy hats.

"I told you they like you," Maggi said and giggled.

Chapter Six

The contest went on for hours. When the end finally came, Rick had won the competition. The natives carried him on their shoulders, dancing and singing old nursery rhymes.

After that, they wined and dined him. Actually they didn't serve any wine, just fruit juice, but to Rick it tasted like the finest wine.

When Rick politely asked how they came to know all these nursery rhymes, they told him about an Earth ship, which crashed on their planet many years ago. Only one little boy survived. They raised him, and he taught them all these wonderful songs and riddles. He lived with them for many years, until one day a trader from Earth took him back home.

Where did they get all those hats?

"Oh, we traded them for worthless rocks," one of the natives sniggered and his friends laughed, pounding their bellies. "Some traders are not very smart."

"May I see some of those worthless rocks?" Rick asked, just to be polite.

One of his new friends ran and came back a few moments later, carrying a handful of rocks. He deposited them into Rick's hands. "Here, Honored Star Person, you can keep these." He grinned, his large teeth gleaming yellow in the rays of the setting sun. "This is a present because we like you."

When Rick studied the rocks, he discovered he held a handful of diamonds. Some of them as large as plums.

Things hadn't turned out badly after all. He felt smug, but he knew he would have never won without Maggi's help. She knew the answer to every question, every equation, every riddle they asked him.

He squeezed her hand as they slowly walked back to the ship.

The natives were delighted with the shipment of goods. Rick didn't even know what he had carried. His orders were to unload the whole shipment and bring back fifty cases full of native artifacts. They only told him to refrain from telling the natives that the company was not remotely interested in the artifacts, as beautiful as they were, but in the material that the natives used to make the artifacts.

Emeralds, rubies, sapphires and a score of precious minerals not even found on Earth.

He turned one last time to wave goodbye.

The natives waved back, standing there, dressed in shorts and black boots.

He couldn't keep from laughing. "Where did they get those outfits?"

Maggi giggled beside him. "From you. That's the merchandise you carried. Now you know the reason I told you to dress the way you did. You see, they like to mimic, but you have to prove to them that you are worthy, and I have to say, you managed it splendidly. In their eyes, you are like a god. They think you are a little peculiar though. Talking to the air and things like that. And now you even gave them all those beautiful things and only took worthless artifacts in exchange."

She hugged him.

"They love you, Dear. And so do I."

The End

Vania Starborn
By
Herbert Grosshans

The Golden Warrior Girl

Oh lovely girl with skin of gold,
with sword in hand and eyes so cold
On your neck, you carry the serpent's sting.
Death is the only gift you bring

Only the Dead are Lucky

Chapter One

Squinting against the glare of the twin-suns, the girl lifted the heavy bow and released the arrow. She smiled proudly when she saw the large Hys-buck falter and stumble as it tried to get away. It crashed to the ground before it reached the protection of the forest and lay motionless.

She whistled softly. Her steed came galloping toward her from its hiding place, where she left it before stalking her quarry. The blanket it carried on its broad back proclaimed it as a domesticated animal, otherwise it could easily have been mistaken for a wild Hys, or at least a cousin of the buck she just brought down.

Snorting happily at seeing her, the animal shook its antlered head and almost knocked her over.

"Easy, my impatient friend." She laughed and gently stroked the long neck. Then she swung on its back and dug her heels into the soft flanks. "Come, let's get down there and claim our prize before somebody else does."

She rode slowly down the gentle slope into the valley. There was no hurry, and yet, she felt a sense of urgency. Warily, her emerald eyes searched the boulders that lay strewn across the ground and the few tall, thick Ora-trees for signs of movement. She was far from her home, in foreign territory, and didn't know what dangers lurked in the forest or in the barren region surrounding it.

Just before she reached the fallen animal, a loud piercing cry from the forest on the other side of the valley made her stop and reach for an arrow. When she heard the sound of many hoofs pounding the hard ground, she sighed.

She knew trouble was on its way.

It was a large group of riders. She counted maybe two times her fingers as they came racing toward her across the dry land, the hoofs of their riding-animals throwing small rocks and gray dust into the air.

Tarks.

She had not met them before, but she knew of them.

Short, stocky yellow skinned people, wild and cruel, with no sense of honor. They were well known to her people.

The first one to arrive, a young arrogant looking fellow with a long, ugly scar across his bare, hairy chest, pulled hard on the reigns of his steed, making it rear up on its hind legs. A huge grin stretched across his broad face, and his black eyes sparkled maliciously. He stopped directly in front of her, while his companions formed a circle around them.

"Who gave you permission to hunt on our grounds?" he said, his voice unusually deep. When he spoke, his wide upper lip curled up in a sneer, displaying two sharp fangs. He held a short, broad-bladed weapon casually in his right hand. She knew how efficient these people used this one-sided keen-edged blade.

She drew herself erect and looked into his black eyes. "I hunt wherever and whenever I feel like it. You have no claim on the wild animals."

His laughter sounded like the bellowing of a Rock-lion. His eyes traveled over her lithe body, lingered on the swell of her breasts. She knew what he saw, and the shadow of a smile tucked at the corners of her full lips.

She was tall and slim, with generous curves. Her buttocks were round and firm, her waist narrow and her hips wide. She kept her body strong and in good shape, not only because the males liked it, but also because it made her feel good. A halter made from soft leather, with holes in the front to leave her nipples bare, covered her ample breasts. Her long, golden hair spilled over her honey-colored shoulders and down her back.

She was different from the people of her tribe, who had adopted her as a small child. She knew she came from another species. Whereas her skin was golden, the people of her adopted tribe were silver-skinned, with black, straight hair. The females had six breasts, two large ones and four smaller ones.

She only possessed two breasts, a trifle too large for the tastes of the males in her tribe. She also lacked the pointy, tufted ears and the small sharp teeth, and she wasn't considered beautiful. Yet, remembering her parents, she didn't believe herself ugly.

Her father had been tall and wide-shouldered, and her mother, almost as tall, slender and curvy, with soft, golden skin. Many times, she'd heard her father call her mother *the most beautiful woman on this forsaken ball of dirt*, and he had told her she'd be as beautiful as her mother some day.

They were dead now, murdered by the Star-Devils.

A long time ago.

Her eyes focused on the yellow man. "Finished looking?" she said, mocking him.

One of his heavy brows went up. "You are either very brave or very stupid," he said. "It is obvious, you are a stranger, for I have never seen anyone with skin like yours. Who are you, and what are you doing here?"

"I am Vania Starborn," the girl answered. "On my way to Cheb."

"It seems your journey ends here," the Tark grinned. "You will warm my bed tonight."

Some of the other men laughed, drawing closer.

Vania looked around, deciding what she should do. She felt confident she could possibly kill five or six, but the rest would bear her down. There were too many of them.

When they tied her hands behind her back, she let it happen. Two of the men gutted the Hys-buck, skinned and quartered it. Then they wrapped the pieces into large skins and tied them on top of four pack animals.

Taking the reins of Vania's steed, the leader of the small band let out a piercing cry and took off. The girl had to clamp her long legs around the belly of her mount to keep from falling off.

They galloped down the valley toward the forest at reckless speed. Once the young Tark looked back, grinning, but she saw the beginning of respect in his black eyes.

She smiled. Not many could ride a Hys like Vania Starborn. Even the males in her tribe, who were practically born on Hysback, could not outride her.

They entered the forest and followed a narrow trail. Riding single file now, the men slowed down. Sometimes they were forced to stop to remove a fallen tree from the trail. The thick branches of the Ora-trees and Gnar-trees hung low, and Vania, who was taller than the Tark-men, kept low against her steed's long neck.

Finally, the trees became sparser, and the trail widened, until they finally left the forest behind. The terrain ahead of them was hilly and covered with tall, purple-hued grass. Slender Mesa-trees replaced the thick Ora and Gnar-trees.

The twin-suns lost their brilliance as they prepared to dip below the horizon. To the south, Gamba, the Lone Wanderer, began climbing into the sky, washing the darkening land with its pale, reddish glow.

Vania could make out the roofs of low buildings far ahead, as the light of the dying suns bathed them with a golden fire.

"We'll be in Dange soon," her captor told her. "I hope you like our hospitality." He grinned wolfishly, and some of the others laughed.

"I might," Vania replied, "if you untie my hands."

The Tark gave a short, barking laugh and pressed his heels into the flanks of his mount. "Let us enter our fair city like the brave, successful hunters we are," he called to his men, "and not like a bunch of tired old women!"

They reached a wide and well-traveled road. The dust swirled around them as they sped, shouting and whistling, toward the city.

Chapter Two

The houses, which stood on both sides of the dirt road, were small, with low roofs. Narrow window slits in the rocky walls admitted little light inside. The roofs were covered with a thick layer of dried grass.

A few people sat in front of the open doorways, watching silently as the riders rode by.

Vania wrinkled her nose as the acrid stench of food and human waste assaulted her senses. She was used to the fresh air of the wide, open tundra, where the air smelled sweet and clear.

They rode past a marketplace. Shopkeepers started to move their wares back into their shops.

Finally, they came before a huge, wooden gate set into a high wall built from giant boulders. One of the men banged his fist against the gate. A few moments later, a voice called from the top of the wall, demanding identification.

"Open the gate before I break it down!" the leader of the hunting party shouted with his big, booming voice. "You know who it is."

The gate swung open, the rusty hinges grating loudly, and they entered a large courtyard. Two guards with long spears stood on either side of the gate, lifting their hands in salute.

"Welcome home, Lord Granton," one of them greeted them. "Did you have a good hunt?"

The young Tark grinned. "I always do, Los. How is my father?"

"Lord Kapkor is as he always is," the guard answered, smiling.

Laughing, Granton winked at him. "As miserable and grumpy as ever, I guess," he said, moving on. He looked at Vania. "Come, let's meet my father, the Mighty Lord Kapkor."

They dismounted, and a few young boys came running to take away the animals.

"Make sure they get fed and rubbed down properly," Granton told them.

The boys bowed, their eyes downcast. "Yes, my Lord," the tallest of them said. "They will be taken care of properly. I'll vouch for that."

Granton laughed. "You are very brave, Harkes, to stick out your scrawny neck by vouching for your peers, but I respect that. Maybe

I'll make you my own personal slave."

"Thank you, my Lord. Nothing would please me more."

"Idiot," Lord Granton murmured as he walked away. He looked at Vania, grinning. "That young stable boy has ambitions not healthy for him. He'll never be more than a stable boy, like his father and brothers, but he has a beautiful sister. I bedded her a few times. She must have bragged about it to her family. Now Harkes believes I favor him before the others."

"Perhaps he believes you want to bed him also," Vania suggested.

Granton threw her an angry look. "You have a sharp tongue, wench, and a foul mouth." Then he grinned. "I will have you put it to better use than just uttering irritating words."

"I also have sharp teeth," she warned him.

They stopped in front of a low, squat building with thick walls and a flat roof. Entering it through a heavy wooden door, Vania noticed that the roof was constructed from heavy timbers and then covered with layers of clay to keep out the rain. Heavy iron bars, imbedded in the rock, reinforced the windows, which were made from transparent rock.

She looked around thoughtfully. *This place is a fortress. Impossible to enter and even harder to leave, once inside.*

Walking across a large entrance hall, they stepped through another thick wooden door into large room, this one richly furnished, the walls covered with expensive draperies and a deep-piled rug on the stone floor.

Padded benches behind low tables ringed the outside walls, leaving the center of the room empty. A few men sat on the benches, large goblets in their hands. Most of them looked up when Vania and her escort entered. She could see the intense stares and heard the lewd comments the men made.

"Look who has finally decided to come home again," said a deep, sarcastic voice from the end of the room.

Vania looked at the speaker.

Even sitting, he presented an imposing figure. Wide-shouldered, his muscles bulging under the tight-fitting shirt, he was an older version of the young Tark standing by her side. However, when he rose from his chair and came down from the raised dais, she saw that he was taller than Granton.

"Lord Kapkor. Father." Granton made a mock bow and walked

toward the older man. "I have brought you a present."

"You've captured a girl. How brave you are. Have you bedded her already and found she was no good, so now you give her to me?"

If the snide remark insulted the young man, he didn't show it. Smiling, he said, "Give me more credit than that, Father. I never touched her…not yet. I thought you might want to talk to her first, ask her what she is doing here. We found her hunting south of the Tarsa-forest."

"Hunting?" Lord Kapkor gave the girl an inquisitive stare. "You are a stranger," he said and came closer. "I have never seen a girl with skin like yours. Where do you come from?"

"South," Vania answered, giving him an innocent smile.

The older Tark looked at her thrusting breasts, exposed nipples and small patch of leather covering her pubic area. "Our females dress a bit more…ah…modest, unless they're slaves."

Vania shook her golden hair from her face and laughed. "The females of my tribe usually don't dress like this either, but I am also a warrior."

A huge grin began to form on Lord Kapkor's broad face, but then he drew his bushy eyebrows together and stared at Vania's partly exposed shoulder. Stepping closer, he brushed her long hair aside and grunted. "Turn around!" he commanded sharply.

Vania obliged and smiled when he parted the hair behind her back. She heard his sharp intake of breath.

"You imbecile!" he barked, turning toward his son, who had been watching him. "She's a Varden, a *Child of the Serpent*. She could have killed you and most of the other idiots with you, and you dare to bring her here, into my house?"

Granton laughed hesitantly. "What are you talking about? She's only a girl, and besides that, she doesn't even look like a Varden."

"Then look for yourself, look at the image of the writhing serpent on her shoulder and at the puncture marks in her neck. She bears the mark of the *Great Serpent-Mother*."

With a doubtful expression, the young lord stared at the two scars, and then he stepped back, shrugging his shoulders.

Angry at his son's indifference, Lord Kapkor lifted one hand. "You dim-witted fool! Cut her loose!"

Chuckling, the girl moved her arms. The strong bonds, which seemed to cut into her soft flesh, snapped with an audible crack. "No sense pretending anymore," she said, rubbing her wrists. "I was getting uncomfortable anyway."

"I apologize for my son's ignorance," Lord Kapkor said, "and for the inconvenience he's caused you." He waved a hand toward one of the tables. "I welcome you as my honored guest. Sit and refresh yourself."

Clapping his hands, he called one of the slave girls over to bring a pitcher and a platter heaped with food. "Have some wine, fruit and succulent morsels of skewered meat."

Vania sat down with a sigh. She noticed with satisfaction that Granton and his companions left the room, but not before throwing her angry glances. "I am hungry," she said, reaching for a chunk of steaming meat. Lord Kapkor sat down across from her and watched her eat and drink.

"What brings you to our country?" Lord Kapkor asked in a friendly tone, but she sensed the tenseness in his voice. Wiping her mouth with the back of her hand, she leaned into the cushions. "There is talk about a stranger from the sky, who has crashed with his sky wagon in these parts."

If Lord Kapkor knew what she talked about, the expression of his face didn't betray him. "A stranger from the sky?" he asked. He drank deeply from his goblet, his dark eyes on her face. Putting down the goblet, he motioned to the slave girl, who stood beside his chair. "Bring more wine for my guest."

Vania watched the young girl hurry away with the empty pitcher. She was dark-skinned, with short-cropped white curly hair. Clad only in a short skirt, her breasts were bare. A deep scar ran across each of her breasts, proclaiming her a slave. She was no Tark, her people lived somewhere in the northern countries, where the twin-suns burned much hotter during the long summer.

Vania frowned, anger clouding her emerald eyes. She did not believe in slavery. To be free was very important to her. She remembered her parents, heard her father's words.

Freedom is a precious gift, child. Never take it for granted. Since beginning of time, people have fought and died for it. Even the lowliest creature strives to be free. That is the reason we came to this primitive planet. To keep our freedom. Out there among the stars are evil men, who want to enslave us because we are different. They want to use our powers for their own evil purposes. We'd rather die than serve them. Better dead then to be a slave.

The return of the black girl brought her back to the present. Vania held up her goblet, watched the girl as she filled it with an expressionless face. Lord Kapkor stroked the girl's round buttocks and put his hand between her legs. The girl gave him an empty smile, but she couldn't mask the hatred in her dark eyes.

"When you treat them right, they are always loyal," the old Tark said to Vania, who watched, disapproving, but she stayed silent.

"Did you come alone?" he asked casually.

"Yes," she lied and noticed the flicker of satisfaction cross the lined face.

He stood up and walked away from the table. "In that case," he said, smiling, "you shall tell us more about yourself and why you came looking for a stranger."

From behind a thick curtain stepped a score of bowmen, their bows drawn and their arrows aimed at the golden girl's heart.

"I would hate to see that beautiful body of yours pierced by so many arrows, but if you make a wrong move you are dead!"

Chapter Three

Keeping her hands on the table, Vania chuckled, showing her white pearly teeth. She had seen the bowmen behind the curtain the moment she entered the room. Lord Kapkor was no fool. Keeping her pinned behind the table, he had made certain she couldn't move fast enough to dodge the arrows.

"I'm hiding no secrets you'd be interested in learning," she said calmly. "If you want me in your bed, all you have to do is just say so."

"So you can strangle me in my own bed when I'm asleep?" Lord Kapkor smiled grimly. "I've heard about your kind."

Two men came in, carrying heavy chains and iron bands, which they laid around Vania's ankles and wrists. Then they put another iron band around her neck with a chain connected to her bound wrists behind her back.

"Take her below," Lord Kapkor said, "and make sure she's comfortable." His laughter followed her as they led her through a backdoor. She noticed that aside from the two men who held her, four more walked behind them, naked swords in their hands.

After walking down a flight of stairs, she was led through a dark corridor. The floor felt slippery, and the air smelled of rotting timbers and mold. They climbed down another set of damp stairs and entered another corridor. In the gloomy light of oil lamps, she saw heavy wooden doors with small barred windows set into the slimy walls. She glimpsed a bearded, wild-looking face peering out at her through one of the windows and heard moaning sounds from behind another door.

Her captors opened a door at the end of the corridor and thrust her inside a room. While four warriors waited outside, two of them fastened chains from hooks in the stone floor to her ankles. Then they left her alone in the dark cell. Only the weak, flickering light from torches outside fell through the small window in the door.

She sat down on the cold, damp floor, wrinkling her nose. The room stank of human sweat and excrement.

Closing her eyes, her mind reached out, questing. She had sensed a mind like her own close by when she entered the building, but it seemed gone now. Reaching out farther, she finally made contact.

It was Vrok, who answered her call. She felt closer to him than any of the others. She had chosen him to be her first lover.

The contact was faint, and she knew they were still far away.

What happened to you, little sister? His thoughts came in weak but clear. She sensed his concern.

I need you help, big brother, she answered. *I ran into some trouble*. She relayed an image of herself shackled with heavy chains to the stone floor.

She felt him withdraw for a moment, received only silence, then his thoughts came back, angry and stronger than before.

Who did this to you, Starborn?

Vania chuckled. Vrok had a bad temper, which he usually kept under tight control, but when aroused, he was a dangerous man to tangle. She almost felt sorry for the Tarks.

I'm a prisoner of the Tarks. In the city Dange. You will have no trouble finding me. I'll keep myself open.

Just stay alive, little sister. We'll be there soon.

He withdrew but not completely. A minute part of his mind stayed with her. She locked onto it. He would follow their mind link, and no matter where she might be, he'd find her.

She smiled, thinking of Vrok. The very first time she saw him, she felt attracted to him, and she knew he shared that attraction. Because of him, she was still alive. His father found her, dazed and nearly out of her mind, wandering around in the ruins of her parents' home. The fire from the sky-ship had killed her father and mother, along with others of her kind. Only because she disobeyed her parents and gone down to the little creek near their home, had she survived.

Vrok's father took her along because he sensed the latent powers in her, but Vrok touched her mind for the first time, and he was the one who taught her the ways of his tribe.

Even if she differed from them on the outside, inside she was a Varden.

She tried to lie down but found it impossible with her hands tied behind her back. Leaning against the cold wall, she made herself as comfortable as was possible.

She must have slept, because a sudden noise made her lift her head and look around. She found the door to her cell open. In the dim light, she saw a short, squat figure moving toward her. Then someone grabbed her roughly by the shoulder.

"Wake up, spy," said a familiar voice.

Lord Granton.

Two other men entered. They carried torches, which they stuck into rings in the wall.

Grinning, Granton stood wide-legged in front of her. “My father is a fool,” he said. “If you were as dangerous as he said, you would never have allowed yourself to be captured.” He held a cup in his hand, which he put close to her lips. “You must be parched. Here, drink this. I’ll get some food later.”

Even though she didn’t trust him, she drank from the cup after a moment’s hesitation. The wine tasted strong and tangy, but it went down easy. She *had* been thirsty.

“Why don’t you take these chains off me,” she said, trying to stand up.

When he put a hand on her shoulder, she knew something was wrong. Her head felt suddenly dizzy, and her arms and legs began to go numb.

“You poisoned me,” she gasped, desperately trying to keep from fainting.

He laughed and turned her body around, pushing her into a kneeling position. Her knees rubbed against the rough stone floor. She felt him fumble between her legs and remove the small piece of leather that covered her pubis.

“You won’t die,” he panted. “It’s just a harmless drug.”

“I’ll kill you,” she whispered as consciousness faded.

Later she woke, with no idea why Granton had slipped the drug into the wine she drank. Her body was sore but then after being slapped and sleeping on a stone floor, she concluded that any additional injuries were not apparent.

“I promise, I will kill you.” Vania renewed her words and prayed Granton would get close enough for her to kill him herself. She tore at the chains, but they didn’t budge. Then she sat and cursed herself for letting them take her. She should have fought when she had a chance.

Then she heard a silent voice whisper inside her mind.

Little sister, I know you’re hurt. I am coming.

Chapter Four

After resting for a while, the pain subsided. When she heard footsteps in the corridor outside, she stood up painfully, determent not to let them hurt her again.

The bolt moved inside the iron lock, and the heavy door swung open with a grating sound. She expected Lord Granton but then she saw his father, Lord Kapkor, entering the dark cell. Another man came in behind him, carrying a torch.

Lord Kapkor shook his head when he saw Vania, naked and covered with grime. "It looks like somebody took advantage of your predicament," he said, disapproval in his deep voice. "Who did this to you?"

Vania didn't answer, just glared at him.

"Answer me, girl!" Kapkor rasped, stepping closer.

"What do you care?" She spat at him. "It was your brave son and his cowardly friends. Maybe you want to take over where they left off?"

She winced when he hit her across the face. Her foot shot out in reflex, smashed into his chest, sending him sprawling across the floor. Only the chains saved him from broken ribs and serious damage.

"Witch!" he cursed, trying to catch his breath and holding his chest.

He drew his short, broad-bladed sword, and she prepared to die, but then he sheathed it again. "Guards," he called. "Take her into the interrogation chamber!"

He left, still breathing hard.

Four guards with drawn weapons entered the cell. Two of them proceeded to unlock the chains from the hooks in the floor, while the other two stood watching her with alert eyes.

She tried to break free, but the drugs in her system still left her weak, and after one of them hit her a few times, she stopped struggling. Then they dragged her out of her cell, down the corridor into another, much larger room.

She saw many strange devices in the room, all of them designed to torture people. They hoisted her up to the ceiling, feet first, and left her with her head hanging down. One of them grabbed her long hair and tied it around a heavy weight. She spat in his face, but he just laughed. Then he put his hand between her legs and squeezed hard.

She screamed and almost fainted from the pain. Through dazed eyes, she saw Lord Kapkor walking into the room, an evil smile on his face. From her upside down position, he looked like a terrifying demon come out of the darkest pits of the underworld.

"I hope our hospitality finds your approval," he said, taking one of her nipples between two fingers. "Such a lovely body. A shame we have to ruin it."

"What do you want from me?" she moaned. "I told you I'm just a traveler."

Lord Kapkor chuckled. "You know, I've thought about it. I don't believe you're a Varden. You certainly don't look like one. A real Varden would never have been as foolish as you have been. No, I think you are a spy from our neighboring country Marakka, with whom we presently are at war."

"I've never been to Marakka, and I am not a spy."

"We'll find out. Kraco!" Lord Kapkor spoke to one of the watching guards. "Bring the spider worms."

From a corner in the room, Kraco brought an earthen container. Grinning, he opened the lid and poured the contents slowly over Vania's body. She felt the writhing, many-legged hairy things crawling all over her, and she tried not to cry out when the sharp pincers of the tiny creatures dug into her skin.

"You'd better talk," Lord Kapkor suggested, obviously enjoying her plight. "And don't wait too long, or my little friends here will slowly suck the blood from your veins, until they are big and fat, and you are dry."

Vania closed her eyes to shut out his grinning image.

Hurry, her mind cried out. *Hurry, big brother.*

His answering thoughts came almost immediately, savage and strong. She knew he must be close.

We're in the city, Starborn, but we must wait until dark. There are many guards and only four of us.

I'll wait, brother. The girl smiled and opened her eyes to look into Lord Kapkor's puzzled countenance.

"I'll wipe that smile off your face," he sneered, hitting her across her breasts.

She bit her lips to stop her cry of pain from escaping and closed her eyes again. The weight tied to her hair was beginning to hurt her scalp. She relaxed her body, trying to ignore the pain and the sucking crawling spider worms on her bare skin.

She didn't get much time to relax. Lord Kapkor, impatient with his efforts to make her talk and not getting any results, forcefully pried open her eyes. "Look at me, spy," he hissed, his face close to hers. She could see the spittle forming in the corners of his mouth. His fangs gleamed dully in the flickering torchlight. "Maybe I should give Kraco a free hand with your body. He has a way with young girls."

Kraco inflated his deep, hairy chest and grinned, touching the huge bulge between his legs.

The other guards laughed. "She wouldn't be of much use when he is finished with her," one of them said.

"Too bad she's not a virgin," another one said. "He loves young virgins."

"The whores in the barracks are not fond of him. They say he's a pain between the legs, and they have to rest for days after."

"Oh, shut up!" Kraco growled. "I get plenty of women."

"You see." Lord Kapkor smiled. "Maybe you should start talking while there is still time."

"I have nothing to tell you except what you already know," Vania whispered.

Lord Kapkor turned away and walked to the door. Before he left, he turned around. "I want her alive when I return."

They let her down from the ceiling and threw her into a trough filled with cold dirty water, where they kept her submerged until all the spider worms left her body. She tried to get away, but the drugged wine and the loss of blood left her weak, and she only managed to pull two of the guards into the water with her. She kicked one of them in the groin, but the others beat her until she nearly lost consciousness.

They chained her spread-eagled to the floor. She watched horrified as Kraco removed his leather breaches, exposing his erect enormous organ.

While the other guards cheered and watched, their mouths drooling, he moved between her spread legs and, holding his rigid member, he prepared to guide it between her fluffy, golden triangle.

At that moment, the door was flung open, and a tall, heavily muscled figure burst into the room, a long, bloody sword in his hand. The black leather armor he wore was cut in a way to enhance his immense body. His exposed skin shone with a silver hue.

When his eyes fell upon the scene on the floor, he roared angrily.

One giant leap took him behind the kneeling hairy man between Vania's thighs, and, with one mighty sweep of his sword-arm, he brought the big weapon down. The keen-edged blade cut through Kraco's neck, severing muscles and bones. The bearded head toppled to the floor, rolled away to lie grinning at Vania.

The headless corpse fell on top of her, blood pumping from the severed neck over her golden skin. The tall silver-skinned warrior gave it a kick with his foot and pushed the grisly body off her.

She smiled weakly.

I thought you'd never come.

He chuckled grimly and grabbed the heavy chains that held her shackled to the floor. His muscles bulged on his thick arms and wide shoulders, and, one by one, he pulled the iron hooks out of their sockets.

She stood, the heavy chains clanking on the floor.

"That's all I can do for now, little sister," he said apologetically and turned to run his sword through one of the guards who had come up behind him. The other guards were engaged in combat with his three comrades, who had entered the room shortly after him. She recognized Torr, Jork, and Karm.

The Tarks stood no chance against the tall Vardens, who not only towered over them, but who possessed strength more than twice that of the short, stocky Tarks. In moments, the uneven battle was over, and the hard ground soaked up the blood of the slain guards.

"You look terrible, Starborn." Vrok took her into his strong arms. He stroked her golden hair, and she laid her head against his blood-spattered shoulder.

"So do you, Vrok," she murmured, holding him tight.

Chapter Five

They found the keys to the shackles on one of the dead guards and unlocked the iron bands from Vania's wrists and legs. She rubbed her swollen, chafed wrists. "I want to have a look in the other cells," she said to Vrok, who nodded, understanding.

Out in the hall, the bodies of three more guards lay in pools of blood. The Vardens used the keys to open the locked doors. In one of the cells, they found a man lying on a straw-covered bunk. The torn and grimy clothing he wore looked strange, unfamiliar. He lifted his head when the door opened.

In the dim glow of the cell, his face looked blotchy, and when the light from the torch fell on it, Vania saw the fresh scars around his closed eyes. She rushed toward him and bent down to touch his face.

He lifted his arms feebly and tried to sit up.

"Are you finally going to kill me, you filthy savage?" he croaked.

Vania sank to her knees beside him and took his hand into hers. Tears burst from her eyes when she spoke. "I'm a friend. I came to help." She stumbled over the words, not having spoken in that language for such a long time.

His hand went up to her face. His shaky fingers gently touched her cheek. "You speak my language," he whispered. "Are you from Earth?" He hesitated, the fingers of his other hand dug into her arm.

Her mind reached out to touch the mind of the stranger. When she made contact, he cried without tears.

"My God," he sobbed. "You are like me." He coughed, spitting blood.

Don't talk, she said in mind speech, wiping his face to expose his golden skin underneath the grime and filth.

They told me there was a colony here, and I came to look for you. Just before I entered the atmosphere of this planet, a 'Searcher' found and attacked me. I managed to elude him before he could finish me off, but my ship crashed, and I was injured badly. When these natives found me, I was barely alive. I would have made it, but they tortured me, blinded me.

He lay back, breathing deeply. She felt his pain, and she knew he was dying.

Too bad I can't see you. He smiled. *I bet you're really beautiful.*

They made us into perfect specimen when they created us, a genetic experiment that turned out to be more successful than they had planned. Now they want us dead.

His hand went up and touched her naked breast. He pulled it back, surprised, but then his fingers curled around it. She didn't push him away.

You are naked, he said. *Does everybody around here run around like that*?

She laughed. *No, not everybody. I was a prisoner, but my friends freed me.*

Your friends?

She sensed his surprise when his mind reached out and touched Vrok and the others.

I can merge with their minds, but they are different. Who are they?

They are my people. My tribe. The only friends I have left.

I don't understand.

Their enemies from the stars killed my parents and everybody else. I am the only survivor.

"Good God," the stranger whispered. "So few of us left.

She felt his dismay and stroked his cheek. Vrok touched her arm, and she turned to look up at him.

"We must leave, Starborn. More guards are coming."

"Yes," she nodded.

She held the stranger's limp hand, and her mind tried to hold on to his withdrawing spirit.

I am dying. His thoughts were getting weaker. *Maybe it's just as well. Not much to live for anyway. There is a war out there among the stars, you know. You're lucky to be hidden away on this backwater planet.*

He was almost gone. She could barely understand what he said. A spasm ran through his body, and he lifted up. Then he sank back with a deep sigh. A smile played on his lips. His thoughts came very faintly, but she wasn't sure what he said. It sounded like *See you, Beautiful*.

Gently, she released his stiff fingers from her breast and crossed his arms over his chest.

"See you, friend," she said. Then she turned away.

Vrok waited for her in the corridor. She saw the two dead guards the others had killed. Quickly, she ran to the cell where they had kept her prisoner and retrieved her clothing. It took only a moment to dress, and then she joined her friends.

"We'll have to get out of here before they sound an alarm. So far we've been lucky," Vrok said to her, as they climbed the stairs.

"How did you get in without being seen?"

Vrok smiled. "You should know better than to ask that. In the darkness, I am an invisible shadow, little sister. We had some help. One of the guards told us about a back entrance." He grinned. "Very reluctantly though, I should add."

At the top of the stairs, they turned into a narrow, dark corridor, which led to a small door.

Torr lifted his hand. *Movement outside.*

The door opened, and they flattened against the wall, but the guard had seen them already. He called out and backed away.

Torr threw his dagger, buried it in the guard's throat. His scream cut off with a gurgle.

When they stepped outside, a group of armed men waited for them. It didn't surprise Vania to see Lord Granton among them.

He grinned when he saw her. "I see your friends came to free you." He drew his weapon. "Don't worry, you won't be free for long. I don't believe what my father said about your so-called incredible strength. I am a Tark, one of the strongest men in Dange. Just because you Vardens are tall doesn't make you invincible."

He stepped forward, his keen-edged sword reflecting the reddish light of *Gamba, the Lone Wanderer.*

"Come," he taunted, turning his attention to Vrok. "Let my blade drink you blood, big man, so I can go on with the more important task of bedding this foolish slave girl."

When Vrok lifted his broad blade, Vania put her hand on his arm. "He's mine, big brother. Give me a weapon."

Without a word, Vrok handed her his heavy sword. She took it and hefted it easily. The effects of the drug seemed to be gone, but she still didn't have back her full strength. When she advanced toward the young Tark, he shook his head.

"I don't want to kill you, golden girl. A woman's place is in the bed of a brave warrior, not on the battlefield."

"It seems you have a few things to learn about women, and I'm just the one to teach you." Vania smiled without humor. Her body ached. Granton's confidence made her angry, and she rushed him without any further preliminaries. Their swords met with a clang of metal and shower of sparks.

They jumped apart after the first encounter. He didn't give her any time to relax, attacking her with unexpected speed. Parrying his thrust easily, she saw the flicker of respect cross his suddenly serious face.

"I believe I underestimated you," he grunted, pressing closer and reaching around to grab her long hair. He managed to entwine his fingers in a few strands and pulled hard, throwing her off balance.

She brought up her left knee and rammed it into his belly, while her free hand groped for his face. Her nails raked his right cheek, and, with satisfaction, she saw blood flow down his face.

He let go of her hair and touched his face. "Spawn of a *She-Demon*!" he cursed, baring his fangs. "I should have strangled you when you were helpless."

He lunged at her again, and she swept down her sword against his.

For a long time they fought, their swords cutting the air, ringing loudly when they met. Neither of them gave any quarter, but the sword began to get heavy in Vania's hand, and she knew she had to end it soon. She could tell that the battle took its toll on her opponent also. His movements became sluggish, and his reflexes were not as fast as in the beginning.

Both of them were bleeding from numerous superficial slashes, but it was only a matter of time when one of them would be wounded mortally.

He stumbled suddenly, fell and lost his grip on his sword. She moved in quickly, kicked the weapon out of his hand and pressed the tip of her own sword into his chest.

When she hesitated, he looked at her. She read the fear of death in his eyes, but he managed to grin. "You've won, golden girl. You'd better kill me quick before you lose your nerve, and I my honor."

Her anger seemed suddenly gone, and she removed the sword from his chest. "You never had any honor," she said, turned and walked away quietly, the heavy weapon a dead weight in her hand. Fatigue washed through her body, and her knees were starting to shake. Her arms and shoulder ached terribly. All she wanted now was to sit down and rest.

Through a red haze, she heard someone call out, and she dropped from sheer reflex. Something heavy whistled through the air above her and fell to the ground with a hard clang not far from her.

A gurgling sound behind her made her turn and look.

Lord Granton lay on the ground, blood oozing from his mouth, the hilt of a dagger protruding from his neck.

She recognized the dagger. It belonged to Vrok.

He bent to pick up the sword Granton had thrown and handed it to Vania, taking his own from her numb fingers. “This would have been your death,” he said. “Never trust a Tark.”

Then he joined Torr, Jark, and Karm in the fight against Lord Granton’s men.

Vania watched with curious detachment as they systematically slaughtered the Tarks. She was too tired to join in the battle. Her arms felt like two heavy logs attached to her aching body.

It was over soon and Vrok swept her up in his strong arms to carry her across the high stonewall. Steps led to the top on this side, but they used ropes to get down on the other side.

They found their riding animals then galloped down the dark empty street. Hearing the angry shouts of Lord Kapkor’s men behind them, they spurned their animals to run faster and take them out of the city Dange.

It’s going to be a long ride. How are you feeling, little sister?

She sensed his concern and sent him reassuring thought impulses.

I’ll survive, big brother. Just let’s get out of here.

Epilogue

Enjoying the warmth of his body in the chilly night, Vania snuggled closer to Vrok. Looking up at the stars overhead, she wondered which one was Earth, the world her parent came from.

Out there were also her enemies, and maybe some day they would come searching for her.

She remembered the words of the golden man in the dungeon.

You are lucky to be hidden away on this backwater planet. There is a war out there.

She chuckled. If she was lucky here, it must be bad out there among the stars, where the wars were fought with terrible weapons that could destroy whole worlds.

But then…an arrow or sword could kill just as easily as a weapon that hurtled lightning bolts.

No, my friend, I am not lucky. Only the Dead are.

The End

Rhodar, the Barbarian
By
Herbert Grosshans

Naked steel in brawny hand, he came from a far-away land
He walked proud and tall with a swinging gait, a barbarian, he tempted fate

Prologue

Rhodar, the Barbarian, does not exist in our universe. He lives in a different universe, in another dimension.

His world is similar to ours in many ways, yet also vastly different.

Not only humans inhabit his world. There are giants, dwarfs, half-humans, and there are magical creatures.

In Rhodar's universe, we'll meet witches and warlocks, evil sorcerers and conjurers, because here magic works. We'll also meet pretty young maidens in distress (or under other circumstances) and muscle-bound fearless heroes who battle the eternal evil with only their courage and their incredible strength.

Rhodar is one of them.

He may seem familiar and not much different from most other heroes, but he is Rhodar. And that makes him different. He has his own personality, his own past. He is not above killing or stealing, like most heroes, but he lives by his own code of honor and ethics. He would never commit cold-blooded murder, nor would he take from a helpless creature, but then again…he is not above taking another man's woman, if she is willing. Or taking from a thief who has already cheated another victim.

Rhodar is a barbarian, a savage, but in his own way as civilized as any of us. Rhodar is who we secretly would like to be.

So let's enter his alien and yet familiar world and follow him on his journey.

Pythese
Chapter One

"I'm sorry, that one is not for sale." The merchant stepped in front of the small golden cage and put his hand on the tall man's bare chest. He pulled it back hastily when he looked into the stranger's steely blue eyes. "No offense, noble sir," the little man cried, "but I cannot sell you that creature. It would bring you only ill luck."

"You have aroused my interest, keeper," rumbled the big man, one brawny arm pushing the merchant aside. He bent closer to inspect the small caged animal. It was small enough to fit into his cupped hands…a reptile, the body covered with fine, blue scales. Its head was narrow and flat, and from its shoulders sprouted a pair of leathery wings.

There was something in the way the little creature looked at the two men that attracted the stranger's curiosity.

"How much?" he asked.

The merchant wrung his pudgy hands. "It is not mine to sell," he whined. "It was given to me for safekeeping by someone whose name I'm afraid to even speak."

"I'll give you fifty *kaales*, which is more than enough for an animal that size."

"Fifty *kaales*?" said the merchant, greed suddenly showing in his eyes. "How about a hundred?" Licking his fat lips, he looked at the stranger's shabby leather kilt, the worn dusty boots. Obviously, this man was a barbarian, who probably didn't have enough money to buy his next meal. His eyes also noticed the long knife, the two long daggers, and the huge battleaxe strapped to the wide back.

The barbarian smiled. "I have the money, if that's your worry. I'll give you seventy-five."

Relaxing, the fat merchant held out a hand and sighed. "Give me seventy-five then, and I'm sure I can justify the sale."

Fishing three large gold coins from a purse at his belt, the stranger threw them on the greasy counter. "You're a hard man to bargain with," he laughed, "but this isn't my money anyway." He took the small cage down from its hook and turned to leave.

"Oh, one word of caution," called the merchant after him. "Don't open that cage, ever, or you'll be sorry." He watched the big man walk out the door, the lean muscular body moving silently with the litheness of a large feline.

There was power in that lean body, but not just power. He sensed the ferociousness of a wild desert-cat in that barbarian when he had looked into his cold blue eyes. If he never saw him again, there would be no regrets. He shuddered when he thought of that huge axe wielded by those sinewy arms.

With the stranger gone, he rubbed his hands and grinned. "He'll be sorry," he murmured, "he just doesn't know it yet."

* * * *

The tall barbarian walked across the dusty street, heading for the inn, where he had rented a room. He shouldered his way through the crowd of mostly short and dark-skinned people, who cast curious glances at the tall, half-naked outlander.

He seemed to walk without a care, but his blue eyes were restless, studying the people in the street with the watchfulness of a wild beast. The proximity of so many people made him uncomfortable; the noise and the reek of sweat, human waste, food and spices assaulted his senses. He preferred the vastness of the plains, where the sky was high, and the air smelled sweet with the fragrance of growing things.

Chanth-Kir was not a large city. Grown out of the ruins from an ancient city, its buildings were a mixture of architectural styles. It was not an unusual sight to find four-story stone structures looming over small wooden shacks.

This was not the best part of town, and the inn was as shabby inside as it appeared from the outside.

The big man pushed open the heavy wooden door and headed for an empty table. Setting the small cage in front of him, he called out for ale. When the serving girl brought a foaming mug, he patted the chair beside him. "Come, wench, sit down beside me and keep me company for a while."

She smiled, accepting the coins he handed her then pulled away from his grasp. "My master would be angry," she murmured, studying him from behind lowered lashes, "but maybe later."

There was promise in her midnight-eyes, and he laughed good-humoredly. He watched her as she moved between the tables, light on bare feet, her legs flashing golden in the light that streamed through the barred windows.

His smiles vanished, and his steely eyes narrowed when he heard shuffling footsteps stop beside his table. A grimy looking individual stood grinning at him, while scrawny hands reached for a chair. "Mind if I take the weight off these tired legs?"

"You're a poor substitute for the company I'm seeking," growled the barbarian.

"I admit I'm not as comely as that little wench, but if by chance you should seek information, I'd be the better choice."

"What would I be looking for?"

"I don't know," grinned the little man, sliding into the chair, "but you must be searching for something. Even a blind man would know you for a stranger."

The barbarian took a swig from the mug and wiped his mouth with the back of his broad hand. "What do they call you, little man?"

"I'm known as Gerrus, Son of Gars, and what name do you go by?"

"Friends and enemies alike call me Rhodar."

"Rhodar, hmm. No clan-name?"

The blue eyes clouded for moment. "No clan-name," the big man rumbled. "Just Rhodar."

As if by chance, the little man's gaze fell on the small cage. "Yours?" he asked casually.

"Just bought it," nodded Rhodar. "Why?"

"I've never seen a *Cloud-Dragon* before, but there are legends." The little man searched the barbarian's face. "I wonder if you know what you bought."

Emptying the mug, Rhodar set it down and smiled. "You tell me," he suggested.

"They're only legends," Gerrus said cautiously. "Like I said, I've never laid eyes upon a *Cloud-Dragon* before. One legend says if you gauge out their eyes when Seal and Rumos join in the sky, the eyes turn to precious jewels. Another says if you boil their…"

Rhodar chuckled and lifted up a hand. "Enough, Gerrus, Son of Gars. I don't put much value in old wives' tales."

"They're not old wives' tales. And you have not heard the most important one…"

"I said *enough*!" growled Rhodar.

The little man opened his mouth but closed it tight, when he looked into the barbarian's steely cold eyes. "You are easily aroused, outlander," he murmured. "I'm only trying to help." His tongue flickered over dry lips as he longingly looked at the empty mug. "My throat cries out for liquid. Is there a slight possibility you might spare a coin or two for a small mug of ale?"

Rhodar laughed when he looked at the little man, who desperately tried to look honest and humble. He ordered two more mugs, gave the serving girl a little tweak on her round buttocks, to which she only giggled, and pushed one of the mugs in front of the little man. "You're a thief," he told him, "and maybe I should have thrown you out by your scrawny neck."

Gerrus sipped slowly, his eyes lingering on the small animal in the cage then back to the weathered face of the stranger, moved on to the shiny double blades of the huge battleaxe leaning beside the barbarian's chair. Undoubtedly, this weapon could tell many tales, none of them pleasant.

Rhodar leaned back in his chair; he seemed relaxed, uncaring, his eyes half-closed.

Like a viper waiting for its prey, Gerrus thought.

A thief, thought Rhodar, as he watched the little man. *Wouldn't trust him as far as I can spit. He'd probably slit my throat if I gave him the opportunity.* He opened his eyes and laughed suddenly, making Gerrus sputter into his ale. "Drink up, friend," he roared. "I'll buy you another one."

After the third mug Gerrus felt his head spinning and seemed to have trouble focusing on the big man across from him. "Had a string of good luck?" he suggested, when Rhodar fished some coins from a fat purse to pay for another round.

"Reward for a job well done," the barbarian said, blue eyes resting on the little man's narrow brown face. He didn't seem to be effected by the brew he had consumed.

"What kind of job?" Gerrus asked.

Again, Rhodar laughed his big, booming laugh. "I murdered a wealthy merchant and his family," he said, winking.

"Murdered?" Gerrus choked out.

"Yes." Rhodar leaned forward, his voice a whisper. "You must know many rich merchants in this city, ripe for the plucking. We could become wealthy, you and I."

"No, no!" The little man looked around the room. "I may not be above relieving a man of some of his leftover money…but murder? Not for me."

"Come, come," Rhodar growled. "You and your friends would have no qualms killing me."

Suddenly sober, Gerrus put down his mug. “My friends? I don’t know what you’re talking about.” His eyes followed Rhodar’s gaze and fell on the three men at a table in a corner. Dressed in garbs that had seen better days but adorned with long knifes hanging from their belts, it was not hard to guess what business they were in.

Deep in conversation, they didn’t seem to notice the barbarian looking at them.

Gerrus sighed. “I don’t know those men,” he said. “Not personally. They are cutthroats and thieves. Not the kind of people I would associate with.” He tried to stand up. “I think I must leave you now.”

Rhodar pushed him back into his chair. “Sit!” the big man ordered. “You drank away my hard-earned money…now answer me a few questions!”

“Anything, my friend.” Gerrus shrank in his seat. “You want to know where you can find willing virgins? A wealthy and lonely widow? Maybe a treasure, guarded, but for someone like you child’s play?”

“Don’t be a fool, Gerrus! Tell me, where can I find the *House of Arguss*?”

“You don’t mean *Arguss, the Sorcerer*? Nobody seeks him out.”

“I do. Where can I find him?”

“He lives three days ride to the east, deep in the mountains. The journey is treacherous. There are wild beasts, wild men, and…” he made a sign in the air, “…magical creatures in the mountain forest.”

Rhodar grinned. “I fear no one.” His hand touched his axe, stroked it. “*Singar* has met magic before.”

“Can I go now?” Gerrus sat still, black eyes flickering in his scarred face.

Rhodar nodded and watched the little man stumble out of the door, but not before he looked at the three men in the corner. Rhodar’s watchful eyes had not missed the movement of hands. Grinning, the big barbarian emptied his mug.

* * * *

The girl stirred in his arms, opened her eyes, smiled. Her naked breasts felt warm and soft against his hard chest.

“I must go soon,” she whispered.

He rolled on top of her, between her parted thighs. Her hand reached between them, and her fingers curled around his hard pole, guided it toward the dark triangle below her flat belly. He felt himself sliding easily into her warm moistness, for the third time between short periods of rest. She gasped, moved against him, her pelvis twisting with sinuous movements. Keeping his weight off her soft body, he tried to be gentle, but she seemed to ask for more. He crushed her against him then, took her with mighty thrusts.

She met his plunges with equal force, hammering her hips into his, moaning loudly every time he entered her fully.

They moved thus for a long time, until she finally lay still, whimpering, her nails raking his broad back, her thighs opening and closing, squeezing hard, dousing him with her warm discharge. He erupted inside her, growling like a wild *Swamp-Leopard.*

Shuddering one last time, he left her and rolled onto his back beside her. They lay silent for a long time, the sound of their ragged breathing loud in the room.

"You are a beast, barbarian," she said, when she had caught her breath.

He laughed, his hand squeezing one of her ample breasts. "And you're a vampire, girl. You've sucked me dry, and you're still asking for more."

She giggled, stroking his muscular chest. "I've had all I can take, beast-man, but there is still tonight."

She slipped from the bed, padded across the wooden floor to the washbasin, poured water from a pitcher and started washing herself.

Rhodar watched her silently, appreciating her voluptuous figure. She'd be fat some day; her breasts were already starting to sag, but she still had many years left. Her face was pretty, her hair soft and long, her body strong and her fleshy thighs willing to open.

She dried herself and slipped into her clothing then she came over to him and kissed him briefly. Before she closed the door, she turned around and asked, "What is your name, beast-man? I am Ainah."

"I am Rhodar," he said. "It was a pleasure, Ainah."

Giggling, she blew him a kiss and closed the door. He sighed, and his eyes fell on the little creature in the cage.

The yellow eyes of the *Cloud-Dragon* watched him silently, and there was something in the unblinking stare that sent small shivers down the big man's spine.

Chapter Two

It was going to be another hot day. Rhodar looked into the cloudless sky, squinted at the glaring sun and steered his horse into the protective shade of a *Sec-tree.*

"Let's rest for a while, Nightwalker."

The big black animal snorted and started nibbling on the grass that was growing sparsely around the smooth trunk of the tree.

Rhodar set the small golden cage on the ground. Pouring some water into a shallow, narrow earthen container, he pushed it between the bars into the cage. "Here, quench your thirst, little one."

The small creature gave him a yellow-eyed stare and dipped a long tongue into the water. As Rhodar lifted the water bag to his own lips, his sharp ears picked up the sound of stealthy footsteps.

Moments later a familiar figure stepped from behind a boulder. "Rhodar, my old friend, we meet again."

"Gerrus, old friend," Rhodar responded, freeing his battleaxe and hefting it easily, his corded muscles rippling on his arm.

The little thief stepped closer, his hands open. "Is that how you greet a friend? With a weapon in your hand?" His eyes shifted nervously, lingered for a moment on something to the big man's right.

The barbarian moved suddenly with the unexpected speed of a *Sand-Lizard,* a glittering object left his hand as he rolled away from the spot where he had been standing.

A gurgling cry then angry surprised shouts. The little thief ducked behind a boulder. The barbarian followed him, but he never reached the little man. A thrown club tripped him. Roaring angrily, he rolled again, landed on his feet and, with a blood curdling battle cry, he charged his attackers.

He counted seven of them, two more a short distance away on horses, another one on the ground, the hilt of Rhodar's dagger protruding from his neck. Among the seven facing him, he recognized the three men from the tavern.

Whirling his huge battleaxe, he brought it down, splitting the head of his first assailant. A club caught him in the back, sent him sprawling. Falling, he swung the axe upward, pushed aside a descending mace and buried the blade in the rogue's chest.

The others pulled back a little, their ugly faces suddenly afraid.

Rhodar stood swaying, his broad chest covered with blood and gore.

"Get him!" someone yelled.

The barbarian swung his weapon, blood dripping from the gleaming blades. "Come," he taunted, grinning. "Come, let *Singar* drink your blood."

"Give us the Cloud-Dragon, and we'll let you go."

Rhodar looked at the golden cage in which the little creature crouched, its yellow eyes on him. He moved toward the cage. "No!" he said.

He had almost reached the cage when they rushed him. One attacker came at him with a sword. Rhodar caught the long blade with a twist of his axe, swung again, felt it bite deep into the man's neck.

Blood gushed.

A sharp pain in his thigh stopped his movement; his leg gave away. He fell, reached for the cage. Something smashed against the side of his head.

While darkness descended, the axe dropped from his grip. Clinging stubbornly to the last fragments of consciousness, his groping hand found the golden cage and with one last desperate effort, he ripped it apart, threw it away from him.

"Fly, little one," he whispered. "Fly and live!"

* * * *

There was a dull pain in his left leg. He tried to move it, gave up when the pain became worse. Something wet and cool touched his face. He opened his eyes a little, suddenly aware of the throbbing pain in his head.

His vision blurred; he tried to focus on the face above him.

A girl.

Black long hair fell into his face.

"Ainah," he croaked, his throat raw and dry.

"Hush," she said softly. "Here, drink this."

He swallowed the drops of cool water, coughed, tried to sit. She pushed him back gently. "Just lie still," she said. "Let me tend to your wounds. You've lost a lot of blood."

She dabbed the side of his head.

He looked into her golden eyes. "You're not Ainah," he mumbled.

She laughed with a silvery, tinkling sound. "The girl from the tavern? No, I am not she."

"Who are you?" For the first time he saw her clearly. Her skin was light, with a slight golden tint. Long black lashes in a delicate face framed her golden eyes, and he knew he must be dreaming.

"You're not real," he said, closing his eyes. "No wench is this beautiful."

She laughed. "I'm not a wench. I am Pythese."

"Even your name doesn't sound real." He opened his eyes again, touched the side of his head and groaned when he felt the caked blood.

"Be careful," she warned. "Your wound might open again."

He watched her as she tied some large leafs to his thigh. She was slender, with a tiny waist, lovely shaped buttocks and not overly large, but beautifully formed breasts. Only now he realized that she was totally nude.

She smiled unabashedly when she felt his gaze on her. "I have stopped the bleeding, but we'll have to find some *Cin-leaves* to keep the wound clean."

"Who are you, wench? A sorceress come to claim my body for some unholy purpose? Is that why you are nursing me?"

She looked at him with her golden eyes. Her red lips still smiled, but her words were serious. "I'm only repaying a debt."

She finished her task, stood up. She was of average height, he noticed, possibly a little taller. Her legs were long and well formed, just like the rest of her slender body. He looked at her smooth flat belly.

"You have no navel," he observed. "You are no mortal woman."

He noticed that her pubic area was bare and smooth, without the slightest fuzz of hair.

Smiling, she knelt down beside him. He saw her white even teeth, as well as the two needle-sharp thin fangs.

She kissed him, her lips teasing his. Her warm breasts rested softly on his chest. "When you're strong again I'll show you how much woman I really am," she whispered. "But for now, rest."

* * * *

Things were a little clearer when he awoke a second time. The girl knelt beside him, watching him.

"I am still dreaming," he croaked, closing his eyes.

He heard her quiet silvery laughter and felt something cool and moist pressed against his lips. Opening his eyes, he grabbed her wrist and looked at the piece of tree bark in her hand.

"Eat this," she encouraged him. "It will help speed up the healing."

Suddenly, he was aware again of the throbbing pain in his thigh.

"I found a small spring with clear water not far from here," the girl said. "Also, there is more protection. Let's try to make it there."

A dark shadow loomed suddenly beside him, and something wet touched his cheek, followed by a snort.

"Nightwalker." He stroked the horse's long head. "I'm glad they didn't get you."

The big black horse whinnied and threw back its head, one hoof pawing the ground.

Rhodar groaned when the young woman helped him up. He shook away her hand. "I can make it by myself, wench," he growled, grabbing his steed's thick mane. His head swam, but he managed to climb onto the horse's broad back.

"My axe, wench," he cursed, looking at the weapon lying on the ground.

"You should have thought of that before you crawled on your horse," the girl said patiently, but the barbarian detected a flicker of annoyance in her soft voice. "Maybe if you apologize for being so rude and if you ask nice, I might get it for you."

"The *Seven-headed Demons* will devour my body before I apologize to any wench," Rhodar growled.

"My name is not *wench*," the girl flashed at him. "It is Pythese! Remember that, you thickheaded barbarian."

Rhodar laughed, despite the pain in his head and leg. "I think I'm going to like you, wench. There is a lot of fire in you."

She stomped her foot. "Ah, what's the use? If it weren't for the debt I owe, I'd let you rot." She bent down to pick up the weapon. Straining, she managed to lift up the handle, but the double-bladed head stayed on the ground.

"What kind of weapon is this?" she wondered, dropping the handle.

Rhodar chuckled good-humoredly. "There is a spell on it, which makes it as light as a feather for its owner, but heavy for anyone else. My father gave *Singar* to me. Since he gave the weapon to me freely, I can wield it, but the spell will not last much longer. Already it is heavier than it used to be. The sorcerer who once a long time ago gave the axe to my father must renew the spell. It is my quest to seek and find Arguss, so I can become the true master of *Singar*." He looked at the battleaxe. “Leave it here until I come back to get it. It will be safe.”

Pythese led the horse down a narrow winding path until they came to a small valley. There was a narrow stream passing through it, with shade trees growing on both sides. They found a place, which offered protection from the sun, and Rhodar slid off his steed.

Grumbling, he lay down under the wide branches of the tree. He didn’t object when the girl made a pillow from grass and put it under his head. But when she washed his face with water from the stream, he growled, “Don’t fuss so much, wench. I am not an infant.”

“No, but you act like one,” she scolded. “You’ve been seriously wounded, and you have lost much blood. And your leg is bleeding again. You must lie still.”

He watched as she examined the wound. She was chewing on a weed, which she spat into her hand. Then she began rubbing the green paste into his wound. It stung for a moment, but suddenly most of the pain seemed to subside.

“A healing compound and a painkiller,” she explained. “I was lucky to find some.”

He closed his eyes and sighed. “Too bad I feel so weak,” he mumbled, his hand groping for her naked thigh. “I think you could arouse great passion in me, wench.”

“Pythese,” she said, but she was smiling.

Chapter Three

He must have slept, for when he looked around again, the sun was low in the sky. Searching for the girl, he found her sitting cross-legged in front of a fire, roasting something on a spit.

"You're awake." She smiled. "How are you feeling?"

He sat up and discovered that most of the pain seemed to be gone. His head was clear, and when his fingers probed his thigh, he felt only a dull soreness. His thigh was wrapped with a band made from woven grass. The female stood up and came over to him. There was something different about her, he saw.

She wasn't naked anymore. She wore a short skirt, woven out of long strands of grass, around her hips. A narrow band made from the same material covered her breasts.

"You have a talent with your hands," he said.

She giggled, a mischievous light flickering in her golden eyes. "I have many talents with different parts of my body," she said. "Maybe I'll let you find out."

He growled, getting to his feet. When he put weight on his wounded leg, there was hardly any pain.

"Be careful," she warned. "It is almost healed, but too much strain might open the wound again."

Sniffing, he looked at the fire. "I am so hungry, I could eat a *tree-goat*. What are you roasting?"

"Only a hare." She laughed, taking the spit from the fire. "I think I burned it a little."

He grinned at her. "I guess you're not perfect in everything after all."

"I never said I was perfect," she said. "I said I have many talents." Smiling, she handed him the spit. "It is still edible."

He wolfed down the slightly charred meat. When he was gnawing on the bones, he suddenly seemed to remember something. "Have you eaten, wench?" he asked, a little sheepishly. "I seem to have forgotten my manners."

"I doubt you ever had any, barbarian," the girl said, but then she smiled. "Thank you for thinking of me, but don't worry, I have eaten."

He let out a loud belch and stretched his sore muscles then he walked down to the creek and began washing his face and upper torso. Looking at this reflection in the water, he thoughtfully rubbed the stubbles on his wide chin. "How long have I slept?" he wondered aloud. "This feels like many days' growth."

The young woman, who had followed him, nodded. "The sun has set three times since last you were awake. I gave you a sleeping potion to let your body heal faster."

"And you stood guard over me all this time?" Rhodar looked at the girl. He walked over and touched her lightly at the shoulder. "I am in your debt, Pythese," he growled. "Why are you doing this?"

She smiled happily, put her slim arms around his neck and looked into his blue eyes. "You called me by my name," she said. Then she pressed her lips against his. "Now I'll show you some of my other talents," she whispered, slipping out of her grass skirt.

His hand slid under the band that covered her breasts and pushed it up.

"Don't tear it." She smiled. "It took me some time to make it." She removed it herself, and then her hands pushed down his leather kilt. Her fingers traveled down his taut belly, found him more than ready.

He groaned when she wrapped her slim fingers around his manhood while he fondled her firm buttocks, squeezing them gently. She moved her hand slowly back and forth the length of his thick pole, causing it to become even harder and larger in her small hand.

"It's not only your muscles that are huge and hard," she said softly into his ear, letting go of his member. Lifting up on tiptoes, she moved forward and captured his big mast between her soft thighs. Gently snapping her hips back and forth, she rubbed the swollen lips of her female organ across his engorged maleness.

"Do not play with me, wench," he growled, his breath coming faster. Her buttocks moved softly in his hands.

She laughed and put her hands behind his head, pulled his face close to hers. Then her warm lips pressed against his. He opened them when he felt her tongue probing his teeth and let her into his mouth. She tasted sweet, like the fruit from a *Fer-tree*.

With a sudden quick movement, she pulled up her long legs, wrapped them around his lower torso and pushed her pelvis forward. Her wet and tight sheath easily swallowed up his hard organ.

She moved furiously in his grasp, using his arms like a swing to snap her hips back and forth.

"I must put you down," he moaned after a while, "my leg is

beginning to hurt me."

Without uncoupling, he sank with her to his knees and put her onto her back. Her bent legs opened wider, and he moved slowly and lazily between her spread thighs. She cried out as an orgasm shook her body, began writhing wildly underneath him.

"Do not move in such crazy fashion, wench," he growled, his breath catching. "I will not be able to hold back my seed."

She calmed down but kept milking him with gentle force. His breathing became ragged and, with a loud shout, he pushed deep into her, held her tight until he was finished spilling his seed.

When he tried to leave her, she shook her head, kept him prisoner inside her tight sheath. Squeezing her inner muscles around his member, she stroked him back to hardness. "Now it is your turn to move slowly," she whispered.

They moved like that for a long time, and their soft sighs and groans gave testimony to the pleasure they experienced.

The two night suns *Seal* and *Rumos* were already in the sky, when they finally dropped into an exhausted sleep, lying in each other's arms.

* * * *

When they woke, it was daylight. The girl stretched and yawned, and then she rolled onto her back and smiled up at him. "I think you should get rid of that hair in your face. It makes my skin itchy."

Rhodar laughed cheerfully and cupped one of her breasts. "You were right," he said. "You do have many talents. My legs feel still weak. Don't tell me it comes from loss of blood."

She giggled, snuggling up to him. After a while, she slipped out of his embrace, ran down to the creek and dove into it. "Come," she called. "The water is refreshing."

He followed her and walked into the water until it came up to his knees. He watched her as she swam back to him, her slender body cutting the water like a fish.

Laughing, she came up in front of him, shook the water from her eyes. "Let me rub your back," she said. "You shouldn't get your wound wet. Not yet."

As she stood in front of him, his eyes traveled over her trim body, from her lovely face, over her taut round breasts, down to her flat stomach, to the fleshy area between her slim legs, back to her smooth belly. He stared at the spot where her navel should have been. "You are so beautiful," he told her, "but you are no human woman."

"More woman than you might be able to handle, barbarian." She smiled, her white teeth gleaming in the bright light of the sun.

Again, he was aware of the two needle-sharp fangs, but he said nothing. She splashed his back, ran her hands over his body. He stood without moving or talking, letting her rub him down, enjoying her closeness, the touch of her soft hands.

When she was finished, he took her in his arms and kissed her. "You must have put a spell on me, wench," he breathed into her ear. She looked down and giggled, her hand following her gaze. He carried her out of the water, stretched her on the ground and fell between her opening thighs.

He took her roughly, like an animal, but she didn't seem to mind, matching his powerful thrusts with equal force. After his first explosive release, she made him pull out so she could turn around then kneeling in front of him, she pushed up her lovely rump. He moved into position behind her, fumbled between her soft cheeks, found her moist entrance and slid back into her tight canal.

She began pumping her hips back and forth, let out an almost anguished sounding cry when a powerful orgasm shook her. He held her hips in his big hands, steadied her erratic movements, shouted harshly when his own release made him quiver, his hard belly pressing tightly against her soft buttocks.

She collapsed beneath him, her breath coming in ragged gasps. He lay on top of her, his pole still inside her softly pulsing sex-organ, his chest heaving from the exertion. Then he pulled out and rolled onto his back. She slid on top of him. Smiling, she searched his face. "Am I woman enough for you, Rhodar?"

He chuckled, stroked her round buttocks. "I still say you are not human! Who are you? What are you?"

"I am Pythese," she answered, laying her head against his chest. "Isn't that enough?"

He didn't answer, just held her tight.

* * * *

They made love four, sometimes five times a day, spending most of their time in the shade of the trees or splashing in the water. They both couldn't get enough of each other. Every time was more exciting than the time before. The girl was always happy and cheerful, and most of the time she managed to wipe the ever-present scowl off the barbarian's face. However, after five days Rhodar became restless. His leg was almost completely healed, aided by the herbal compounds

Pythese had mixed for him. It was time to move on.

The young woman didn't try to talk him out of it, when he told her he had to go back to Chanth-Kir. The thieves had taken everything he owned, except for his horse, his axe and his kilt. He was determined to get revenge.

"I may not be able to recover all of my money," he growled, as he mounted Nightwalker, "but I'll get back some of it."

The girl swung up behind him and put her arms around his lean hips. Rhodar carried his huge battleaxe in one hand, seemingly without effort now and, clucking softly, he gave Nightwalker the command to get going. The horse was as restless as its master, and with a neigh, it trotted off in the direction of the city.

As they passed the spot where the rogues had ambushed Rhodar, he threw one last look at the shattered remains of the small golden cage and felt a stab of regret over the loss of the little *Cloud-Dragon,* hoping the little creature was safe.

Above, the bright sun burned down on them from a cloudless sky. The piercing cry of a *Dew-Hawk* made Rhodar look up, and he pulled back his lips into a humorless grin. The sight of the giant bird of prey was a good omen and, shouting a loud battle cry, he dug his heels into Nightwalker's soft flanks, spurning the big horse into a fast gallop. He was anxious to get back to the city

They reached Chanth-Kir in the late afternoon.

Looking at the shabby sign of a tavern, Rhodar rumbled, "Where will we spend the night? We have no money."

Pythese slid off the horse, picked something from the ground and handed it to the barbarian. "Pay with this."

He looked at the small pebble in her hand. "A rock," he said. "Have you lost your senses, wench?"

"Look again."

Rhodar blinked and stared at the glittering crystal. "A gemstone! What witchery is this?" he cursed under his breath. "With a gift like that, you can have anything you want."

"The spell lasts only a short while," the girl warned. "By tomorrow night this will be nothing more than a piece of worthless rock."

The barbarian laughed, reaching for the gem, but the girl pulled her hand away. "No," she said. "I must give it, or the spell is useless."

While Rhodar went into the stable in the back, Pythese entered the tavern to rent a room.

The innkeeper looked at her strangely when she handed him the gleaming jewel. “I don’t want no riff-raff in my rooms. This is a respectable place.”

“I can see that,” the girl said, looking at the scruffy customers sitting around shabby wooden tables. “This must be the meeting place of the *Five Lords.*” Turning back to the innkeeper, she said, “I am no whore, and I have no intentions of inviting any of your lordly guests to my room. Besides, I’m expecting company. Now…bring me two large mugs of ale!”

She sat down at one of the empty tables, ignoring the stares and lewd comments of the men watching her. When the big barbarian walked in and joined her, they stopped making remarks but kept looking.

Rhodar leaned his battleaxe against the table and drained his mug. “Ah,” he sighed, “I’ve missed this. I have a mind to sit and drink all night. Wash the dust out of my guts.”

“You’ll do no such thing!” the girl scolded him. “We have more important things to do.”

Rhodar laughed and called for another mug. “I perform much better with a keg of ale in my belly,” he chuckled. “It slows down my reflexes.”

“Might also get you killed,” Pythese said, suppressing a smile.

When the barman brought the foaming mug, Rhodar told the girl to give the man another gemstone and said with a loud voice, “Give all your honorable patrons a pitcher of ale on me, for tonight we drink and are merry. Tomorrow my trusted weapon will split the skulls of the rogues who waylaid me and robbed me of my possessions, leaving my body for the vultures. But they didn’t know that Rhodar is invincible.” He stood and lifted his mug. “Drink up, friends. It is free.”

A few cheered; some started whispering to each other. After the fourth round, everybody was happy and joined the barbarian in a lusty battle song. Even though Rhodar was swaggering and seemed drunk out of his mind, he never left his back unguarded; his hand was never far away from the handle of the big double-bladed axe.

He had not missed the fact that two of the men drank little, and he watched them slip out of a backdoor. Leaning over to the girl, he whispered, “Time to leave.” He grabbed her around her waist and called, “Take me to my bed, wench, before I become useless for tonight.”

Winking, he dragged her away. The men around him laughed and gave him a few hints, telling him how lucky he was to have such good fortune with women and money.

As they staggered up the creaking stairs, Pythese whispered fiercely, “You fool, to call attention upon us. Half of those cutthroats will try to break down our door after we are asleep.”

“I don’t believe that,” Rhodar said, his voice now without a slur. “There is honor even among thieves. But then again, there is also always the exception.”

When they reached their room, Rhodar held up his hand. By the dim light of the flickering oil lamp on the wall the girl saw what Rhodar had already noticed.

The door to their room stood slightly ajar.

“Too much ale,” he said with a drunken voice, “my legs are weak. I just want to sleep.”

He hit the door as if he had bumped into it. “Help me, wench,” He mumbled loud enough for anyone in the room to hear. “I can barely walk.”

Then he kicked open the door but didn’t enter. There was a sharp outcry from behind the door as it slammed into an object. From the other side, a shadowy figure rushed toward them, swinging a heavy club.

The barbarian’s heavy fist smashed into a bearded face. With a loud sigh, the body of the assailant collapsed to the floor. Rhodar only dimly saw another figure advancing in the darkness. Something glinted in the man’s hand. A knife. With a cry, the rogue rushed him, the knife aimed at the barbarian’s bare chest.

Rhodar kicked it out of his hand, rammed the wooden handle of his axe into his attacker’s belly. The man screamed, went down.

Pythese was suddenly there, carrying a burning oil lamp. By its flickering light, he studied the two on the floor. One was out cold; the other one writhed on the floor in pain, clasping his belly.

The barbarian grabbed him roughly and threw him on the bed. “I’ve seen you before,” he growled. “And fought you before.”

“We left you for dead,” the wounded man said hoarsely then his body convulsed with retching sounds. “My belly,” he groaned. “I’m dying.”

“You’ll live,” Rhodar said coldly, “unless I decide to kill you.”

“We only wanted that creature in the golden cage. We weren’t supposed to kill you.” The rogue looked at him slyly. “Anyway, you're alive. So everything is forgiven?"

Rhodar laughed without humor. "Where is my money?" he demanded.

"Money? We took no money from you," the man whined. "You'll have to speak to Gerrus. He's the one who arranged everything."

"Gerrus, huh?" Rhodar gave the unconscious man on the floor a kick. "Take your quiet friend here with you and get out. Count yourself lucky I'm in a good mood tonight."

The man scrambled from the bed. "Thank you, noble sir. I won't forget this."

"I'm sure you won't." Rhodar grinned. "Your aching belly will remind you."

Barring the wooden door from the inside, he turned to Pythese who lay already naked on the bed.

"Come," she pouted. "We've wasted enough time already."

Ripping off his kilt, he moved between her spread thighs. Her hands worked her magic on the weapon below his belly, and, with a loud satisfied sigh, she sheathed its full length.

"I hope you spoke the truth when you said ale slows down your reflexes," she moaned into his ear, "because you should prepare for a long night."

He growled deep in his throat, grabbed her hips and snapped his pelvis with forceful strokes between her clutching slender but strong thighs.

"The rogues did not kill me," he grunted, "but I have a feeling you just might succeed where they failed. My battleaxe is of no aid against the weapon you possess."

"I was not aware that you and I were locked in battle." Her hot breath washed over his face, and her voice came in ragged gasps.

He crushed her to him, held her tight as waves of pleasure rushed through his body. She laughed softly, milked him forcefully. "I hope you have more left," she whispered when he was finished.

He lay motionless for moment then began moving again, much slower this time. "I can go on all night, if you so wish," he said softly.

Giggling, she pushed up against him. "I so wish."

Chapter Four

The next morning, while Pythese searched for some descent clothing, Rhodar searched out the inn where he had spent a night before. There were only a few people in the bar. As he had expected it wasn't long before he spotted a familiar face.

The little thief saw him at the same time Rhodar did. Seeing the entrance barred by the large body of the barbarian, his dark eyes shifted to the backdoor. Calculating his chances, Gerrus shrugged and grinned. "I heard you were back, Rhodar, old friend," he called.

Two other men sat with the thief, but they were strangers to Rhodar. One of them stood up and left hurriedly, when the big barbarian advanced toward their table. The other one sat still, his eyes shifting nervously from the huge battleaxe in Rhodar's hand to his grim face.

"Sit," the little thief said. "It is my turn to pay."

"With my money," growled Rhodar, holding out his hand. "My belt!" he demanded.

With shaky fingers, Gerrus took off the broad belt and handed it to the big man. "I took the liberty of spending a tiny sum, but most of it is still there."

Rhodar checked one of the belt pockets, saw the coins and grinned, satisfied. "You're a bigger thief than I thought, Gerrus. You didn't even share the loot with your friends."

Gerrus shrugged. "They never asked for a share."

"Where are the rest of my things?"

"That's all I have."

Rhodar grabbed the little man by the throat. "Was it your idea to come after me?"

"No, oh, no," choked Gerrus. "Actually, I wanted no part of it, but Kathar insisted we get back the *Cloud-Dragon*."

"Who's Kathar?"

"He's the man you bought the creature from?"

"The merchant!" Rhodar cursed, letting go of the little thief. Gerrus rubbed his throat and coughed violently. "You're not a gentle man, friend Rhodar," he said hoarsely.

"Give me one good reason why I shouldn't split your head," the barbarian growled, hefting the axe.

With an ashen face, Gerrus lifted both hands. "I didn't lay a hand on you Rhodar. When you lay mortally wounded, it was I who pulled you into the protective shade of the trees."

In spite of his anger, Rhodar had to grin. "Even in the face of death you still lie, Gerrus. I was under the tree when your friends beat me unconscious."

"They're not my friends, only acquaintances."

Rhodar sighed, lowering his weapon. "You should choose your acquaintances more carefully, Gerrus, Son of Gars." He turned to leave when a girl's voice called out, "Barbarian?"

It was Ainah, the serving girl. She rushed up to him and threw her arms around his neck. "You left without a word," she pouted. "There was so much I still wanted to show you. Will I see you tonight?"

He disengaged himself gently, thinking of Pythese. She would be furious to find him in this position. "Keep it open. One never knows what might happen," he grinned. Then he planted a loud kiss on Ainah's mouth.

She wiggled her hips. "I'll be waiting, beast-man."

* * * *

The fat merchant turned around when he heard the sound of the opening door. His eyes widened when he saw the barbarian. "I was told you're dead," he gasped. His hands reached for something on a shelf. He came up with a dagger.

"I believe that belongs to me," Rhodar said grimly. "That and a few other things."

"And you have something that is mine." Kathar wiped the sweat from his bald head.

"The little flying dragon?" Rhodar said. "I paid good money for it, and thanks to you the little creature is gone."

"You freed it yourself. I warned you not to open the cage." He waved the dagger threateningly when Rhodar took a step toward him. "Stay away, wild man. I know how to use this."

The barbarian laughed. Two long strides took him around the counter, and his big hand grabbed the fat man's wrist. The dagger cluttered onto the countertop.

"You don't know what you've done, you ignorant fool," whined the merchant. "That creature is loose now, preying on innocent victims."

"You're the fool, Kathar," growled Rhodar. "That little creature cannot do much harm to anyone."

"But you don't understand!" Kathar cried out, when Rhodar shoved him against the wall. "What do you want from me?" he wailed.

"I want my seventy-five *kaales* back, plus everything else your henchmen brought you."

"I'll get it. Just don't hurt me." He slumped to the ground when Rhodar let go of him. Wheezing, he lay there for a moment. "I'm not a well man," he moaned. "This excitement will kill me."

"There is nothing you deserve more," the barbarian said. "Now stop groveling, and get my things. I don't have much time."

The merchant pulled his fat body up, grabbing onto the counter for support. The grating sound of the opening door made him look up. When he saw the girl, his lips began to tremble, and he made a mad dash for something on one of the shelves.

Rhodar turned toward the girl, watched her lift both hands. Like a wild beast, he crouched in a fighting stance, a growl left his throat and he felt the hair in his neck stand up.

A blinding flash left the girl's open hands, followed by a clap of thunder. Her mouth was open, displaying her needle-fangs. "You should wear the amulet around your fat neck, Kathar. It does you no good on the shelf," Pythese hissed. For a fleeting moment, her golden eyes burned with an intense fire then it was gone.

The merchant screamed, rushed past Rhodar and the girl and fled out of the door.

Rhodar looked at the girl, his blue eyes narrow and watchful.

"How do you like my new outfit?" Pythese asked, a sweet smile on her delicate face.

Rhodar didn't answer. Behind her in the open doorway stood a score of uniformed men, naked swords in their hands.

Enforcers.

* * * *

Pythese sat on the only cot in the otherwise bare cell, her long legs crossed. "You should have fought them," she said with an accusing stare.

Rhodar growled something, while walking the floor like a caged *Rock-Tiger*. He looked through the iron bars at his battleaxe. It was leaning against the far wall in the guardroom. Half a dozen men were needed to carry it into the guard station.

"They are the law," he explained. "If I kill an Enforcer, the Guild will hunt me until I am caught and executed."

"The law!" she exclaimed. "Do you really believe the Guild follows the just law?"

He shrugged. "They have the power. They *are* the power." He gave her a brooding look. "Why didn't you hurl your lightning bolts at them?"

"My power is limited. There were too many guards. Besides, those lightning bolts don't kill. They only render my opponents unconscious for a short time."

He stood in front of the girl, his arms folded across his deep chest. Scowling, he said, "How did you get the money to buy those fancy clothes you're wearing?"

Laughing, she jumped lightly to her feet and did a little pirouette in front of him. The silky long skirt swirled around her slender body. He caught a glimpse of a naked leg. "Do you like me in it?"

"How did you get the money?" he persisted.

She pouted. "What does it matter? I just sold some of my gemstones."

"I thought so," he growled. "We're in deep enough trouble as it is."

He lay down on the cot and closed his eyes. "I'm going to sleep. Maybe I'll finally wake up and discover I'm still in bed with that wench Ainah, and this is nothing but a dark dream."

"Ainah!" Pythese exclaimed. "You prefer her to me?"

He opened his eyes when she lay on top of him, her clothes rustling, as she peeled them off. "Come now, wench," he rumbled. "Is that all you can think of?"

"Isn't that what you always want?" she purred, her hands stroking his chest, her teeth nibbling on his lower lip.

"Only when we're alone, and not in a place like this. How can you even think about coupling right now?"

"Now you're angry."

"Angry, yes, but not at you, Pythese." He held her against him for a moment. "Just let me sleep until I can think of a way to get us out of here."

She smiled, kissing him gently. "You're like a *grarrl-root*, barbarian," she whispered. "Rough and bristly on the outside, but when you peel off the tough skin, there is nothing but tenderness inside."

"Stop talking nonsense, girl," he growled, "and go to sleep."

* * * *

The sound of voices awakened Rhodar. Instantly alert, he slid off the cot, dropped into a crouch. Then he realized where he was and relaxed.

He must have slept through the night. From the barred window, bright sunlight spilled into the cell, illuminating the heap of flimsy clothing on the clay floor, beside the empty cot. Looking around for the girl, he failed to find her.

Then his gaze swung back to the opening cell door.

A guard stood there, the large keys dangling in one hand, a sword in the other. Beside him stood a robed figure. Rhodar could see it was a woman by the way the robe hugged the slender body. Well-formed, too. A cowl covered her head, and her face was hidden behind a veil.

"Is this the man?" the Enforcer asked.

She nodded silently.

"Out!" barked the guard, waving his sword.

Rhodar followed the man's order slowly, watching the guard with narrowed eyes. He walked ahead of them, down the narrow corridor, toward the guardroom.

He counted seven Enforcers. They were sitting around a rough wooden table. One of them threw a handful of numbered *appa-sticks* into the air. As they fell, all of them bent eagerly across the tabletop to see how the sticks had fallen.

When Rhodar walked into the room, one looked up, grinned at the barbarian. "You have rich friends, outlander. You are free. One word of advice. Don't stay too long in Chanth-Kir. You have made enemies."

As Rhodar reached for his belt that the Enforcer handed him, the door was flung open, and a familiar figure rushed into the room.

"That's him!" the innkeeper yelled. "He was with the woman who paid with these." He threw a handful of pebbles on the table. "Rocks," he said. "Worthless rocks. She made me believe they were gemstones."

Without a word, the captain of the Enforcers pulled a leather pouch from a pocket and emptied its contents. A number of brightly sparkling gems rolled across the table.

"Like these?" he asked, scowling.

"Just like those," nodded the innkeeper and pointed an accusing finger at Rhodar. "He is a thief. I want him punished."

The captain took a step toward the robed woman and pulled back her cowl, exposing her thick black hair. Then he ripped off her veil.

"Pythese!" Rhodar cursed, staring at her pale face.

"It's the girl," said the innkeeper. "She gave me the stones."

"Put them back into the cell!" ordered the captain, a puzzled look on his face. "How did she get out in the first place? I don't remember releasing her."

"You can't hold the likes of her for long," came a voice from the open doorway. A hooded figure stepped through. The newcomer pushed back his black hood, exposing a wizened old face, with cold black eyes.

The Town Sorcerer.

Pythese uttered a loud shriek, shook off the guard's hand and tried to rush past the dark-clad sorcerer. Before she reached him, he made a sign and lifted his arms. In his open hands appeared a golden light; it expanded into a large net and settled on top of the girl. She screamed and struggled to free herself from the golden web, but she only managed to entangle herself more.

Rhodar's sharp eyes saw the fine golden thread that connected the web with the sorcerer's hands.

Driven by intuition, he sprang toward the wall where his battleaxe leaned, grabbed the weapon and with one mighty swing he severed the connection to the net.

A bright flame engulfed the enchanted blade where it met the golden thread then the web disappeared.

The sorcerer uttered a strange guttural sound. His hands moved in an intricate pattern; another web began to take shape, but as it started to engulf the girl, her robe suddenly lost its substance. Shapeless, it flowed to the ground. Before the net completely enclosed the apparently empty fabric, something moved inside. A small blue-scaled creature fluttered swiftly past the sorcerer through the open doorway.

The Enforcers called out with astonished voices, rushed to the door.

In the confusion, Rhodar bolted down the corridor, past the cells, looking for another way out of the prison.

He found it in the back. An unbarred window high above the ground.

One mighty leap took him to the window's ledge. He pulled himself up, smashed the glass with his axe and crawled through.

He landed easily on his feet then crouched to see if anyone had witnessed his escape. He was in a dark alley, and there was no one in sight.

On light feet, he trotted through back alleys toward the inn to get his horse. While he ran, he noticed the heavier weight of the axe in his hand. The last encounter must have drained some of the protective spell.

It was time he finished his quest.

Unobserved, he got Nightwalker. The horse whinnied softly when Rhodar stroked its long head. "Quiet, Nightwalker," Rhodar murmured and led the animal out of the barn into the back lane. As he mounted the horse, his ears detected the flutter of tiny wings, like those of a bat. Then a small dark shape descended from the sky. Before it touched the ground, it seemed to grow, took on more substance.

A moment later, Pythese stood in front of him, naked, a shy smile on her lovely face.

"Need company, barbarian?" she asked a little breathlessly.

"I knew you were no mortal woman," Rhodar growled. "You're the little *Cloud-Dragon,* and you are a *Shape-shifter*."

"Do you mind?" She stood uncertain.

He sat unmoving, only his cold blue eyes roving up and down her shapely body. Then he grinned and shrugged, holding out a hand.

She gave a merry laugh, took his hand and swung up behind him. "You won't be sorry," she whispered into his ear.

He dug his heels into Nightwalker's soft flanks. Galloping down the alley, Rhodar burst into a lusty song, enjoying the feel of the cool morning air on his bare upper torso and the smooth warm naked skin of the girl snuggled close against his back.

"I can think of nothing better than a strong horse between my legs, a warm wench at my back, and the weight of my beloved battleaxe in my hands," he shouted. "It is good to be alive and free."

Sarah's Gift
By
Herbert Grosshans

A woman in a cabin the hunter did find
Her love would forever haunt his mind

Ever since the death of his wife, Thanksgiving had lost its meaning for Jake. What did he have to be thankful for? Now the holiday was just an excuse to take some time off from a stressful job and lose himself in the little bit of wilderness that was still left.

There was talk that the turkey hunt might be suspended for a few years to give the birds a chance to recover. Hunting pressure had become too great in the last ten years.

It wasn't like it used to be when he went hunting with his dad. He couldn't remember when they didn't have a turkey for Thanksgiving, but this year might just be that year.

Then again…what did it really matter if he got one or not? There was no pleasure in eating a turkey by himself.

The weather was turning chilly, and he shivered inside his camouflage outfit. His fingers, which held his bow, were getting cold and stiff. The temperature must have dropped at least ten degrees within the last hour. He could smell the snow in the crisp air.

Looking into the sky, he saw the clouds moving in fast. *Chances of me getting a bird today are getting slim. Animals are smart. They know when a storm is coming, and they'll disappear, searching for cover.*

His daydreams were interrupted when he heard the soft cluck. Then he saw a big gobbler strutting into the open.

Jake had done this too many times, and he reacted without thinking. He had been ready for this moment all morning, and when he released the arrow, he knew it would not miss the target.

It was almost anti-climactic when he picked up the limp carcass of the big bird. A quick check of its beard and then he stuffed it into his backpack. Again, he looked up at the rolling dark clouds and realized he had to get back to his vehicle as fast as possible. It looked like a snowstorm was going to hit soon. Unusual for this time of year.

Picking up the rest of his gear, he started walking back along the trail. It was a good hour's walk to his truck and another hour to the highway. He wanted to be out of the woods when the storm hit.

The first flakes began to fall less than fifteen minutes after he started walking. Gently at first, but after another fifteen minutes he could barely see the trail. Just to be sure he was still on the right trail, he checked his compass and put it away, satisfied he was headed in the right direction.

Listening to the howling of the wind above the treetops, he knew this storm would be a bad one.

After walking for over an hour, Jake had the feeling he was going in circles, but the needle of his compass assured him he was still following the right trail. When he couldn't find his truck after two hours, he realized he was lost.

His warm clothing was in his truck, as was his camping gear. He wasn't dressed for spending a night outside, not in this kind of weather. When he tried his cell phone, he got nothing.

Damn! How could he have been so careless? He didn't panic. He'd been an outdoorsman far too long and knew that panic was your worst enemy when lost in the woods.

He didn't remember taking another trail, but he must have, even though according to his compass he had not. There was no sense floundering through the bush, so he kept on walking.

The trail ended suddenly, and it almost seemed as if the veil of whiteness began to lift. There appeared to be a light ahead and he walked toward it. Coming closer, he saw the outline of a building. A log cabin.

Thank God. At least I found shelter where I can wait out the storm.

He pounded against the heavy wooden door. When no one answered, he pounded again. After a moment, the door swung open a crack, and he stared into the muzzle of a rifle. Above it was the face of woman.

"Who is making all this racket?" she asked.

"Sorry to bother you, ma'am, but I'm lost. I was hunting turkeys when I got surprised by this freak snowstorm."

"You hunt turkeys with a bow and arrow?"

He smiled. "Yes, ma'am. Regulations, you know. Wouldn't want to break them."

"Are you an Indian?"

"Not as far as I know. But I haven't checked my ancestry lately." He grinned in an effort to ease the tension.

"Haven't seen you around these parts. Where do you come from? Are you a drifter?" Her rifle was pointed straight at his chest, but he noticed a slight tremor.

"No ma'am. I come from the city. I'm a lawyer. You might have heard of my firm *Dupont and Son*." He smiled. "I'm the *Son.* My father passed away a couple of years ago."

"A Big-City-Lawyer and a Frenchman to boot. I don't trust either."

"Neither do I." He gave her his most disarming smile. "Listen, ma'am, I'm freezing, and my clothing is soaking wet. Just let me rest for a while, and I'll be on my way again."

"Well, all right." She hesitated. "But I'm not afraid to use this." She opened the door and stepped back to let him enter. He stomped his feet to get rid of the snow.

When the door closed behind him, he shrugged off his bow, quiver of arrows and his backpack and let them slide to the floor. A fire crackled in the fireplace, spreading welcoming warmth. The place was neat and clean, but he had the strangest sensation that everything he saw somehow didn't look right.

The pots and pans on the big woodstove were scrubbed clean, but they looked old, like something you'd find in an antique store. There was a large table and four chairs. On one side of the room stood an old couch. A couple of wooden boxes served as end tables. Preserves on shelves in the kitchen and bunches of onions and garlic hanging from the ceiling added to the eerie feeling.

"I have some hot cider on the stove," the woman said. "You look like you could use some."

"Thank you, ma'am, I sure could."

"Stop calling me *ma'am.* I'm Sarah."

He took a seat and watched her fill a large mug with the cider. He was surprised to see how young she was. From her mannerism, he had thought she was an older woman, but when she stood close to the lantern on the table, he got a better look at her face. It was pretty. Her dark eyes were large, and her lips full. She had a way of tilting her head when she poured the cider that he found quite appealing.

She can't be older than twenty-eight or twenty-nine.

A faded picture of an older man holding an antique rifle sat on the mantle above the fireplace. Black and white. One of those old-fashioned pictures one could get made in souvenir shops.

"Is that your father in the picture?" he asked.

She looked at him for a moment. "No, my husband."

"Where is he?"

"Dead. Tree fell on him a couple years back."

"Sorry to hear that. Was he a hunter?"

She laughed. "He couldn't hit a barn door, but he did manage to bag an elk every winter. Wasted a lot of bullets though." She handed him a mug then poured cider for herself before sitting down across from him. "How about you? You said you went turkey hunting. Get one?"

He pointed with his chin to his backpack. "In there. A nice big tom."

"What you gonna do with it?"

He shrugged. "I don't know. Give it away, I guess. In exchange for an invitation to dinner."

She gave him a calculating look. "It's Thanksgiving today. I'd invite you if I had a turkey."

He stared at her. "You want that turkey?"

"You said you'd give it away. Might as well be me who gets it."

"Are you asking me to stay?"

She lifted her shoulders. "You ain't going nowhere else today. Looks like I'm stuck with you."

"Then we'd better get that bird prepared."

"We?" She chuckled. "I'm afraid it'll be my chore. A city slicker like you probably won't wanna get his hands mucked up with turkey-guts."

"Listen, lady…"

"Sarah."

"Sarah. All right then, Sarah, listen now…I've been hunting since I could hold and aim a rifle and a bow. My dad taught me well. There are certain unwritten laws, you should know. A real hunter takes care of his game."

"Well, who would have guessed?" She smiled, got up and went to the cupboard to take out a lantern. She lit it with a shake she pulled out of the fire. "Can't do it in here, but there is a shed in the back." She walked into the other room, came back with a thick wool shirt. "Here, take off you wet shirt and put this on. It should fit you."

He pulled the turkey out of his backpack, took the lantern and went back outside. He had no trouble finding the shed. It was roomy enough for what he needed to do, even though it was cluttered with all kinds of things, like rolls of thick rope and even some barbed wire. The tools hanging on the walls belonged into a museum as far as he was concerned. Nobody used those anymore these days.

He hung the lantern from a hook in the ceiling and gutted the big bird. Since there was no way to pluck the feathers, not in the cold shed and without hot water, he skinned it. Disposing of the guts and feathers didn't present a problem. He left everything in the forest behind the shed. It wouldn't last long. Birds or possibly a coyote would find it soon enough.

When he came back into the cottage, Sarah was busy peeling potatoes. She looked up and smiled at him. "Well, let's get it into the oven."

"Is there anywhere I can wash up?" he asked.

"In there. I've already got some water heated up."

There was a small wooden tub, barely large enough to sit in, partially filled with warm water. He stripped and climbed in, sat for a while and let the heat of the water warm up his frozen body.

He turned when he heard the creaking of the opening door. Sarah walked in with a towel and a washcloth. "I'll scrub your back," she said matter-of-factly.

He didn't object and enjoyed the feeling of her soft hands.

"You have a fine body," Sarah murmured. "One would think a lawyer who doesn't do any physical labor would have a soft, flabby body."

"I work out." He smiled. "One of the few pleasures I still have left."

"A man like you must have a lot of lady friends. Is there a special lady in your heart?"

"I'm afraid not. I don't go out much."

"Aren't you lonely?" Her hands lingered on his broad shoulders.

"Not usually but..." he said with a low voice, "maybe on days like today. Holidays are a drag."

"I'm lonely, too," she said softly, leaning forward. Her breath was warm in his neck. "I haven't been with a man since Edward died." She kissed him on the forehead, on his cheek, and then her lips touched his.

Surprised by her forwardness, he was slow to respond, but then he kissed her back with a hunger he had suppressed for a long time.

When they broke apart, she gasped and said, “Forgive me. I don’t know what came over me.”

He smiled and rose from the tub. Dripping water, he stood naked in front of her. Her gaze traveled across his muscular body, down to his manhood.

At first, she gasped, and then she smiled. “My…one little kiss has that effect on him?”

Jake reached out and pulled her into his arms. “He hasn’t been with a woman for much too long. He’s very anxious.” He took her face between his large hands, looked deeply into her dark eyes.

“I hope he’s gentle,” she whispered.

“Very.” He kissed her full lips. Then he picked her up and carried her into the next room. Gently, he put her onto the bearskin in front of the fireplace. He lay down beside her and kissed her again. Undoing her apron, he began to unbutton her dress.

“Let me help,” she whispered when he fumbled with the buttons.

“I’ve never been good with buttons,” he murmured, nibbling on her ear.

Once the dress was off, he practically ripped off her bloomers, wondering fleetingly why a young woman would wear them.

“Be gentle,” she whispered again when he lay between her thighs. Her hand reached down to take hold of him, guided him into her dark thick triangle.

A loud gasp escaped her lips when he entered her. Her need must have been as great as his because it wasn’t long before she reached her first orgasm. “What is happening?” she cried out. “I’ve never felt like this before.” Warm fluid gushed out of her.

He was ready to climax, but he held back, not wishing to end for this moment. He crushed her soft breasts against his chest, covered her face with kisses. She came again. Whimpering and clinging to him, she clawed at his back with sharp fingernails. He couldn’t hold back any longer and came inside her with a series of loud grunts.

Then they lay in each other’s arms, both of them breathing harshly, spent and satisfied.

He lifted his head and looked at her. Her hair had come undone and framed her pale face like a black veil. “You are so beautiful,” he said, studying her closely for the first time.

She smiled. “How can I be? I must look awful with my hair frizzy like this.”

“It’s in style,” he said. “Every woman wears her hair like that these days. I love it."

"I don't even know your name, Mr. Frenchman."

"It's Jacques Dupont, but everybody calls me Jake."

Startling him, she suddenly sat up. "Oh my god. I forgot about the potatoes!" Naked, she rushed to the stove and lifted the cover off one of the pots. "I hope you like your potatoes black," she said with a laugh.

He looked at her, standing naked in front of the stove, enthralled by her lovely body. "You must be the most beautiful woman I have ever seen," he said. Even in the dim light of the oil lamps, it was evident that she was blushing.

"Don't stare at me like that, Jake Dupont. It makes me uncomfortable. A lady doesn't like to be stared at, especially with no clothes on." She reached for another apron.

"Don't," he said softly. "I want to remember this moment forever."

"That's a long time." She laughed and wrapped the apron around her. "I think we should eat. Make yourself useful, and put some more logs on the fire."

After eating, they lay again on the bearskin. She didn't object when he ran his hands over her body, or when he kissed her breasts, her belly, her thighs, and when he put his tongue into her cleft.

"No man's ever done this to me," she moaned, "but it feels wonderful."

He made her climax several times before he entered her again. They moved against each other for a long time.

"I love you, Sarah," he said. "I don't want this to end here. I will come back for you."

She kissed him gently. "Promise?"

"I promise." Pulling a ring from his little finger, he took her hand and put in on her finger. "I had this ring made for my wife, but she died before she could wear it. I want you to have it as proof of my love."

"Are you sure?" Her lips were warm on his.

"I'm sure."

"It's a beautiful ring." She reached behind her neck and removed a thin silver chain. There was a locket attached to it. She put the chain around his neck. "Here, this is my gift to you."

He held her in his arms as they drifted off to sleep.

* * * *

He awoke chilled to the bone and found himself lying naked on rough floor planks. Sitting up, he looked around the room.

"Hello," he called out, but there was no answer. He was alone. Alone in a room empty of any furnishings, except for an old, rusted stove with some rusted and dented pots and pans.

The rough stones of the fireplace were crumbling, and the hearth was covered with dusty cobwebs.

He saw his backpack and bow and arrows lying on the floor by the rotting wooden door. The backpack was empty. Then he spotted a neatly folded bundle on the floor beside him…his underwear, camouflage shirt and pants. When he picked them up, he was surprised to find his pants and shirt completely dry.

Light filtered into the room through the web-covered window. The silence outside caught his attention. The storm seemed to have died down.

Shivering, he put on his shirt. He stopped when he felt the thin chain around his neck and lifted the small locket away from his chest. As he did so, he realized the ring from his finger was missing.

"What the hell!" he cursed, trying to piece together the happenings of the previous day and night.

Maybe he'd knocked himself out somehow. A trauma like that would produce hallucinations. His memory seemed quite clear, but had that woman been real?

He opened the silver locket and stared at the picture of a woman. "Sarah," he whispered. "What happened to you, my love? I couldn't have imagined you."

Grabbing his things, he stepped outside onto a blanket of fresh snow. He didn't see any footprints.

The rising sun made the snow-covered tree branches sparkle with millions of tiny diamonds. It was a beautiful day, and he didn't have the foggiest idea where he was.

Rummaging in his backpack, he found his cell phone and dialed 911. He'd better get to a hospital and get checked out. Maybe he suffered from a brain tumor or something.

When the dispatcher came on line, he explained that he was lost, and she gave him the number of the Sheriff's office. He told the officer who answered about his problem and was surprised when the man said, "I know where you are. I'll have someone pick you up. Just don't go anywhere."

He had no intentions of leaving, but he did have a look around the property.

There was a rotting shed in the back. Beside it were two weathered wooden crosses.

One read: *Here lies Edward Williams, husband of Sarah Williams, 1840-1889.*

The other one made him crouch down to get a better look. What he read left his head spinning: *In Memory of Sarah Williams, beloved Mother and Grandmother, 1861-1940.*

He touched the wooden cross in disbelief. How could that be?

He turned when he heard the truck pull into the snow-covered yard and watched as an older man in uniform climbed out. Walking slowly, the man came up to Jake and smiled. "So, you're the feller who got himself lost on our property?"

"This is your place?"

The older man nodded. "Yup, but nobody lives here, obviously. It's the old homestead of my Great-Grandmother Sarah Williams. The new house is a couple miles down the road."

"Sorry about trespassing, Mr. Williams."

"Oh no, it's not Williams. My name is Robert Dupont. Sarah named my Granddaddy after his real father, a Jacques Dupont." He chuckled. "Funny story, actually. Great-Grandma Williams, I never knew her, of course, she died before I was born, but I know the story. Apparently, our Great-Grandfather, a Monsieur Jacques Dupont, he was French, you know, got lost while hunting turkeys for Thanksgiving. He stumbled into Great-Grandma's place and, well…you can guess the rest."

"What happened to this Monsieur Dupont?"

The older man shrugged. "Who knows? They had their little fling, and he disappeared. Left Sarah brokenhearted. They say she never got over him." He winked. "Rumor has it he was a French nobleman from the big city. Sarah was just a simple country girl." He slapped Jake on the shoulder. "Come on, we'll take you back to civilization."

"Give me one more moment." Jake took one last look at the wooden cross and the name on it. It seemed as if an icy hand was holding his brain prisoner.

"Is my father boring you with the story about the origins of the Dupont family?" a woman's voice said behind him. "The man she shacked up with was probably just a drifter who took advantage of a lonely woman's generosity."

Jake turned and stared at the speaker.

"What's the matter? You look like you've seen a ghost, mister."

"Sarah?" Jake managed to say with a brittle voice.

"That's my name all right," she said, tilting her head. "Do you know me?"

"You look familiar," he stammered, still staring at her.

"Probably seen my picture in the local paper. It happens to me often. Anyway, I was named after good old Great-Great-Grandma Sarah." She lifted her left hand. "I even inherited her favorite ring."

He stared at the ring, words stuck in his throat.

"I never did catch your name, mister."

"Dupont," he said, "Jake Dupont."

"You don't say? Hey, maybe you and I are related."

The End

Look for Herbert's books at
www.melange-books.com

The best-selling Xandra series (Three books)
Seeds of Chaos, Book One, Eden's Gate
Seeds of Chaos, Book Two, Hell's Gate
Stardogs, Book One, Return to Redsky
Stardogs, Book Two, Redemption
Orion—The Hunt
Cliffs of Time
Outpost Epsilon
Orion, Symbiont of Passion

Visit Herbert's website: http://hegro.blogspot.com/

Cross the threshold into the World of Dreams and Imagination.
Warning: Adult material. Some people may be offended.
Enter at your own risk.